Praise for Derek Marlowe's

A DANDY IN ASPIC

'He writes like John le Carré at the top of his form' *Yorkshire Post*

'A classic of the cold war spy stories - one of the earliest and one of the best. Marlowe's Eberlin/Krasnevin is on the run from himself on different levels and in different places: the evocations of London and Berlin in the 1960s are superb.' Piers Paul Read

'Characters and settings make it near-compulsive reading with the tension rising to an exciting finale in Berlin' *Daily Mail*

'A Dandy In Aspic is a great spy novel: beautifully written and with a melancholy soul beneath its wry humour, it's high time it came out from the shadows again' Jeremy Duns, author of the 'Paul Dark' novels

'Nicely told, with occasional wit and considerable irony . . . A most promising debut' *Sunday Times*

'A very well written, intelligent spy thriller' *The Observer*

ALSO BY DEREK MARLOWE

Memoirs of a Venus Lackey

A Single Summer with L.B.

Echoes of Celandine (also published as The Disappearance)

Do you remember England?

Somebody's Sister

Nightshade

The Rich Boy from Chicago

Nancy Astor

ABOUT THE AUTHOR

Derek Marlowe was born in London in 1938. He was a novelist, playwright and screen writer. *A Dandy in Aspic*, his first novel, was originally published in 1966 and became an international bestseller. It was translated into 15 languages and Marlowe himself adapted the book into a film starring Laurence Harvey and Mia Farrow. He was the author of eight further novels, including *The Disappearance*, which was originally published as *Echoes of Celandine* and became a film starring Donald Sutherland. Marlowe had one son, Ben, and died in 1996 at the age of fifty-eight.

First published in Great Britain in 1966 by Victor Gollancz Ltd and in the USA by G. P. Putnam's Sons, New York
This edition published by Silvertail Books in 2015
www.silvertailbooks.com

1

A catalogue record of this book is available from the British Library

Typeset in Ehrhardt Monotype by Joanna Macgregor
Printed in the UK by CPI Group (UK) Ltd, Croydon, CR0 4YY
ISBN 978-1-909269-23-1

A DANDY IN ASPIC

DEREK MARLOWE

SILVERTAIL BOOKS • *London*

FOREWORD

I wonder what happened to my first edition of *A Dandy In Aspic*. I must have been careless about lending it when it could no longer be bought. Derek's succeeding novels, from *The Memoirs of a Venus Lackey* (1968) to *The Rich Boy from Chicago* (1979), are in their place on my bookshelves; seven titles, lacking the first and ninth. The last novel, *Nancy Astor* (1982), based on his own screen-play, had passed me by. But it was *A Dandy in Aspic*, written in four weeks in a flat he shared with me and Piers Paul Read just off the Vauxhall Bridge Road in 1965, that changed Derek's life.

Derek, Piers and I were friends but not a trio. We each had a room and kept to it. We had a kitchen but seldom ate communally. I was sharing my room with my future wife, Jose. It was the year of 'You've Lost That Loving Feeling' by the Isley Brothers: Derek played it on a loop. He went out most days because he had some kind of a job, and there were indications of an exciting life elsewhere. He'd met some people who had a rock band, and the band became The Who.

I'm writing from memory, an increasingly fallible resource, but my memory recalls that when Derek told us that he was writing 'a spy novel', we were sceptical. Surely that band-wagon had passed by? *The Spy Who Came in from the Cold* had been published years ago! But what I do remember is that when Derek told me the basic premise for his novel (a spy with two identities who is ordered to kill his other self) I thought: now, that is an absolutely brilliant idea.

By that time, Derek had delivered his riposte to our scepticism. Gollancz, he announced one day, had accepted his book. The American rights and the film rights followed. By our lights, Derek was rich. Success had arrived.

The flat in Vincent Square was the third chapter of my times with Derek. We had met as tenants of bedsits in a house in Blenheim Crescent just off Ladbroke Grove, Notting Hill. Today those houses change hands for millions of pounds but back then, 1961 to 1964, Blenheim Crescent was the wrong side of a frontier between respectable Notting Hill and Rachmanland, so named after a notorious landlord whose fiefdom was rife with drugs and prostitution. London was getting into its famous 60s swing, and Derek, a romantic figure in dark clothes, had a life of which I (a country mouse in the big city) knew little. I don't think I was aware until later that he'd had at least a couple of plays modestly produced in London. But in 1964 we were independently invited, as promising young playwrights, to spend a few months in West Berlin with a group of young writers and film-makers, a 'Literarisches Colloquium' funded by the Ford Foundation. That's where we met Piers. Comfortably installed in a substantial house on the shore of a lake, the Wansee, we young writers were left to do pretty much as we liked (to work, as was hoped). This extraordinary perk culminated in a kind of graduation evening of performances of the results of our fitful labours. My dim memory of Derek's play suggests that it might have been the same piece, titled 'The Scarecrow', mentioned by Wikipedia as having been produced in London the same year. All I recall is the scarecrow and the unexpected (and effective) intrusion of a recording of 'I Won't Dance'.

From the first meeting in Blenheim Crescent to the last day in Vincent Square there were three or four years during which our lives conjoined. I think of him as slightly mysterious, slightly withdrawn, mostly keeping his thoughts to himself. But perhaps that was me. I have to concentrate to recall his laugh. Later, as married men, we saw each other at intervals at each other's houses. Three of my copies of his books are inscribed, from 1970, 1976 and 1980.

In the late 70s, perhaps (I don't keep a diary), I stayed with Derek and his wife Suki at their baronial mansion in Gloucestershire (subsequently sold to a Rolling Stone). After their divorce he moved to Los Angeles, in 1989. One day in a bookshop on Sunset Boulevard, I saw him for the last time. He was, as ever, laconic, smiley, quiet, and darkly good looking. I should say something about that. Whether by his choice or by his publishers', the early novels come without an author's photograph. Among my 'English firsts', there is no photo until *Somebody's Sister* (1974), his sixth novel. I remember Derek making a deprecatory remark about his looks, to the effect that he had a funny-looking face. I thought he was beautiful, with full wide lips, dark creased eyes, and a neat head of hair around a slightly flattened face, as if he'd run into a wall in a cartoon. It was a hipster look which in itself didn't give much away, but the mind behind the face was, and is, an open book; literally. The epigraphs of the novels come from Browning, Hart Crane, Blaise Cendrars, Ford Madox Ford, William Empson, Walter de la Mare, C P Cavafy, Malcolm Lowry, Edward Gorey. Can one call the list disparate? To me, it evokes an aura of doomed romanticism in different guises. The names of characters – Mallory, Dowson, Hallam, Lytton, and others – seem not so much made up as borrowed from the same period piece, a scrapbook of country-house England before 1914. Derek's favourite novels were *The Good Soldier* by Ford; and (the exception that proves the rule) *The Great Gatsby*.

Hemingway versus Fitzgerald was an argument we had more than once. Derek was a Fitzgerald man, and the books made the case for him, especially *The Rich Boy from Chicago*. Even the title sounds like Fitzgerald. That book's epigraph is from a poem by Henry Bax, and perhaps it's not fanciful to suppose that the four lines spoke more for Derek than did Browning and the rest …

> In all forms of endeavour, private and public,
> there are only two poles: sex and power.
> Between these poles is a line called the equator.
> It is an imaginary line.

… because Henry Bax was imaginary, too.

It has been a fast fifty years since I used to hear Derek typing his way through *A Dandy in Aspic*, long enough for a reputation to wax and wane, and wax again. To be out of print is not a value judgement in itself, more like a hazard of the writing life. The novels were well received when they were new, and it's good to see the first one back again. It will find and please new readers for a graceful writer and a graceful man who died too young.

Tom Stoppard
13 August 2014

When she got back to the Cheshire-Cat, she was surprised to find quite a large crowd collected round it: there was a dispute going on between the executioner, the King, and the Queen, who were all talking at once, while all the rest were quite silent, and looked very uncomfortable.

The executioner's argument was, that you couldn't cut off a head unless there was a body to cut it from; that he had never had to do such a thing before, and he wasn't going to begin at his time of life.

The King's argument was that anything that had a head could be beheaded, and that you weren't to talk nonsense.

The Queen's argument was that, if something wasn't done about it in less than no time, she'd have everybody executed all round. (*It was this last remark that had made all the party look so grave and anxious.*)

The Cat's head then began fading away, and soon it had entirely disappeared. So the King and the executioner ran wildly up and down looking for it, while the rest of the party went back to the game.

LEWIS CARROLL,
Alice's Adventures in Wonderland

APOGEE

1

Amontillado Caroline

In the Country of the Blind, the One-Eyed man is probably in a circus.
–ALEXANDER EBERLIN

The surest way to be out of fashion tomorrow is to be in the forefront of it today.
–ALEXANDER EBERLIN

EBERLIN ate alone as usual. Returning to his apartment at about six o'clock, he would shower in silence, change into something less comfortable, and sit down to a dinner-for-one prepared by an aged, yet untalkative, valet who let himself in at four o'clock every afternoon and let himself out at eight o'clock every evening. No words were ever exchanged between master and servant but "Good evening" and "Good night," except on one garrulous evening when the valet apologized, with uncontrolled discretion, for the wine. It was a happy relationship and Eberlin wouldn't have it otherwise. He was a quiet man by nature, to such an extent that an honorary member of Brook's, a jovial fellow and consequently shunned by all, remarked to an acquaintance that the reason why Eberlin was inarticulate was because he was born with a silver spoonerism in his mouth. It was an inaccurate statement, but nevertheless this pleasantry was taken up by all the fashionable wits of the town and earned Eberlin a mysterious reputation as an outsider, a man to claim and cultivate as one's own. In no time, feasted, toasted and courted by a bevy of open-mouthed sycophants from all the right schools, Eberlin was guest of honor at the best parties and functions in London, a situation that made not the slightest difference to Eberlin's personality since he attended none of them.

Instead he would spend his free hours locked in his rooms at 24 South Street, contemplating the view from the rear window, occasionally reading a book from his library–he was now halfway through *Pelham*–or taking a slow walk across Hyde Park until he reached the Serpentine and then returning home. Once a week, on a fine Sunday morning, he would walk under Park Lane and emerge on the central island where Byron sat, all bronze and pigeonsmeared, and would read all the newspapers without discrimination, and then leave for South Street, throwing the wads of news into the trash bin outside the Dorchester Bar; and then, like this evening, he would, as usual, eat alone.

The wine was awful. The valet had bought it cheap from a supermarket, knowing from experience that his master was apathetic about the acquired bigotry of vintages and bouquets. It came out of the decanter like sludge. Eberlin drank it unconcerned, as he leafed through the letters on the table. There were ten of them, mostly unsealed invitations from S.W.1, which were usually dropped on sight, unopened, into the wastebasket. But this evening, Eberlin opened all, glancing quickly at Who or What was At Home, and then stopping on a small white card which stated simply:

Caroline Sue Hetherington requests your pleasure
at 14 Ruston Gate S.W.3
for some of her Amontillado Sherry.
Seven P.M. *12 August.* *R.S.V.P.*

Eberlin tucked the card into his wallet and left the table. He walked slowly into the white-walled bedroom and studied a large map of London lying on the bed. Then he folded the map together and put it in the bedside table drawer.

The valet was waiting in the hall, arms extended, holding up, with professional foresight, a deep blue, blue-silk-lined overcoat. Eberlin put it on, felt the pockets for keys and money, and then strolled back into the dining room, closed the door, turned off the light and looked out of the window. The street was empty of people. He stood there, hands in pockets, for a long while. The valet was in the next room, washing up plates with the minimum of noise. Eberlin was just above average height, thin in the body and, much to his disdain, thirty-six years old. He considered it an uncompromising age, lacking the finesse of earlier years and the authority of later. Never one to consider his life of any great importance, he had endured the years of his youth with the frivolous abandon of a monk, retiring further and further from his fellow men as the months passed, until he reached the point when he contemplated celebrating his thirty-sixth birthday in the high manner of Captain Oates. But he didn't.

Obliged, by a quirk of fate long since regretted, to play out his role, he blundered on into the dawn of middle age, a hermetic dandy, surrounding himself only with the fetish of himself–predominantly his clothes, which he chose with exquisite and envied care, his books, his three double-barreled fowling pieces by Manton, and his collection of old Sèvres porcelain locked in a vault in the V and A–and an utter lack of envy for his fellow man. He had that noble selflessness of a man who cares for no one but himself. Brummell, a man he admired unashamedly, had that. Until he went mad.

A plate bounced off the edge of the sink in the next room, cracked in midair, then split into pieces on the floor. Eberlin made no reaction, but turned suddenly from the window, crossed the dining room, entered the hall as the valet appeared shamefaced from the kitchen, and left the apartment. It was a cool summer evening, pleasant in that part of London with the park and the mews houses and the small squares. Eberlin considered walking, not because of the weather, but because his car, a Maserati Mistrale 3.7, was at present disemboweled and eight feet in the air at Cuchet's Garage, twenty kilometers from Lyons. A taxi man stood ten yards down the road as an elderly man and his wife dithered over the fare. Then the roof sign lit up once more, just as Eberlin had decided to walk.

"Ruston Gate," he said quietly to the driver. Then he closed the door and settled back into the seat of the taxi.

* * *

"Don't you think bottoms are the most super common denominators men and women have?" she said with a strident brashness that fanfared her virginity.

It was a large room on the first floor, decorated fashionably in

Art Nouveau colorings and bric-a-brac from side-street boutiques, and carried the confused weight of self-consciousness with admirable dignity. Not one square foot of the carefully chosen wallpaper was evident behind the melee of assorted musical instruments, reproductions, bookshelves and Victorian kitchenware. Lady Hetherington called it her *conversation room*, with all that implied, and had been known to amuse the Montagus of Beaulieu in this very room by hanging radiators of vintage cars around the portrait of Prince Rupert as a special treat.

The music was loud but no one danced. The eleven people instead posed awkwardly around the room clutching warm, empty glasses in their hands and made polite comments about absent guests and the state of the Crown. In one corner, huddled on a brown velvet-covered couch, three out-of-work actors sat talking about themselves, like three Gorgons passing round the I from one to another. A small, fat man, in a three-piece suit, stood, hands clasped behind his back, staring at the spines of the books on one wall, now and then reading out a title aloud with mock surprise to an incredibly plain girl with fat legs whom Caroline had chosen as her best friend, being herself blessed with the fragile translucent beauty of a corner angel. She (Caroline) was now squatting on a footstool at the feet of two of her male guests, dressed in a simple violet sleeveless sweater and tight deep-velvet trousers, her slender arms clasped under her thighs, her head on her knees, gazing fixedly at a whippet who was asleep by her feet.

"Balls," she said suddenly and looked up, frowning, at Nigel, a childhood friend, who was caressing her back with his hand, "why doesn't John marry Mummy and get it over with? I mean, it's not as if she's unattractive or anything. All he wants to do is sleep with her and take her to Brinkley's on Sundays and all that horrid routine. I feel for her sometimes, but she won't listen. Don't you think it's unfair?"

Nigel's fingertips had now reached Caroline's bottom and were resting on the thin pile of the trouser material with breathless apprehension. He said, "Oh I agree" quickly and slid his thumb under the cotton belt and onto the warm skin of her lower back. Caroline pulled a face, moved away, and woke up the whippet as Eberlin entered the room.

He stood at the door and looked around at the other guests. "Too late for whisky and the sherry's awful, but if you hang on

for a while, James is bringing along a pipkin," said a small pink-faced young man in a petulant tone and a honey corduroy suit.

"Caroline never has enough in the house, does she?"

Eberlin ignored him and walked across the room toward the fire as Caroline jumped up with a smile and tugged at the sleeve of his overcoat.

"I'm awfully glad you could make it. Sherry's not too good though, I'm afraid."

Eberlin nodded and took out a cigarette from a light leather case and lit it.

"Do you want to be introduced around or would you rather be stuffy and ignore them? I recommend being stuffy and ignoring them because they're all very dull and boring, except for Mark and he's in Canada."

She was a short girl in her bare feet, five foot one or two perhaps, but precociously attractive, and had had mild affairs with a dozen or so middle-aged men in the four years since leaving finishing school. All had proposed marriage and all had been refused in the nicest possible way, and all remained ardent enemies of her, meeting in public and condemning her as nothing more than a whore, and phoning her in private, hopefully, in the early hours of the morning from the bar of their club. She wore her blond hair straight, curling up only within chewing distance of her wide, pale-painted mouth, and stood invariably with her small stomach forward, looking up out of violet eyes at all and every self-respecting man who longed to put her under his arm or over his shoulder and into his bed. All except Eberlin, who barely glanced at her, but surveyed the room openly, studying each guest in turn without expression and taking in, in detail, the absurd fracas of the décor. The fat man in the corner stared at him, waiting to catch his eye, then opened his mouth in expectant greeting when Eberlin did, but remained gaping as Eberlin flicked his eyes to a framed print of a Modigliani *Jeanne* above the man's head, then over to a nineteenthcentury oboe that hung, impotent, in pieces, over the armoire door.

Caroline said, "Stop it!" loudly to the whippet and glanced at Eberlin, but he took no notice and looked for an ashtray, catching sight of the fat man's reflection, still studying him slyly, one hand toying with a plaster dog, in the long, gold-framed, delicately carved mirror over the mantel. He threw the cigarette into the fire.

"Don't you want to take your coat off?" Nigel remarked, giving Caroline an overt peck on the cheek. "It's awfully hot in here." Eberlin took off the coat and handed it to Nigel who hesitated, then plonked it on the edge of the couch and shouted "Michael!" Eberlin picked it up again and carried it, draped over his arm, out of the room to the entrance hall and laid it on the chaise longue, and then returned to the room by another door, entering behind everybody, and taking a book off a table, opened it and considered the first paragraph.

Two more guests arrived; one, carrying a large metal pipkin of beer, was presumably James. The other, a big-boned girl with black curly hair, praised everything in the room with exaggerated gasps of contemporary slang and then left quickly after ten minutes with a blue apothecary bottle which Lady Hetherington had brought all the way from Tunbridge Wells. One bold zealot had put Purcell's *O Come Ye Sons of Art* on the record player and was hushing members of his tightly knit clique of two every time the counter-tenor reached a disturbingly high octave. Caroline herself retained the attention of the more imaginative members of the group by demonstrating her appealing ability to touch her toes without bending the knees, while her best friend muttered miserably alone under the base shelf of *The Collected Works of Dickens*. The fat man offered Eberlin a Will's Whiff, which he refused curtly, crossing to a vacant hamlet chair that was conveniently out of everyone's way near the window. It was now one minute to nine. He sat down at an angle from the other guests, facing an elderly man who gave him a nod and said, "What an excellent suit," and nodded again. The music stopped abruptly with cries of "Shame!" and "God!" then the more modish sounds of a pop group hit out at all-comers. Eberlin considered abandoning the whole sorry affair altogether and returning home, when a soft white arm, wrist jangling with Persian charms appeared over his shoulder clutching a full glass of Chivas Regal, and Caroline whispered in his ear:

"I saved this especially for you in the hope that you might arrive. It seems silly to introduce myself now, but I'm Caroline."

"How do you do," he said, taking the glass and drinking it slowly.

Standing behind him, she rested her arm on his shoulder and whispered again: "The fat man in the corner asked me if I knew you. He seemed terribly interested when I said you might come. Do you know him?"

"No."

She leaned forward, smelling heavily of Amontillado and *Numero Cinq*, so that her hair irritated his cheek, and smiled at him. Eberlin got up, walked across the room, and appreciated Prince Rupert.

"The Duke of Marlborough," said a male voice behind him and another said, "No, it's Prince Rupert," and a pretty girl in a trouser suit said, "Prince Rupert," and then the fat man said, "My name's Copperfield."

Eberlin turned and looked down at a beaming round face, squint-eyed behind spectacles. His hair was sparse, his tie Winchester, and sweat hung around his obese cheeks. "How do you do," and he extended a chubby hand.

"How do you do," said Eberlin quickly and returned to the painting.

"You're Eberlin aren't you?" Copperfield said quietly. "I've heard a lot about–"

"Excuse me." Eberlin returned to the hamlet chair and sat down again and picked up his drink. It was now twelve minutes past nine. Caroline was standing with a group of men near the piano and was listening to none of them. She looked steadily at Eberlin over her shoulder and smiled, and then walked across the cluttered room toward him.

"I do hope you're not bored," she said. "A little."

"Would you like to see the rest of the house? It's not much but you might like it. I'll show you."

Copperfield stubbed out his cigar and stared at the two of them. Michael, an ex-lover of Caroline's, muttered in his ear and he smiled and they exchanged glances and another man laughed. Then Copperfield came up behind her and hovered his splayed fingers under her bottom and the two men chuckled, and he winked over her shoulder at Eberlin who said "All right" to Caroline and left the room, treading on Copperfield's black, neatly polished, patent leather toe.

There were only three other rooms in the house, besides bathroom and kitchen. One was a form of study where the late Lord Hetherington had begun every year his definitive biography of Edward the Confessor, contemplated his butterfly collection, and had made love twice, with blatant exertion, to his wife three days before their wedding. It was now never used except to store Caroline's old dolls and her mother's copies of *Elle* and *Vogue.* The other two rooms were bedrooms, decorated in a ridiculous shade of yellow, with paper grapes cut out and stuck over the ceiling by an earnest designer friend of Lady Hetherington's, long since forgotten. The sexual undulations of Lady Hetherington were, in fact, well known in her section of London society, as well as on a small but impishly pert Greek island in the Adriatic. She had, it seems, lost her virginity at an early age and had been offering herself as a reward for its recapture ever since.

Eberlin stood on the white carpet of Caroline's bedroom and glanced at his watch.

"Well, that's about it," she sighed, "except for the John, and that's in a horrid puce color. Some odd whim of Mummy's after she spent the weekend at the Chestertons'. I'm glad you came. I feel very privileged."

He looked at her as she sat on the edge of the bed chewing the inside of her mouth.

"I expect you're fed up with my saying that, aren't you?" "Not at all."

She gave a quick laugh and pulled at her hair.

"I don't really want to go back down there yet. I know it's my party and all that but it's awfully dull. They always are. Oh dear."

She pulled her left leg at right angles onto her other leg and toyed with her toes. She was indeed an eminently seductive girl, being small-breasted in the right manner and wide-mouthed and pleasantly apathetic about everything important. Eberlin moved a step nearer and she looked up at him with a wide smile and returned in inviting concentration to her foot.

He had met many attractive women in his life, and despite his lack of apparent interest, had retained his boyish surprise at the infinite variety of beauty there was in this narrow sphere. He had had a few affairs of no import in his early twenties with various fashionable girls of small minds. And then at twenty-five had prolonged an affair into a confined relationship that had broken the back of his cynicism toward women and had left him, after the full final cymbal-crash of the breakup had faded, with a profound respect for the opposite sex, an abject disenchantment with himself, and a darkhaired young son called Jesse. He had tried vainly for the last weeks of the affair to alchemize the horrendous quarrels into something better but, mostly through his own fault, it all collapsed around him; except for the final pathetic attempts to establish himself, like a struggling spiritualist slipping her card into a passing coffin.

At first, after they had lived apart, he would visit her and his son with a shifting uneasiness, buying small presents like colored bricks and bibs. And then as the months passed, he found himself being pushed further away, until the very district where she lived, with new friends and new patterns of speech, began to bear the exclusive properties of a sanctuary to all but himself. His visits became rarer then as he steeled himself to blunder through the looks and questions of *his* strangers and *her* intimates, until he abandoned it altogether in a morass of self-pity and bitterness. After five years he never saw her again, though he read somewhere, or somebody told him, that she had married a property owner and was living in grand style somewhere near Bath. The end of the affair had been made official, and yet even now, at thirty-six, he felt an involuntary pang at oblique reminders of her–her name, walk, gestures, phraseology echoed in someone else, the inevitable comparisons when bores praised their lovers, the whole, sad, enviable, incredible monolith of the affair.

Once he had found an old letter of hers in a neglected book, and had sat staring at it without reading it for a quarter of an hour, blocked in the whole agony of the moment. He couldn't bring himself to destroy it, yet he feared rediscovering it on some unexpected day in the far future. And so he tried to lose it, leaving it around negligently, hiding it amongst a gallimaufry of rubbish, pushing it under things, out of sight and between things. Finally it did disappear and he spent three frightened hours in his pajamas one night looking for it feverishly, but it never turned up. For two months afterward he never touched an object that didn't readily come to the eye, and then the letter gratefully slipped into the back of his mind and he relaxed.

Eberlin still regretted one thing above all–that he could never be sure if he should have married her. His antipathy began in fear but went on into something more inexplicable that he never resolved. He didn't marry her and henceforth nurtured a bitterness at all married people, as he had watched contemporaries marry and assume that marital hat, that middle-class insular smugness which seemed to be the hallmark of the pedestal they had erected. And so he abandoned them and lived with himself, suffering only the briefest of relationships with women, preferably none at all. Each month his bank would send a check to his ten-year-old son, whom he wouldn't recognize in a small room, and each year he became more attractive to women in general and more forgotten to one in particular. Eberlin hated it all. He stood studying the crown of hair of this girl, this child sitting before him, this small, inconsequential creature whose narrow life had hardly yet begun. He felt old.

"Aren't toes funny things when you think about them, which I do never," she said suddenly, then looked up and caught his expression. "What are you thinking? Awful question."

Eberlin smiled and turned away toward the window. It was now nine forty.

"I don't suppose you remember ever meeting me before," she was saying, "but I saw you when I was with Mummy in North Africa, last month. You looked all sort of brown and distinguished and very English in a nice sort of way, and very super, and I asked someone who you were and they said your name was Eberlin and you were in the Ministry of something. All very mysterious really. Mummy fancied you like mad."

"What part of North Africa was that?" said Eberlin quietly. "Oh, Tripoli. Mummy's got this thing about Dido–you know,

the jolly old queen of Carthage. That's Tripoli, isn't it?" "Yes. Near there."

"Mmmmm."

A sigh and a pout. "What *do* you do?"

"Nothing very dramatic. A desk job."

"Oh, I can't believe that. I bet it's all swish and underhand and night flights to Budapest," she gurgled, and stared frowning at Eberlin's back. He had to stay there eleven more minutes now at the least. It was a slight discomfort, but with an attempt at Stoic resolution, he could probably last out. She was quite a sweet girl but so very young, and would probably say, any minute, something like "Do you find me attractive?" He lit another cigarette. Smoking too much, Eberlin.

"Do you think I'm attractive–I mean, sexually attractive?" she said suddenly, standing up and thrusting out her jaw as if it were the most serious matter on earth. Which to her it was. "Mummy's incredibly sexy and is always having it away all over the place. No end of lovers. I'm not at all seductive though," and then, "Am I?"

Eberlin inclined his head slightly toward her and replied: "A little. But it doesn't disturb me."

"Oh."

She looked down at herself, prodding her stomach, casting a scrutinizing look every now and then at Eberlin, then at a mirror on one wall. Someone downstairs shouted, "*Caroline*!"

"I suppose you're right." She frowned finally, staring into the mirror. "I'm not really what you might call–*voluptuous*, am I?"

Eberlin laughed and said pleasantly, "I wouldn't pay too much attention to your reflection. I've always thought that in this modern age of scientific advance, it was about time someone perfected the art of making the common mirror. In all my life, I have not encountered one that has interpreted my image correctly."

"Caroline! Caro-*line*!"–it must be Nigel–"that dog has messed all over Michael's coat and he's furious!"

There was a long pause, and then Caroline shrugged and walked slowly to the door.

"I'd better go down. Are you coming?" "Not yet."

She nodded thoughtfully, gave a sudden smile and went out quickly. He heard her running down the stairs and someone saying, "Where have you been?" and the reply, "Oh, shut up–I've been in the john, for Godsakes!" Eberlin walked out of the room, paused on the landing and entered the musty dark study of the late Lord Hetherington. He closed the door, sealing out the social whirl, and studied the objects on the desk, then glanced out of the window. London was a cold city at the best of times, but retained a casual indifference to its inhabitants that was comforting. He could see the dark shape of a domed building–couldn't be St. Paul's, could it? Brompton Oratory more likely–and the lighted windows of the Georgian houses opposite. No one particular in the street. He was about to turn and leave when a voice behind him said:

"Oh there you are."

Copperfield entered quietly, shutting the door behind him. "I thought you'd gone."

He stood, smiling fatly up at Eberlin, a dead cigar still in his mouth. Eberlin dropped the heavy curtains back into place and, pulling a chair out from under the desk, sat down, crossed his legs and waited. Copperfield wandered around the room irritatingly, picking up irrelevant objects like a chunk of Dover chalk labelled DOVER CHALK, and a rolled-up rubbing of the Black Prince rather badly done. He moved heavily, breathing emphatically as if from asthma and now and then humming an odd tuneless mnemonic of music to himself. No words were exchanged for three whole minutes. Eberlin listened to the strained highlights of music and noise below and thought of nothing at all. There was a sudden thump as Copperfield dropped the unfinished Chapter One of *Edward the Confessor, A Portrait* onto a small side table, took the cigar from his mouth, and remarked casually to a print of the Magna Carta, bought from H.M.S.O., that was hanging on one wall:

"Pity about Nightingale."

Eberlin pulled at, imperceptibly, the crease of trouser above his knees and made no reply.

"Did you ever meet him?" "No."

"Funny chap," said Copperfield.

Eberlin swung around in the chair and stood up. "I'm afraid I must leave."

Copperfield glanced at him carefully, then crossed deliberately to the door and leaned on it, facing Eberlin and fixing him with a cherubic smile of utter complacency.

"I've heard a lot about you, but never had the pleasure of meeting you before. Frazer thinks very highly of you."

Eberlin stood in the center of the room, deadpan, and stared at a spot just above Copperfield's indecently covered scalp. There was no impatience or insolence in his attitude; he was just someone passing the time by standing still. The fat man gave a quick tug to the points of his waistcoat and picked at some imaginary fluff on his lower jacket.

"I've always felt that you were being wasted tied down to the office. It suits me because I'm a lazy sort of chap, not one to go running around. But you ... always surprised me ... you sticking it there. No ties or anything," and then looking up through his silly little glasses, "have you?"

"No."

"No, I thought that. No ties. I'm a married man myself–well, I look it don't I? Married. You must have gathered that from the way I was ogling the sexy little hostess. A man of your perception must have noticed that. It's very obvious. But I can't help it. I go to strip clubs on the sly. I'm that kind of man. I even have a collection of pornographic magazines at home, hidden away. Untouched photographs–they show everything. You know? He gestured. "Well, you can tell I'm the type who does things like that–by just, well, looking at me. I get the magazines from a friend of mine in C. and E. He's not really a–you speak Russian, don't you?"

"Yes."

"Well?"

"Yes."

"Say something in–no, that's silly. I speak it too but not too well. French, yes–but Russian, not too good I'm afraid."

He looked up quickly and appraised Eberlin with a diminutive smile. Eberlin stared back calmly and then said:

"Do you mind moving out of the way? I'm leaving." Copperfield did mind and ignored the question. "You were in North Africa recently, weren't you?" No answer.

"Tangiers, wasn't it?" "Tripoli."

"Oh yes. Tripoli. Of course. I don't know why I said Tangiers.

Nightingale, I suppose.... Speak Arabic at all?" "No."

"No. Well, who does nowadays?"

Copperfield was suddenly propelled forward into the room and away from the door he had been leaning on, as it was pushed open from the outside suddenly and Caroline stood staring in, lower lip under top, at the two men in the study.

"Oh, I'm sorry. I didn't know–"

She turned to move away, when Eberlin stepped forward smiling.

"It's all right. I was just leaving."

She caught Copperfield's sudden look of anger as he turned quickly back toward the door.

"Do you have to?" she asked.

"I'm afraid so. I have some work to do."

He brushed past her and made quickly for the top of the staircase. Copperfield shouted after him:

"Can I give you a lift? I heard you pranged your car in France."
"No, thank you."

And he was down the stairs, carefully, followed by a breathless Caroline, and picking up his coat from the chaise longue, and down the second flight toward the front door and into the street. He pulled the coat on, glancing around him. Caroline ran out after him in her bare feet.

"I'm sorry you have to go. You will come round again, won't you?"

But he didn't answer, leaving her gazing after him as he strolled cautiously down the road to the main junction. At one point he glanced back and caught signt of Copperfield quickly pulling away from the study window, and then a taxi lurched into range, and he was running toward it. It was nine fifty-five and he was late.

* * *

He sat in the taxi thinking about Copperfield. It was inconceivable that *he* was the reason that he was asked to attend the party. But who else? What else? Hardly jolly old Caroline and the ghosts of Mummy's lovers. Copperfield then, with all his innuendos. It had to be him. Not a very subtle encounter whichever way you looked at it–but then these things rarely were. A cryptic message by a recognized route, with the words *Amontillado Caroline* on it, and one is supposed to play along with the whole infantile absurdity of the affair. Eberlin would gladly opt out of the whole business tomorrow but it wasn't that easy. He leaned forward and told the driver to change direction and go to the rear of the New Victoria cinema, by way of Hyde Park Corner. The taxi demonstrated a smart right turn into Montpelier Street, and then eased into the Brompton Road. A street clock opposite Harrod's said ten five but was probably fast.

It had all started when he arrived in Fngland for the first time to attend Oriel College, Oxford. His public life–though that was hardly the word; it was more private than his private –was predestined from then on. A first class Honors degree and a postgraduate course in Medieval Warfare, of all things, and then straight into the Ministry, after all the necessary pulls and pushes and committed dinners were finally over. He had spent four years in Africa, based in Entebbe, doing nothing. The British Government was admirably tolerant at his lack of duty there. To them, the very effort of surviving outside

England for a length of time was an art in itself. Eberlin would send letters back reporting the state of the banana crop and the decline and fall of the okapi. Once, in a mood of utter depression, he had copied a whole letter, word for word, from one of Evelyn Waugh's books, about that wretched fellow who was sent to Africa as a correspondent. Eberlin had picked it up in the nearby NAAFI and found cold comfort in the story. Two days after sending the copied letter, he received the reply: MESSAGE RECEIVED, GOOD WORK. B. Then followed six months in Berlin and four months alone, except for the wild horses that took him there, in Abadan. He was now back in London and destined to be lodged there permanently, it seemed. One year ago, he had written *Ex Libris* on the flyleaf of his passport, and burned his suitcase.

The taxi stopped outside the cinema, blocking the narrow road. Eberlin paid the driver, walked quickly through the narrow corridor into Victoria Station and across the cold expanse of platform and then out onto the front of the station, and climbed into a second taxi and headed south of the river.

Twenty minutes later he was sitting, hunched up against the night wind, on a bench on the South Bank, staring across the Thames at Charing Cross Embankment, a cigarette clenched in his teeth. It was ten thirty-five and he was five minutes over the time. He glanced around, but there was no one in sight on the tiled public terrace except two lovers on a neighboring bench, a lamp exhibiting them to the world. Eberlin stared without interest at the man's face peering over the girl's shoulder. The girl had her eyes closed, head back, legs angled, while the man, sitting next to her in a green duffel coat, seemed to be exploring the crotch of the girl with his left hand

and, as Eberlin saw it, picking his ear with his right. Eberlin stared blandly at the common tastelessness of it all, ignoring the man's furious glares, wondering if the people he had to meet had come and gone. He got up and walked to the edge of the embankment and stared into the river. Perhaps he should leave now. He turned away, throwing his cigarette into the Thames.

Ahead of him was Hungerford Bridge, and he peered into the dark shapes of concrete flower beds and dark recesses of buildings and trees as he approached it. He reached the bottom of the long flight of stone, steep steps leading up by the Festival Hall, and began to climb them, his footsteps resounding on the concrete, pulling himself up with the aid of the metal rail on the wall. It was quiet now and dark and his horizon had suddenly been reduced to a square block of starred sky at the top of the steps high above him. He reached the top of the first slab of stairs and then he saw them. They were standing in the darkness of a small alcove, halfway up the flight, and were staring down at him, white smudges of face in the gloom. Eberlin hesitated, then the two Russians began to descend the steps, and in thirteen seconds they had met. They stood leaning against the right, high wall, breathing heavily, and offered around cigarettes. One of them remarked that he had just been reading the placards outside the Hall and that Ravel's *Piano Concerto in G* was to be played on Tuesday. His companion said that he liked that very much, especially the piano sequence in the second movement. It was agreed that that was indeed a fine piano sequence. Eberlin said nothing but stared, depressed, down the steep steps toward the concrete plateau of benches and flowerpots below. The couple were still there, performing their digital pas-de-deux under the spot of yellow light. A ship sounded off on the Thames behind him, and one of the men said:

"You were late."

Eberlin accepted a light for his cigarette and nodded.

"When you hadn't arrived by half past ten we anticipated your movements and waited here. You were watching those two on the bench."

"Yes."

"Mmmm."

Eberlin gave a quick shudder and said, "Do you mind if we walk up the steps?"

"Not at all."

They began to climb the steps in silence, Eberlin between the two men. When they reached the top and stood twenty yards or so away from the base of the bridge, one of them said:

"Krasnevin?"

"Yes?" Eberlin replied.

"Why did you want to see us?" "Not you."

"Pavell refuses to discuss it further."

"I would still like to talk to him myself." "It is out of the question."

And the second man said, "Utterly."

Eberlin sighed. He walked a little behind the others as they approached the first few wooden steps of Hungerford Bridge. A train rattled endlessly over the bridge above their heads, shattered lights picking out the web of steel by the side of and under the lines. He looked up. One of the many things he admired about England was the bridges. Not that he was interested in engineering in any way, but as a child in Russia he had read a book about how one of the bridges of London was once covered in houses, like a living umbilical cord between the two parts of the city. Was it Waterloo Bridge? *Waterloo Bridge is falling down, falling down*–no, that couldn't be it. What does it matter? He caught up with the two men and said:

"I only want to speak to him for ten minutes. He can't refuse me that."

The men didn't answer. One of them began to climb the steps of the bridge, but the other stopped him and shook his head. They crossed instead under the steps and into the shadows.

"What did you think of the party?" "Not Copperfield?" asked Eberlin. "To a degree."

"He works for Brogue." "The Negro?"

"Yes." "Important?" "To a degree." "Of course."

"It's imperative that I meet Pavel." "Why?"

Why? They might well ask. Big Ben struck ten forty-five and they heard someone above them running down the wooden steps, and a different sound as a man came into view on the concrete and hurried away from them, not seeing them, and disappeared behind the building. Eberlin trod on his cigarette.

"I at least should be worth something more than a couple of zombies like you."

The men laughed. Eberlin had said the word *zombies* in English, which amused the men. They laughed again and repeated the word. Eberlin felt sick. He swore loudly, broke out of the darkness, and began to walk toward the bridge. They allowed him to reach the first step, then one of them, an impish little man who had fought at Stalingrad, ran after him and said quietly:

"Comrade Krasnevin."

Eberlin stopped and looked at him. "Pavel is waiting for you in the car."

The man beamed with self-pleasure and Eberlin controlled a further expletive.

"Where?" he asked.

"Where else?" was the answer.

His companion joined him and the two men walked quickly up the steps over Eberlin's head, leaving him alone again. He stood holding his breath until he could hear them no more, then nervously lighting another cigarette, he walked quickly in the opposite direction.

* * *

"Who are you now–Krasnevin or Eberlin?" "I don't care."

"Well, are we to speak Russian or English?" "As you wish."

"I thought this was important?" "It is."

"Well then."

Eberlin sighed heavily, slumped farther down in the seat of the car, and stared fixedly out of the window at the night outside. The small Volkswagen was parked in a dark lane ten miles north of London. The main road to Oxford and the North was behind them and below them and they could hear the low rumble of heavy night lorries commuting back and forth. Pavel was sitting next to Eberlin in the front seat, in front of the wheel. They didn't speak for a long while, then Pavel said casually, his hand reaching toward the radio:

"Do you want some music?" Eberlin shook his head.

"It might clear the air."

"No," Eberlin replied. A silence and Pavel drummed lightly on the rim of the steering wheel, avoiding Eberlin's eye. Finally, he lowered the window on his side, leaned slightly out of it on his elbow and said quietly:

"You mustn't think that I'm against you. I'm not. I understand you more than you think but–"

"I don't want understanding. I don't want to be treated like a sick child or some naïve idiot who has to be humored–"

"I'm not humoring you."

"What else are you doing then?" "I've told you–I'm–"

"Throwing platitudes at me like rice at a wedding." "Well, what else can I say? You know I can't–" "It doesn't matter."

"Yes, it does."

"No, it doesn't. And close the window before we invite an audience."

Pavel did so. He glanced at Eberlin. "I'm sorry."

"That's all right," replied Eberlin quickly. "It's my fault." "No, it was mine."

"No, really, it was–" Eberlin stopped and smiled. Pavel relaxed and took a Schimmelpenninck *Duet* from the glove compartment with his left hand and put it in his mouth. Eberlin lit it with a silver lighter.

"Attractive lighter," Pavel remarked. "German."

"Is it? You surprise me. I didn't know they made such–" "*West* German."

"Oh, I see."

Pavel was a small man, thin on top and in the body. He was ten years older than Eberlin and had known him all his life. They liked each other very much and regretted bitterly the fact that they could never risk meeting together socially for a drink or idle conversation. Pavel had been married once, to a Hungarian girl whom he had met during the war. They had lived first of all in Budapest and then after the war moved to Leningrad, a town they both had loved very much. However, when Pavel was established in Soviet Military Intelligence, he was posted to Moscow, often not seeing his wife for a period of months. Inevitably, the marriage began to break apart and one day, returning home, he found nothing but his own few possessions and no note. He never inquired after her whereabouts nor even sought a divorce, but merely asked to be posted somewhere else. They sent him to Berlin, where he met Eberlin once more, and then to London. He never saw his wife again.

"Why exactly *do* you want to return to Russia?" he said suddenly.

"I've told you."

"No, not that. I know you too well. It's more than love of the old country and all that."

"Everything is too out of proportion now," said Eberlin softly. "The whole thing. I'm not objecting to what I do–no, that's a lie, but we all feel that. No. I feel caged in. It was all right at the beginning when I was younger and keen and just working for Kuzmich, but it's not that anymore. I'm working for the British as well–up to here. And it's all getting out of hand...."

"You knew that. You didn't go into it blindfolded."

"Not blindfolded perhaps, but I had something then. I had ..."

Eberlin turned away and stared at the dark fields outside and the black trees blocked around them.

"*What* did you have?" Pavel asked. "Enthusiasm," Eberlin replied, "enthusiasm."

There was a silence in the car, then Pavel said very clearly and without emotion:

"You know what you are saying, don't you?"

Sensing the tone of the voice, he turned and caught Pavel staring at him coldly. Eberlin pulled a wry face and laughed.

"Oh, come now–I'm not thinking of defecting or joining the British or anything like that. Is that what you're thinking?"

"I wasn't sure...."

"You know me better than that–my loyalties haven't changed.

Only my attitude to my job, that's all."

"Has the killing of Nightingale anything to do with it?" "No. Yes. No–I don't know. No, of course it hasn't." "What about the other man? He neither?"

"Killing those men isn't the heart of it. To me it was just an expediency. No, not that. Everything's just snowballing in size every second and I don't think, if it gets any bigger, that I'm the right man to cope with it. For my sake and for the sake of everybody, I ought to be sent back to Moscow."

He opened the car door suddenly and got out into the lane and closed the door behind him, leaving Pavel sitting inside. Eberlin walked onto the damp verge and over a ditch and into a sloping field that stretched down toward the highway. His shoes squelched as he trod carefully over the wet grass to the brow of the field and stood looking down at the shifting headlights below, like a broken, dejected scarecrow. It wasn't long before he heard the dulled slam of a car door and then, shoulders hunched forward, Pavel made his way over the grass too and joined him, and they both stood silently looking at nothing. Then, with a light touch on Eberlin's sleeve with his hand,

Pavel said quietly, "We'd better get back."

They both turned and returned to the car and sat back in the seats. The doors were shut. Pavel reversed the car slightly, nosed it toward the main road and then eased into the traffic. There was a roar and an E-type Jaguar hurtled past, and they both stared at the receding white rear of the car highlighted in the headlights and then it was gone. Pavel switched on the radio and late night BBC music petered out into the stillness of the car.

"You've been in England sixteen years now, haven't you?" asked Pavel after a while.

"Eighteen."

"Eighteen? As long as that? You must be–thirty-five, thirty-*six* now. Thirty-six?"

"Yes."

"Time passes. Have you still got that odd little man cleaning up for you?"

"Yes. But he's not a cleaner, he's a manservant." "Oh really?"

Eberlin smiled.

"Well, well," murmured Pavel, and then, "This is a nice piece of music, don't you think?"

Eberlin had come into the country at the age of eighteen with a trunk of textbooks, ink-stained exercise books with essays ranging from *My Holiday* to *The Great Vowel Shift and Its Effects*, photos of himself and other schoolchildren standing before the Taj Mahal, and one of him holding the ear of an elephant near Delhi, slightly out of focus. He had entered Oriel College with an impeccable background, filled with Kiplingesque memories of British India. It was a façade he had enjoyed, for he had never been near India in his life. At the age of sixteen, he had entered an offshoot of Pugachev, the Soviet Military College near Kiev, and had graduated from there immediately to Oxford to assume the identity of the fictitious English boy, Eberlin. The foundation work was faultless. It was part of a system instituted as long ago as 1927 by Stalin, who even then saw Communism as an international movement of subterfuge and infiltration, and the operation could roughly and badly be translated as *Wine Cask Fill*–a clumsy expression of which the nearest English equivalent might be "New Wine in Old Bottles." At times, even, a preselected English child of the right background was trained in England from birth, and then at a certain age, after establishing roots in relevant sectors, was transported to Moscow or, as it was later, Kiev, to be replaced by a trained Russian complement, who would pick up the roots and carry on. On paper it looked fallible. In practice, it was without error. Eberlin himself knew of a Tory M.P. of a northern constituency whose loyalties ranged much further than the House of Commons. He had met, as a pupil in Pugachev, a brash, ebullient young fellow called Dubrovsky who had been a year ahead of him, and whom he knew now to be a Republican general in the U.S. Army. He had met him once vaguely in the Fish Room at the White House, during a cocktail party of Eisenhower's in 1960. Eberlin couldn't stand either of them. He had met Senator John Kennedy there too, and had liked him as a man but despaired of his implicit trust in his associates. The assassination three years later came as a shock but as no surprise. On the day of it, he received a bottle of Haig tied in a blue ribbon, from a member of the Ministry. He poured it, nauseated, down the sink. The next morning, he received a message from Pascal that read simply: AM WEARING A BLACK TIE UNDER MY RED. Eberlin, like many liberal Communists, questioned much of their dogma, but adhered to its basic tenet passionately. If asked, Eberlin would not admit to it, but in essence he was an ultra-extreme Socialist in the English sense. But it all, brought down in the final analysis, had no point whatsoever.

"What you said about not caring …" said Pavel. "It's the wrong word, but I can't think of a better."

"Well anyway," Pavel added, "I won't say anything about it." "I had to tell you."

"Yes, I appreciate that, but I think it wise if I … forgot all about it. I'll tell Kuzmich that you would like a transfer back home and advise him accordingly, but I must say this–I don't think he'll agree. You're too valuable here."

"Or not, as the case may be," uttered Eberlin with a trace of bitterness, and switched off the radio.

"I'm sorry," said Pavel after a pause.

Eberlin glanced across at him. "I wish I didn't have to involve you in this."

"I'd be hurt if you didn't," and then: "Oh by the way–how was Caroline?"

"Caroline who? You're driving too fast."

"Didn't you attend her party tonight–or is it yesterday now?

Yes, yesterday."

"Oh. Oh yes. Did you know Copperfield would be there?"

"I wasn't sure. There's a frantic turmoil there, as you've probably gathered. Might be something to do with your killing Nighingale."

They were now approaching the outskirts of Central London and leaving the main highway.

"He wore a toupee." "Who? Copperfield?" "No. Nightingale."

"Oh yes? Have you met that Negro fellow recently?" "Brogue? No, not for a week or so."

"He's an interesting man but unlikely to go very far. A desk man. Weak. He's a pederast, you know."

"So you told me."

"They've been making inquiries about you," remarked Pavell casually. "Oh, pretty harmless, but with probings here and there. You know the sort of thing."

"Heston-Stevas took me for a drink for the first time in years. I rather like him."

"Interesting. Out of simple curiosity, what *did* you think of Caroline Sue Hetherington?"

"Why? Do you know her?"

"No. But I've met her mother, who is adorable." "You'd better leave me near Kilburn."

"As you wish."

They arrived in the small dark streets of North London at one fifteen in the morning. The car stopped in a quiet side street and the engine was cut.

"When will I hear?"

"I'll talk to them first thing tomorrow. You will know in the morning."

"Edwards?"

"Yes. Krasnevin–"

"I know. The answer will be no." "I can't promise otherwise."

Eberlin pulled the coat from the back of the car onto his lap. "Still the dandy," remarked Pavel with a smile.

“My only vice,” replied Eberlin, “and all on Ministry salary.” “I should hope so. Anyway, if you ever do return east, you’ll be

a rich man.”

“Ah, but there I won’t be able to advertise it so easily.”

He held out his hand to Pavel and they shook hands warmly. “I’ll do all I can,” Pavel said quietly and turned away to start

the engine of the car. Eberlin looked at the long-nosed profile of his friend, then opened the car door quickly and closed it behind him without looking back. The Volkswagen drove off abruptly and Eberlin stood in the chill August night for a moment, then put on his coat, glanced around and walked casually toward Marble Arch. After fifteen minutes he took a taxi to Charlotte Street and then another–God! how he missed having the car–back to Park Lane. From there he walked the few yards to South Street. In ten minutes he was undressed and in his large double bed, and slept soundly for all of half an hour of the remaining night. Coming out of a sweat of irritation and into the dryness of oncoming slumber, he was brought fully conscious by the penetrating jar of the telephone, nine inches from his ear. He opened his eyes and was horrified to find not only that it was eight thirty-five, but that it was sunny as well. He picked up the phone.

2

80E 944776

Copperfield is a pathetic creature. I swear if you trained him as a cobbler, children would be born without feet.
–ALEXANDER EBERLIN

THE voice on the other end of the line was high-pitched and asthmatic. Eberlin recognized it at once.

"What do you want, Copperfield?" he said irritably. "Eberlin?"

"Yes."

"At last. I phoned you three times last night."

Eberlin pulled back the bedcovers with his foot and lay on the bed gazing at the ceiling. He tucked the phone under his chin, and reached for the cigarettes. What day was it? Must be Friday. He glanced at the bedside table. Friday it was. And the damn thirteenth as well. Ah, well.

"Eberlin? You still there?" "What do you want?"

Eberlin had a profound resentment for the telephone. One was compelled to look one's listener straight in the eye.

"Did I wake you … or anything?" "Copperfield–will you tell me what you want?"

"Well it's not me really. It's Brogue. He wants to see you this morning."

"And?"

"You're sure I'm not disturbing you? You must have been out late last night, because I phoned at–"

"What time does he want to see me?" "Ten thirty."

Ten thirty? Too early. He wouldn't know by then. Perhaps eleven. No, that was cutting it too fine.

"I'll see him at eleven fifteen," he said.

"He rather hoped you could make it earlier."

"I'll be in the office by eleven fifteen. Good-bye." He put down the phone.

Eberlin sat up and twisted his legs around, sat on the edge of the bed and stared at a Beardsley print on the far wall and considered the day. Two decisions or nondecisions lay in store. Both on the surface unfavorable, and yet perhaps of slight importance in the plan he had resolved on during the night, a decision of utter selfishness and consequently full of the purest integrity. He stood up and drew back the curtains. The sun hit him with the force of a tank, a situation that was not altogether favorable. And so he drew the curtains together again, put a record on of *Les Temps Difficiles* by Léo Ferré which some Parisian bore had sent him and which, much to his disdain, he found he liked, and began the morning ritual.

Stripping off the white silk pajamas, he walked with growing confidence into the bathroom, and showered in ice-cold water, in a shower built to a design he had seen in Berlin. The bather sealed himself into a glass coffin and was impaled by bolts of water thrust at him, at infinite velocity, from every angle. After three minutes one felt fit for anything. Or nothing. After five minutes Eberlin felt fit, if not for anything, at least for Kuzmich and Brogue. He dried himself on a rough towel and began to dress. Normally the procedure of shaving, massage and clothes took seventy-five minutes, but today, due to the hour, Eberlin had to complete it all in half the time. At nine forty-five he was fully dressed, more composed and looking for his hat. He never breakfasted, since his metabolism was of a nature that denied him such a luxury, tending to make him feel sluggish and heavy after a first meal. He made do with one glass of pure orange juice, four cups of black instant coffee (paradoxically, though he was petty and particular over possessions and clothes, he never pruned his taste buds, considering food nothing more than a basic necessity to be completed as painlessly and quickly as possible), three cigarettes and one apple. By nine fifty he was in South Street and walking east into Farm Street, then through to Berkeley Square, and across around Grafton Street into Albemarle. By ten fifteen he was at the Bank in St. James's fearing the worst.

It was a small bank, with one of those odd exteriors, half-mock, half-genuine bizarre, that impressed on one the right air of guilt and self-consciousness as one entered the heavy swing door. In time the

whole corner block was to be demolished and replaced by glass-walled offices, and already various tweedy subordinates from the Council had visited the spot with note pads and cameras and studied the site from all angles, then gone away to prepare plans. Eberlin, when told of it, regretted the change, having acquired over the years a deep affection for the exterior of London. To him, there were two almost unique capital cities left in the Western world–Lisbon and Vienna, and perhaps Moscow, but then he hadn't seen that for twenty years. He entered the bank.

There were two men standing before the only available counter, one patiently watching the other being served. The teller's name was written in gold capitals on the open window. It read: MR. J. K. EDWARDS, who, as Eberlin knew, was a small, sad-faced man who favored his hair parted in the middle and wore large white stiff collars and broad-lapelled suits. Together with his long face, seemingly perpetually in a state of wonder, he reminded one of a Mack Sennet bit player. Eberlin saw with comfort that the clock was now ten nineteen, so he walked to the queue of two and waited, gazing idly at the clerks on the far side of the second partition. Brogue came into his mind for no apparent reason, and he wondered for the first time why he was actually required. It all seemed slightly disturbing, especially since Brogue's department was concerned with off-base direct action, an area he had so far, on the British side, been kept well away from. The prospect of entering into a field of British Intelligence directly complementary to his work for the K.G.B. was, if nothing else, slightly unnerving. But anyway, Brogue hadn't the authority to put forward such a proposition. He was only–

"Yes, sir?"

Mr. J. K. Edwards was looking up at him with an air of pained interest. Eberlin realized that the queue was now behind him. He approached closer to the counter and said:

"Could I have a check, please?"

The teller replied, "I presume you have an account here, sir."

"Yes, I have," Eberlin said and pushed two pennies across the counter. The teller glanced at them, then put them on one side, on their own. He handed over a blank check with a thank you, which Eberlin took with a counter thank you and a nod, and walked with it to a table. Using a bank pen, he filled in the check for ten pounds to be paid CASH to himself, and signed it *Alexander Eberlin.* Drying it, he returned to the counter and handed over the check, received ten single-pound notes from Edwards, and walked out of the bank. It was then ten twenty-three. The simple procedure had lasted three minutes only, and in a further fifteen Eberlin was back in his flat, locking the front door and the bathroom door behind him.

With growing apprehension, he laid the ten pound notes on the bathroom shelf and checked the numbers, dismissing them in turn until he reached the eighth. The number of that was: 80E 944776. Eberlin returned the nine other notes to his wallet and took the selected one over to the sink. He slowly filled the sink half full with cold water, added some prepared hypo, and floated the banknote on the surface until both sides were lightly wet. Holding it by one corner, he then held it before the strong shaving light above his head, and studied the central circular design for Kuzmich's answer. It was there, carefully hidden, but there, and Eberlin's pessimistic fears were wretchedly confirmed. Printed in small neat capitals barely an eighth of an inch high, in the maze of repetitive BANK OF ENGLAND, was the simple and definitive word–NIET.

Eberlin cursed loudly, emptied the sink, rinsed it out, destroyed the note, slammed the front door and strode angrily up South Street to No. 4 Chesterfield Street, staring straight ahead and acknowledging no one. When he arrived at eleven ten, Copperfield and Heston-

Stevas were waiting in the outer office with silly grins on their faces, like two bashful suitors in the court of Du Barry.

* * *

Miss Heather Vogler was an appreciative girl at heart, a fact that was rather unfortunate since her body was designed by Praxiteles.

Moreover, there was a sweetness about her face, a seductive texture that made her a cynosure, pleasant to be seen with at all but the most austere public and private occasions. She had discovered at an early age that men who were interested in women's clothing were rarely interested in women, whereas men who really liked women never noticed what they wore. And so, she never peacocked herself with the latest fads and kinks of fashion, but dressed imperceptibly simply, and was never without a lover. An intelligent girl by any standard, she therefore never revealed her intelligence to a man, but cosseted him by being impartial, never flattered him for the sake of it nor praised him in public, never treated him with a laughing toleration nor embarrassed him by being too familiar before others.

She could neither include him in talk of future days nor let him think that she would not be there, if he wished it. She respected his work, so never opened discussion on it, and respected his friends and so never demanded to be accepted by them. And for the time she was with him, whether it be one night or a thousand and one, she cared for him above all She gossiped never, talked little and never lingered over people known only to her, nor did she discuss ex-lovers, either hers or his, but always retained an independence that insured their security. She never, in a slump-shouldered pose, complained of being lonely, neglected, ignored or tired, nor, on entering a man's apartment she had known intimately, did she inspect the dust. Conscious of being a woman, she had learned to cook, dance and make love with a sensible degree of aptitude; and when the affair was over, she never resorted to tears or threats, however subtle, or played on his weaker virtues, in order to further it for another second. She would instead leave without a grudge or offers of platonism, wash her hair and consider again. Mindless and unheeding of the accumulated grouses and misexperiences of woman, she viewed life and love with only the freshness of her own entity, and in that she out-Eved Eve. Miss Heather Vogler was a rare, rare creature.

Then one morning, in late February, quite suddenly, that jewel, that quintessence of all things feminine, that unique girl, was crushed, made distrustful, something broken, a bitter scarred generalization of the mass. For on that day she met Emmanuel Gatiss, and that rare individuality was over. In three months with him, there was little left, and she was transferred, a tragic wreck, to Eberlin's office and he took her in as a secretary, giving her his shoulder and nothing more. Emmanuel Gatiss, self-coded EPSILON/32/Y, highest-paid agent in British Intelligence, was sent by a concerned department to Istanbul and then to Munich, to pursue an operation the office boy could achieve. The trip was partly Eberlin's suggestion, for he had begun to fear him, believing that if any man could reveal his cover and strike home, it would be Gatiss. Neither he nor Miss Vogler, as they stood in the outer office at eleven fifteen that morning, knew that Gatiss was to be back in London the next day. Copperfield knew it, however, and was smiling broadly as he said:

"Good morning, Eberlin, and how are you? I've been talking to Vogler here. We've been having a chat. Heston-Stevas and I have been having a little chat. A little bit of a parley. Haven't we, Vogler?"

He fluttered his eyes, and Heston-Stevas, his face slightly flushed, said, "Hell, Eberlin. I'm afraid I pinched one of your cigarettes. Hope you don't mind?"

Eberlin, quickly glancing into the inner office, said, "Where's Brogue?"

Copperfield looked up, puzzled, then with a smile picked up a typewriter eraser from the floor where Miss Vogler had dropped it, and returned it to her, lingering with a hand on hers. Eberlin walked toward the door.

"Tell Brogue I will see him this afternoon."

Heston-Stevas, flustered, glanced at his companion and put up one hand ineffectually to stop Eberlin.

"He's waiting upstairs now," Copperfield uttered quietly, staring directly at the door, his face wiped clean of earlier pleasantry. "In his office."

Eberlin studied the two men for a moment, then said, quickly, "Vogler," turned and left the office, with Miss Vogler hurrying after him, watched idly by the two men. Then they were left alone. Copperfield lowered his voice, put his arm around Heston-Stevas' shoulder, glanced around and said in confidence:

"There is also the question of Vogler. Tell me, Paul, who has her services if Eberlin goes?"

Heston-Stevas replied self-consciously, "I already have a secretary. Haven't you?"

Copperfield laughed loudly, gulping for air, and left the room.

* * *

They took the manually controlled lift to the next floor, and then walked down the green and cream corridors, bearing left toward the southern corner of the building, she clutching a note pad and pencil to her Jaeger-covered breasts, he avoiding her eye, arms by his side. "Am I walking too fast?" Eberlin said suddenly.

* * *

V

PRI MD WHI

12. 8. 65 KSB 285

FROM MD K FIN/CC/WTG/HOC TO FRAZER CHEST-FLD. LP5/3 CC EBRL. /NB/LAJ

REF YOUR TELEPRINT 800 128 KSB 268 QUOTE CONCUR PM CONCUR HEALEY UNQUOTE. LEAP FORTH. BEANTHALL. /532Z/K/LP

* * *

COL 268 4 4

KSB

PRI JJ LON

"I must admit your references are excellent," said Brogue, taking off his glasses and looking straight into Eberlin's eyes. "You'd better sit down."

The office was large, painted green and devoid of any pictures, ornaments or other personal embellishments except for a portrait of Queen Elizabeth the Second by Annigoni and a print of *Cowper Thornhill's Ride Between Stilton and London.* Behind Brogue's head, Eberlin could see the small square outside filled with trees and no people, pleasant and inviting in the August sunshine. He stood in the center of the room looking down at Brogue who was sitting, swiveling gently from side to side, in the mahogany chair and toying with a bone cigar holder.

"I'd rather stand," replied Eberlin. "It would help you come to the point."

A faint flicker of annoyance crossed Brogue's yellow-brown eyes and then he smiled and glanced at Miss Vogler, hovering indelicately behind Eberlin, all in beige and head down and toes turned in.

"Wait outside, Vogler," he told her.

Miss Vogler turned toward the door.

"Stay here," Eberlin said quietly, "stay in here." He looked casually out of the window.

The Negro took a beat and lit a cigar slowly, taking his time, observing Eberlin intently. Someone knocked on the door, waited, then hurried away. Brogue leaned back in the chair.

"I'm afraid what I have to say is private. I want your secretary to leave."

"She's a private secretary. You have not the position to tell me anything she couldn't hear. We stay."

"I see."

With slow deliberation, Brogue got up and walked to the other side of the room and picked up an ashtray from a corner table. He then stood there, holding the glass object, studying the other two occupants of the room, standing in profile.

"Vogler–how long have you been working here?"

She moved her head in his direction, wide-eyed, a pretty neck emerging from the white frill collar. A delicate nose.

"For Mr. Eberlin?" "Altogether. How long?" "Three years."

"Three. Sit down."

She glanced at Eberlin and he nodded, and then she crossed to a straight-backed chair in the other corner and sat down, crossing her legs, adjusting her skirt. Eberlin remained standing, like a fulcrum, in the center of the room. Brogue walked quietly over the thick-pile carpet and stood behind Eberlin, the cigar in one hand, the ashtray in the other, his great hulk towering over the other man.

"You dress well, don't you?" His voice was curt and insinuating. "If you have called me here for the name of my tailor, he's in

the book."

Brogue smiled and puffed a column of smoke onto Eberlin's shoulder, so that it hung on the weave of the jacket, then circled, dispersed and floated to the ceiling. Miss Vogler sat stiffly away from it all, her hands clasped tightly on her lap, slight sweat emerging in the center of her back and between her breasts. The Negro gave a short deep laugh, slapped Eberlin's back hard, and returned behind the desk, standing there, a huge, self-satisfied grin on his face. He

picked up a red file from the desk, marked CONFIDENTIAL EX. F3, and held it up over his head like a banner.

"This is you in my hand, Eberlin. Ninety-six pages all dedicated to you. Catch!"

He suddenly pretended to throw the file across the room, but held his hand. Eberlin made no attempt whatsoever to receive it, but kept his arms to his side, and then turned to Miss Vogler and said in a bored voice:

"Let us go back." She stood up.

"What did you think of Nightingale?" asked Brogue casually, ignoring Miss Vogler.

Eberlin, his hand on the door handle, paused and replied, "I never met the man."

"No?"

Eberlin sighed. "Your work on the three men who were killed was excellent. You knew of course why they were sent? What they were doing?"

"Of course."

"Did their deaths surprise you?"

"My relations with them went only as far as the inside of this building. I am employed as an organizer, not a guardian angel."

'Yes. Yes, so you are. Please come back into the room. I have very little to say."

Brogue sat down again, throwing the file before him on the desk.

"Cigar?"

"No thank you."

Eberlin moved away from the door and walked to the corner table and poured a drink for himself. A Haig. Miss Vogler sat down again carefully because the chair creaked. The chair creaked.

"I am, as you are well aware, in no position to inform you of anything not related directly to my department."

Eberlin dropped two cubes of ice into the glass and rattled them like dice.

"But I would like to ask you two things."

Eberlin drank the whisky slowly, staring at the print in front of him. Brogue continued, swiveling once again in the chair.

"I want you to attend a d.b. on Monday next at Selvers. Eleven hundred hours. Will you be there?"

"Do I have a choice?"

"From me, yes. From Frazer, not one." "Then I'll be there."

"Jolly good." Brogue paused, then said, "You weren't at Nightingale's funeral, were you?"

"Were you?" "Yes."

"Was I there?" "No."

"Any more questions?" "No."

Eberlin put down the glass and returned to the door. Brogue stood up.

"Thank you for coming." He smiled at Eberlin, who looked at him deadpan and replied:

"It was hardly worth the ceremony, was it?"

The buzzer on the Negro's desk sounded and Miss Vyse's voice was heard to say, "Mr. Frazer is waiting outside, sir." and Brogue replied, "One moment," and flicked down the button and then picked up a silver snuffbox from the desk top.

"Oh, Eberlin, you're interested in this type of thing, aren't you? I bought it from Carter and Beckett."

Eberlin looked at it from across ten yards of carpet and dismissed it.

"I wrote to Carter and Beckett to discover the original owner. You see it has an inscription inside from George B. Apparently this chap George B. is George Brummell. The dandy."

"No."

Brogue gave a surprised laugh and added: "Oh, but yes. Beckett confirmed it."

"The snuffbox you have in your hand was made no earlier than 1880. It is too large, too clumsy and too vulgar to have belonged to George the *Fourth*, let alone George Brummell. On the other hand, it suits you admirably. Good day."

The Negro's jaw dropped down slightly and he stared at the

snuffbox in his hand. Then he dropped it onto the green leather blotter, turned his back on both of them and stared out of the window. Eberlin opened the door and went out as Miss Vogler crossed the office, clutching her notebook.

"Oh by the way, Vogler," Brogue muttered quietly, without turning around, "you may be interested to know that Emmanuel Gatiss will be here tomorrow. He's arriving on the seven o'clock plane."

Eberlin heard the words and hesitated, then caught Frazer's eye in the outer office and nodded, and walked past, walking quickly down the corridor to the lift. He heard Miss Vogler tip-tipping on the stone floor after him, hurrying to catch up, but he was in the lift and slamming the metal doors and pressing the *G* button and lighting a cigarette. His hand shook and he felt as if he was on the threshold of an enormous chasm.

It had been a long, long morning and he needed air.

3

Gatiss

Women, Vogler, are such extraordinary creatures. Their stubbornness never ceases to amaze me. Look at Henry the Eighth's sixth wife. I mean the woman was either a supreme optimist, or she never read the Court circulars.
–ALEXANDER EBERLIN

What do I do? I collect noses from statues.
–ALEXANDER EBERLIN

THE passenger in the rear seat of the BEA Viscount Flight 63 sat staring intently at the back of the Queen's Building through hornrimmed dark glasses, as the plane taxied to a halt at London Airport. He waited patiently till all the other passengers had left the aircraft, then got up and took his carryall from the ceiling rack, said "Good day" to the hostess, and walked out into the sun and down the steps and into the waiting coach. The other passengers took no notice as he sat casually, near the sliding door, arms folded, though the more perceptive might have noticed that he had taken no food nor drink throughout the flight, nor did he smoke or read, but sat still, arms constantly folded, looking out of the window for hours on end. He was a tall man, strongly built and sun-tanned, though it was evident from the ticket stub that he had just come from Munich, and his face was broad-jawed, high-cheek-boned, with an arrogant nose. Blond hair cut stylistically short. No rings, wrist bracelets or tie clips, though his few intimates knew him to have a Star of David hanging low on his chest on a gold chain.

The coach reached the Arrival building, and the man left first now, walking quickly up the glass-enclosed ramp to the Customs room. At the British barrier he showed his passport and was waved on to the Customs officers, who ignored his black leather suitcase, and then the man strolled casually into the long, early-morning waiting lounge and stood before a bookstand, idly gazing at a gardening weekly. Another man, in a pale gray suit, approached him

with a smile and touched his arm and said quietly, "Welcome back, Mr. Gatiss," and shook his hand, and then added, "The car is waiting outside," and the two men walked away through the crowd, walked away unhurriedly toward the exit.

***

Eberlin spent the following two days of the weekend in planned despair. Abandoning all self-imposed codes of etiquette, he banished the valet for three days, shaved never and drank one whole bottle of Emva Cream Sherry he found hidden among the shoe brushes. The full impact of the Friday hit him late the same evening, not that he hated the British plans less, but he loathed the Russian refusal to repatriate him more. He tried twice in blustering exposure to contact Pavel, but all contacts had been severed temporarily. He wandered wearily back to his room, pulled up a chair and sat staring at a point three feet beyond his eyes for two hours until the point disappeared because it had got dark; and he felt like a spoiled schoolboy.

Eberlin had no friends to visit nor did he wish to have them. Partly due to his own acquired self-sufficiency and partly due to the risk of cultivating confidants, he had shunned close relationships. When he was at Oxford, surrounded by dozens of attractive girls who admired him openly (downward smile, sidelong glance, tip of tongue pressed at front of upper palate) and dozens of earnest young men who admired him from afar (repeating his aphorisms, copying his clothes), Eberlin had written in his journal: "I added up my friends the other day. It was a difficult task but finally, after much drastic deliberation, I narrowed the number down to none."

Nor, in the later years, had he gone out of his way to seek the company of his countrymen. Like all European cities, London had its circle of Russian emigrés, mostly of a generation older than himself, and it was not rare for him to encounter relics of Czarist Russia at a cocktail party or a club. The meetings were always brief and impassionate, but he would still feel a pang of nostalgia on hearing that unique attack on the English vowels which only Russians possess, and on seeing faces he remembered in a million towns in the days of his boyhood. Two weeks before taking his degree he had visited the theatre with a fellow undergraduate called Brawne to see the Moscow Art Company in *The Cherry Orchard*. It had been a brutal evening. Later, Brawne had taken him–"You might be amused, Eberlin, you might be amused"–to visit an aged Russian Baroness who claimed a friendship with Chekhov himself. The woman had lived in a large flat in the fashionable part of London, and was surrounded, like Miss Haversham, by souvenirs and memories of her past–faded photos of herself, drapeaux from the court of Nicholas the Second, an icon or two. She had reminisced to them as they sat perched politely on a chaise longue, her eyes filled with visions of her romantic youth. Unconscious of Eberlin's knowledge of Russian, she would break off to talk to her housekeeper in her native language, and once Eberlin heard her say: "These boys are so innocent, so innocent. They think I'm mad, Tatyana, and sometimes I think perhaps I am," and the housekeeper keeper had merely replied, "*Tshay gotoff*." The three of them then had the tea and the Baroness showed a photo of herself as a pretty young woman, sitting in a droshky, wrapped in a fur coat and peering solemnly at the camera. It was a tender picture and Eberlin, for a moment, thought of his mother whom he had never known, and handed the picture back as if it were crystal.

The Baroness talked of Chekhov himself: "A sad, sad man but so kind," and then fell asleep in the chair before them, so that they had to sneak out of the apartment on tiptoes. Outside, Brawne, a normally garrulous man, merely said, "Proud isn't she?"

A month later, Eberlin read in the newspaper that the Baroness had been arrested for attempting to steal a bottle of cooking wine from a supermarket.

And so Eberlin remained in his apartment alone, thinking sometimes about Gatiss and Brogue, but mostly thinking of nothing. Once he hailed a taxi and said to the driver, "Drive east," and the driver said, "How far?" and he had replied, "Nowhere," and had got out again immediately, shamefaced, and hurried away, tripping over the curb edge and leaving the taxi still standing there bewildered. Once, late on the Saturday afternoon, he had visited the V and A and was taken to see his Sèvres collection and asked to be left alone. He sat in the vault surrounded by the samples of his extroversion and his taste, piled high around him, sat like Morgan at Panama among the spoils, sat like Napoleon in the shell of Moscow, sat staring at the porcelain; and then clamored to be let out and returned home again, and phoned back to the V and A telling them to take them, take them all, take everything without money, take them all. Empty the vault.

Once he spent one hour trying on every shirt he had until he tired and stood with the discarded shirts lying around his feet. "My failures," he said echoing Brummell, and left the room.

He got drunk again on Saturday evening. Alone he sat in the bedroom drinking whisky and listening to assorted music on the radio. He found he couldn't get better through the drink nor even music-hall, but slowly divorced himself from his identity and started talking to himself. Full of utter self-pity he phoned the West London Air Terminal and asked the time of the next plane to Moscow. When asked his name, he froze in horror and dropped the phone, sweating, and hurried out of the apartment and stood on the end of South Street watching his own front door. Then he got drunk again, and at ten thirty he phoned Heather Vogler at her apartment. She answered and he asked her what she was doing alone on a Saturday night and she started to cry and then he said he was drunk. She came over and sat next to him on the bed and cried and talked about Gatiss, and then they both sat miserably staring at the wall. Finally Eberlin got up and went into the bathroom and took off his clothes and showered and walked naked back to the bedroom, having forgotten she was there, and stood, staring at her in surprise and muttering "Excuse me," and got into bed.

She stood up and said, "I ought to go," and didn't move, and Eberlin looked at her standing there, the incredibly soiled-pretty flower of a thing, standing there in a white silk shift, standing there before him, and he apologized for himself, saying: "The biological act of procreation has its flaws. I know for a start that someone is walking around with my personality. But if you consider me a gentleman, please go now because I think I ought to sleep with you."

She then walked out without a word and closed the door and he heard her in the street hurrying away, and he turned over and went to sleep. He was waked up in the early hours of the morning by Heather Vogler as she returned and said she needed some things and got undressed and slipped into bed next to him and leaned her body against his back, trying to peer at his face, but he was asleep again. He awoke next morning alone, to the sound of church bells, and then sat around again all day doing nothing, and forgot about the day and went to bed early and woke up to find it was Monday and the day he had to go to Selvers. The damn weekend was over. It was there.

4

Selvers

Madness is constant betrayal.
–ALEXANDER EBERLIN

AT Charing Cross Station, he bought a single ticket to Wadhurst and was told that he would have to change at Tunbridge Wells, a situation he took with good humor. He walked across the platform to a small bar, and waited for the departure time. There were few seats in the room, so he stood clutching a pint of warm, thin beer, looking out of the window at the bustle of the station until it was time to go to the train. Being in a particularly reflective frame of mind and naturally antisocial, he chose a small, corridorless compartment, and sat by the window. He had bought a copy of all the newspapers, plus a *History Today*, a recent *Stern*, and copies each of White's *The Making of the President 1960* and Crane's *The Red Badge of Courage*; the former he always intended to read and the latter, not to reread, but to send to Vogler as promised. He placed the stack of reading matter beside him on the green seat, glanced through them all once, and then never touched them again throughout the journey. As he was slowly taken south out of London past the familiarities of the Festival Hall, and then through the southern suburbs, clean and surprisingly empty in the sunshine, Eberlin, grateful that the compartment had remained empty, found himself considering what might be in store. It seemed frighteningly probably that he would be asked to continue Nightingale's operation, which immediately would put him in a tricky situation regarding his loyalties. His duties to Pavel were not as informer, but, in basic terms, as assassin. Some passing of information had been involved, but he knew that he had been trained to kill the secret enemies of the Soviet Union such as Esau Pretty and Sidney Nightingale, and nothing more. This he had achieved with the minimum of difficulty apart from decapitating the Mistrale on the Route Nationale. If asked then, what to do? Impossible to contact Pavel, for some damning reason, which meant that the decision was in his lap. Eberlin considered taking the train all the way to Hastings and St. Leonard's, changing his name to Smith and abandoning the whole thing: flush it down a toilet, discard it, wash his hands of it, spit it out. But hardly a practical gesture.

The train was stopping at Sevenoaks now, and a man and his wife and two children whom they called Michael and what sounded like Shlemiehl but couldn't be, joined Eberlin in the compartment and ruined his concentration entirely. He took out a cigarette, requested a light from the father, who, red-faced, disturbed the order searching for a lighter, and then lit the cigarette with, "Knew I had it. Knew it was there," and tried to further the conversation. But Eberlin turned away and stared out of the window at the monotonous but beautiful southern countryside. Trees really are greener in England. Another one of those signs in the field. Three cows under a tree. One cow in a field. One horse in a field. A wooden bridge with a hole in it. Two more cows and a horse. Two more cows and a horse and another of those signs in a field. Three oast houses. Gatiss himself would be there without doubt. A row of Victorian houses without shutters but shutter hooks and Monday washing on the line. A blue boiler suit. Poetic working-class man living on the downs? Sounds like a crossword clue. That would be the reason he had flown back from Munich. Emmanuel Gatiss. A new white seat in an empty fields miles from anywhere. And what about Frazer? He too? I suppose a man must have crossed all those acres with a can of white paint in one hand and a brush in the other just to paint the bench. Sublime effort. Another cow in a field. He had never been to Selvers before. Might be interesting. He had never been to Wadhurst before. Let's face it, he had never been on this train before. Narrow life in the Ministry. Fourth one of those signs in a field. Consistent but a failure. Train going too fast to read the damn thing–looks like Watkinson's something. Watkinson's the Opticians? The Mistrale ought to be ready soon. It was entirely his fault but it ought to be ready. Where did he say I have to change? Tonbridge or Tunbridge Wells? Tunbridge Wells. Someone shouted "Tunbridge Wells" and Eberlin got out. Two more stations to go.

The second train arrived at the small Wadhurst station at ten forty and Eberlin got out. He was the only passenger who did. He looked up and down the empty platform and inquired about a taxi.

The Stationmaster smiled and walked away. What does one make of that? He stood gazing at an incredible collection of framed awards on the wall, certifying that this was the best-kept station in the

Southern Region for seven consecutive years except 1957. Slipped up that year, Wadhurst. Can't afford to slack where flowers are concerned. The stationmaster didn't return, so Eberlin walked out onto the gravel driveway outside and decided to walk. He had worked out that Selvers was about a mile from the station, mostly uphill, but it was a fine day and a pretty town, so walking would not be too disastrous. He strolled casually down the drive, past a row of coal bunkers and then up a steep hill toward the core of the town. He had just reached the top, sweating slightly, when a voice behind him said quietly, "Sir?"

He turned and saw a small, dark-haired man in a chauffeur's uniform, smiling up at him. Behind the man was parked a black Zodiac with the two inside doors open, the lower corners touching the banked grass verge of the road.

"I thought I might have missed you, sir."

Eberlin didn't answer at first, unsure, and prompted the chauffeur to screw up his eyes and inquire:

"You are Mr. Eberlin are you not, sir?"

"Yes," replied Eberlin finally, looking down at the station below him. "Yes I am."

The frown faded and the chauffeur smiled and gestured to the car. Eberlin nodded and walked back to the Zodiac and sat in the leather back seat as the chauffeur closed the door and sat in front and swung the car into the center of the road and up over the crest of the hill.

They both sat in silence. The car turned right at the center of the town–a village really–and down and up a long road, flanked by impressive bourgeois villas, and then down, out of the residential area and into the green, undulating farmland, past two converted oast houses and then turning left suddenly at a blue and white cottage and along a narrow lane, the car lurching on poor springs over shifting gravel. Ahead Eberlin could see an old clock tower, reading ten fifty-five, that suddenly emerged from a thick copse in the valley below and invisible to the main road. That must be Selvers. In two minutes the car was plunging down and entering under a red-brick archway and into a small quadrangle and parking neatly between a maroon Rolls Royce and a gray Jaguar Mark 10. Poised in one corner, wheels askance, trunk open, top down, open like an unwrapped parcel, stood a steel-blue Jensen with a dented fender. Gatiss was here. Eberlin climbed slowly out of the Zodiac.

It was very quiet except for the sounds of birds and the lazy far-distant stutter of a tractor, and he looked around. The building surrounding him looked like an old baronial manor or a small exclusive school for the rich. He could see that it was completely cut off from neighbouring farms and bungalows, lying as it was, nestled snug in a dip in the Sussex Downs, and guarded, no doubt, at night by dogs. But not, this morning, it was rather pleasant and he admired the leaded windows and the tall ornate chimney stacks. The chauffeur was suddenly walking away from him and he was left alone in the flower-bordered quadrangle.

There was a click and a small door opened in a corner of the square, and two men in dark suits appeared in the sunlight, screwing up their eyes against the light and talking rapidly to each other in high voices. They both saw Eberlin at the same time and stopped, silent, then the taller of the two smiled and walked toward him across the gravel, hand outstretched, thirty yards away. He was shouting

Hello Hello at him, then reaching him, shaking Eberlin's hand and saying, "So glad you could make it," as if he were welcoming him to a cocktail party or a hunt, and as if, no matter how polite, there had been any option.

"My name is Lake and that is Keats. If you just follow me, we'll take you to the rooms. Did you have a good journey? You've never been to Selvers before, have you? Isn't it a lovely day? Those are freak narcissi, by the way. They should come out in spring, as you know, but they don't. Rather unusual, don't you think? Mind the grass since it's newly seeded just there. What a beautiful day. *What* a beautiful day."

Into the sudden darkness of the interior of the building and along a broad, oak-paneled corridor hung with dull portraits of forgotten ancestors, Eberlin followed the two men chattering to each other ahead of him, and occasionally glancing back at him with a smile and a comment. They reached, finally, a long ground-floor room and entered. It was a billiards room of sumptuous opulence, decorated in pale pink and gold and lit by streaks of blinding sunlight. Dominating it was a white marble, female nude, standing bent forward clutching at frozen, fallen draperies, head on an angle, Grecian-profiled, cold bottom thrust into the air, stomach creased. A broken finger and a damaged toe. She looked with wistful apathy at the expanse of green-baized table at her feet. Eberlin entered the room cautiously and was puzzled to find it empty. He stood by the blackened, hollow fireplace and turned toward his guides. The two men hovered at the door, making no attempt to enter, and Lake said: "Drinks over there in that brown thing. Ought to be some Cinzano left if you like Cinzano. Glasses there, too. No ice, I'm afraid. Cigarettes in box and–

what else? Cigarettes in box. Oh–try to avoid playing billiards if you can possibly help it, because it's not, well, desired. Read a book if you like. Gibbons is there, I know. And some others. Do you like Thackeray? See you later."

The door was slammed and then reopened, and Lake put his head in again.

"Oh, by the way, the statue's name is Daphne. Greek and all that. Don't you think she's awfully passé?"

And the head disappeared as the door shut again and Eberlin heard the two men walking away, talking rapidly to each other once more for a moment. Then there was silence. He had been left alone.

One hour and thirty-five minutes later he was sent for.

* * *

Eberlin stared at Lake's fist. It was poised over the heavy door waiting for a reply from within. They were standing in a small anteroom and had been for ten minutes. Lake had been unnaturally quiet throughout, for which Eberlin was fully thankful since he had begun to shake slightly and was feeling decidedly nervous. Moreover, it was now almost one and he hadn't eaten a scrap of food all day. The door was opened by Heston-Stevas, who smiled self-consciously at Eberlin and stood aside to allow him to enter. Lake, like an irritating usher, stopped Eberlin at the door with a gesture and stepped into the center of the room with a smile.

"Mr. Eberlin, gentlemen," he announced and turned back and waved him in with an impatient flick of his hand. Heston-Stevas

closed the door behind them and Eberlin, steadying his nerves, paused to study the occupants of the room. The thick curtains had been closed so that the eight or nine men seated around a large table were in semidarkness, as if they were forcing mushrooms or taking part in an obscure séance. Lake took his arm and led him to the head of the table.

"You probably know all here, Mr. Eberlin, if only by name. Mr. Quince, Mr. Brogue, Sir Alistair Pond, Mr. Frazer, Colonel Flowers, and at the far end, Lieutenant Ridley and Mr. Moon. Oh, and over there are Mr. Heston-Stevas and Mr. Copperfield."

There were imperceptible nods and grunts and scrutiny, then Lake said:

"Please sit down here, Mr. Eberlin. In the witness box, so to speak. Or is it the dock? Ha ha. Would you like a drink or did you have one downstairs?"

"A very large, very strong whisky would be warmly welcome," replied Eberlin with an attempt at a grin.

"I'll see what there is," Lake said without humor, and left the room. Eberlin sat stiffly in the chair, adjusting his eyes to the gloom, attempting to pick out any telltale expression on the still, impassive blur of faces. He noticed that Gatiss wasn't there, and was somewhat relieved. Copperfield, the perfect foil, broke the silence.

"Did you have a good journey, Eberlin?"

Eberlin looked around and picked out the speaker by the glint of glasses and fatness of the belly.

"Pleasant, Copperfield. Pleasant. A train journey."

"Pity about your car being in Casualty. So useful aren't they?"
"Yes," Eberlin replied, "however I–"

"You've wrecked your car?"

The voice was unfamiliar and bit across the dialogue with searing attack. It had come from Pond, a thin bony man with piercing eyes, on Eberlin's left, who was not asking any idle question. This isn't a tea party, Eberlin thought, not in anyway at all. The question was repeated.

"I asked if you had wrecked your car." "Not exactly wrecked–"

"Speak up, we can't hear you."

"Not exactly wrecked. I was involved in a slight accident while driving through France."

"What do you mean *slight*? Is the car with you?" "No, but–"

"It had to be serviced?" "Yes."

"Then it was not *slight*. Please be accurate, Mr. Eberlin. What happened to your car?"

"The front was smashed in." "You mean the hood?"

"Yes ..."

"A head-on crash?"

"No. I swerved to avoid another car and deliberately drove into a tree. A poplar, I think, but can't be sure. It was a question of expediency."

"Expediency? You deny that it was your own fault?"

"Not exactly, but I could not have avoided the situation. I felt at the time that I did the correct thing."

"And now?"

"I beg your pardon?"

"Do you think you did the right thing now?" "Yes."

"Your whisky, Mr. Eberlin."

Eberlin looked up and saw Lake holding a small glass of whisky. He took it gratefully. He felt all eyes watching him as he controlled himself to sip the Scotch slowly. Colonel Flowers leaned forward and asked casually:

"What type of automobile do you drive, sir?" "Maserati Mistrale, Colonel."

"But that's not an English car is it?"

"Italian," Copperfield said suddenly from across the room. "It's an Italian sports car. Very fast. People race them at meetings."

"I see," said Colonel Flowers thoughtfully, and then, turning back to Eberlin, "Do you race yours, sir?"

"No."

"Yet you drive fast, sir?"

"Yes, but then I consider myself an excellent driver, Colonel."

There was a pause and then Eberlin said distinctly and with careful pronunciation:

"I am quite sure that you have taken every effort to study my file, so could not have failed to have noticed the K109 Report I completed regarding the accident. The facts are all there, gentlemen. But may I suggest that if this barely visible cabal has been assembled solely to discuss my driving qualities, I would be very happy to take each one of you for a short spin and so demonstrate my capabilities at no extra charge."

There was a silence and heads glanced at each other and then: "Have you finished your whisky so soon, Eberlin?" declared

Copperfield, stepping forward on his own cue. Eberlin lit a cigarette with a table lighter. Frazer, sitting opposite him, spoke for the first time.

"No, we didn't ask you here to discuss motoring. On the contrary, if you'll be patient just a little longer, we will tell you all you wish to know. Ridley."

He nodded to Ridley who pressed a button at his elbow, and a rectangular screen lit up on the wall behind Frazer's head. On the large screen was projected the face of a young man, dark hair falling over the right temple, full-mouthed and staring out at the onlookers with surprise through clear, wide-spaced eyes.

"Sidney Nightingale," said Ridley and pressed another button. The screen was wiped clean and a second face appeared, this one obviously taken candidly, for the owner was slightly out of focus and was turning, mouth open, to talk to someone now cropped out of the slide. The face was of a man of about forty, eyes lined heavily, and, Eberlin suspected and knew, usually behind spectacles, a large nose slightly bulbous at the end and underlined by a thin moustache.

"Esau Pretty," stated Ridley.

The face was wiped off to make room for a third. Here was a different man altogether, a more mature man with cunning but intelligent eyes, thinning hair, and a heavy mole on the right cheek. One could see the top of a striped shirt and a Guards tie.

"Ernest Lee Gulliver."

The lights were turned on, dazzling the occupants of the room.

Then turned off again.

"You no doubt recognize the men?" asked Frazer. "Yes," replied Eberlin.

"And know of course that they are all dead. That in fact they were all killed."

"Of course Mr. Eberlin does. A fact like that is hardly likely to escape his–meticulous attention."

Eberlin turned quickly to see the speaker, and saw, with a jolt, that it was Emmanuel Gatiss, who was now sitting straight-backed in a chair against the far wall, arms folded and smiling steadily at him.

"Good afternoon, Eberlin."

"Good afternoon," replied Eberlin and turned away.

"You know Mr. Gatiss of course," declared Lake. "Mr. Gatiss has just returned from Germany."

It was becoming hot in the room and sweat was forming on the men's faces, except for those of Gatiss and Brogue. Eberlin studied Brogue, sitting quietly in profile to him, puffing at a cigar with that ridiculous holder of his. The Negro sensed the observation and glanced out of the corner of his eye but said nothing. He was a man who had learned to keep his place among superiors. There was a strained atmosphere hanging like a catch net from the ceiling, that seemed to affect everybody, for they had become restless and fidgety and Copperfield had even gone so far as to unbutton the top button of his shirt. Leaning over to stub out a cigarette, Eberlin glanced back at Gatiss and found him gazing in his direction with intent scrutiny, a smile on his face of such hidden profundity that in contrast the Mona Lisa was guffawing.

"You are aware no doubt of the details of *Hesperides*?" Frazer was saying, and Eberlin looked up and across the table in overt concentration.

"Yes, sir. As far as my department itself was aware."

"Quite. But I think your T301 files covered almost everything."
"If I may interrupt, sir," Quince interrupted with an ingratiating whimper, "the actual operation itself is really not the meat of our program. It is Top Security and well, there are unauthorized persons present who–"

"I am well aware of that, Quince," snapped Frazer. "I am well aware of that."

He stood up and walked, stoop-backed, toward one of the large windows and drew back a curtain so that the stark daylight highlighted him in the corner of the room. He took out a pipe and lit it

in careful concentration, then turned to the room.

"I would like all but Eberlin, Quince and Colonel Flowers –and of course Gatiss–to leave the room."

Imediately, Lake hurried to the door and ushered the others out into the anteroom. Gatiss didn't move but remained seated against the far wall in shadow. After the door had been shut and the sounds of departure had faded, Frazer straightened his back, said "Now then" very clearly and distinctly, and walked back to the table.

"Would anyone care for a drink? Eberlin? Would you like a drink?"

"No thank you, sir." "Another whisky, surely?" "That would be fine, sir." "Anyone else?"

There was no other demand.

"Quince–get Eberlin a whisky will you? And make it a large sensible one this time. And one for me, too. No point in ignoring Ministry expenses."

There was a slight murmur of polite amusement. Frazer smiled and coughed and tapped the pipe forcefully on the polished veneer of the table.

"Now then, Eberlin, I'm sorry to have kept you hanging about so long in the dark, but you are no doubt well aware that we all have thought very hard before asking you to come to Selvers. I'm not going to go into the whys and wherefores of why you were selected. The very fact that you are before us now should be sufficient. I have long admired your efficiency and, may I say, devotion in your work. Now, as Quince has said, the actual operation *Hesperides* is not the core of the matter. That is of a parallel nature. What *is* the core of the matter, is that the success of *Hesperides* has been severely impeded. Not once but three times. So, in my book, what is required first, before we can reliably send out a successor to Nightingale, is the elimination of that impediment, All right so far?"

Not at all all right so far, thought Eberlin. If they didn't want him to take over from Nightingale, what the hell did they want?

"You mean you don't wish me to follow through with *Hesperides*, sir?"

"No."

"I'm afraid I don't understand, sir."

Quince's voice slithered into the air once more.

"Perhaps I could elucidate more easily, sir, since it is more my–"

"I'm perfectly, capable, Quince. Where is that whisky?" "Oh, here, sir."

He set down a large glass of J. & B. at Eberlin's elbow and before Frazer, then sat down himself next to Flowers who was drawing a horse on his blotter, slightly out of proportion and without a tail.

"We're not asking you to understand completely at first, Eberlin," Frazer continued, "only to listen to what we have to say. I mentioned that we had first to eliminate this impediment. Well, that's right–but we're not going to ask you to do that either. No. What we *want* you to do is find out where the impediment is."

"By the impediment you mean–" "The assassin."

Eberlin set down the brimful glass of whisky carefully, attempting not to spill it. He was suddenly grateful for the semidarkness.

Steadying his voice he said as casually as possible:

"You used the word 'where,' sir. Does this mean that you know who the assassin is?"

"Well, we believe it to be the same man each time. Purely theory of course but a pretty fair guess. You see, we've known for a while that the Russians have been infiltrating assassins into our system, and the man we want is obviously one of these. The choice of victims and methods bears this out, obviously. What we want you to do is go out, find out where he is and let us know. We'll do the rest. We don't even want you to touch him in any way or make yourself known to him, but just keep in the background. You've proved to us how efficient you are in Research J matters, and we believe you'll make a damned good job of it. Moreover it's a fair chance that you're not known to the Russians and so can travel more easily."

"Do you have any strong lead on this assassin, sir?" "No. Not really, except that we know who he is."

The ceiling dropped possibly six inches but still retained its original beauty, though in a modified form, despite the fact that the temperature of the room had just reached boiling point. Restraining himself from mopping his brow, and seeking anxiously for a simple way of asking the frighteningly obvious question, Eberlin delayed the moment by asking Flowers to pass the lighter, then plunged forward with:

"Who exactly–is he, sir?"

"Oh," replied Frazer, almost flippantly relighting his pipe, "does the name Krasnevin ring a bell at all?"

* * *

Quince drew the curtains back and the whole room was filled with sunshine, picking out the layers of tobacco smoke and the intimate creases and lines and formations of the men's faces. A box of cigars was handed around and each man took one, cut it and lit it, passing around a lighted spill from hand to hand. Eberlin leaned back in the chair, holding a cigarette in his right hand and sipping the whisky. He was conscious of Gatiss's eyes boring into the back of his neck. He swilled the drink in the glass in studied contemplation.

"Well," Frazer said, "I didn't think you'd have heard of him, but we have been informed from MNF that Krasnevin is probably our man. He's the chappie we want you to find. Now, don't give us an answer now. Go outside for a stroll, take in a bit of that sun, have a look at the downs and think about it. Remember, you're under no obligation, and let us know your answer in half an hour. All right? Any questions?"

Eberlin could think of a million questions he wanted to ask and so replied, "No questions, sir."

"Good. We can discuss details if and when you decide. Shall we adjourn?"

"One moment, sir–if I may be so impertinent as to ask Eberlin a question myself."

The sharp clipped voice came from the corner of the room and Gatiss stood up and walked slowly to the table and picked up the table lighter and studied it.

"Not at all, Gatiss. Go right ahead."

"Thank you, sir. It's just a point of curiosity." He was not looking directly at Eberlin but seemed to be engrossed in the intricate design around the lighter. With almost impertinent indifference, he said quietly:

"When you were on the way here to Selvers, this morning, did anything of interest occur?"

All heads turned toward Eberlin and he smiled, puzzled. "Anything of interest?"

"Yes, you know? Something that might have attracted your attention. Something unusual, abnormal perhaps."

"Well, not as far as I can … how exactly do you mean?"

"You know exactly how I mean. Was there something that happened that shouldn't have happened, or vice versa? It's a perfectly simple question and shouldn't be too difficult for a trained man like you."

"Well, I saw two cows in a field near Sevenoaks," replied Eberlin with a grin, and the others gave a small laugh in chorus.

"Oh really?" said Gatiss, dropping the lighter on to the table and without a trace of humor. "Were they Frisian or Jersey?"

Their eyes locked at Gatiss looked down fixedly at Eberlin. The other three men straightened their faces and fidgeted. Flowers began to tip-tip and toy with a pencil.

"I'm perfectly serious, Mr. Eberlin. Perhaps I ought to give you a clue if you want to consider this a parlor game. You were met by a chauffeur, were you not? Just outside Wadhurst?"

"Yes, that's right."

"I'll repeat my original question. Did anything of interest happen to you today? Something abnormal?"

"Not that I remember," replied Eberlin steadily, reaching for the drink.

"Then I say you should remember. Did the chauffeur ask you for your papers?"

"No, he–"

"Did you ask him for his?" "No, I did not."

"Why not, Mr. Eberlin? Isn't it one of the first rules of our profession to check every person contacted and never take anyone for granted?"

"Yes, but I took the chauffeur at face value for rational purposes."

"Why did you?"

"Because, Mr. Gatiss, I can't think of anyone else who would know my whereabouts sufficiently to be at that particular spot at that particular hour with a car to take me to Selvers. Do you?"

Gatiss smiled and surveyed the table like a lord at a medieval feast.

"I can think of several, Mr. Eberlin. Several. You would do well to think again," and he walked slowly toward the door, pausing only to turn back to Eberlin and say:

"Let me give you a particle of advice. We're playing a dangerous game, you and I. It is not designed for frivolous thinkers. I insure my health by trusting no one, no one at all. I don't trust you, Mr. Eberlin. Good day." He left the room, closing the door hard behind him.

There was an embarrassed silence. Eberlin knew he had made a mistake and had been ridiculously stubborn about it.

"I'm afraid Mr. Gatiss is right," he said to the others with conscious humility, "it was foolish of me."

"Indeed it was," replied Frazer, "but I'm sure it was a rare occurrence. We are grateful to Gatiss however for bringing it to our attention. Shall we meet here in half an hour and hear Eberlin's answer, gentlemen?"

He stood up and left the room, followed by Flowers and Quince.

Waiting till he was on his own, Eberlin walked downstairs into the quadrangle, breathing in the fresh air deeply, and then out of the square, under the arch and down onto the fresh grass, onto the grass of the fields, and into the peace and comfort of the downs.

* * *

He had visited most of Europe at one time or another and had been taken, a reluctant tourist, to all the natural beauty traps of the countries, and he had failed to discover landscape more idyllic, more soothing and, like echoes of infant fantasy, more evocative than the English downs. In the summer, with the sun an intimate, and a secure isolation from the world, they offered at worst a panacea from care. Eberlin had often driven down from London on free weekends to Kent and Sussex and sometimes farther west, and parked the car and walked alone, like a reincarnated Romantic poet, clutching a slim volume of verse, pantheistic in wooded valleys.

Now he stood on a green, crop-grassed slope staring across at a complementary slope opposite, seemingly out of perspective so that one felt one could touch the other bank of the V of this cornice of valley with a long pole, or a branch or a cane. But it was deceptive. For he would need to make his way down, to that narrow stream beneath him, and walk along till he found a bridge or a narrowing of the bank, and then up the other side until he could turn and look back, across at where he had been ten, fifteen minutes before. Eberlin lit a cigarette and began to walk parallel to the stream toward a row of oak trees left as a natural border in the rotation.

He had barely covered a few yards when he heard his name called. Turning, his eyes blinded slightly by the sun, he could see the shape of a man making his way down toward him from the red brick building of Selvers he had just left. He waited till the man was twenty yards away and saw that it was the thin, ascetic, flushed figure of Heston-Stevas.

"I hope you don't mind my joining you," he panted, reaching Eberlin. "They're all sitting around talking about fishing and other dull things like that."

Eberlin smiled and said, "Not at all," and the two men continued together across the slope.

"I'm glad they asked you down here," Heston-Stevas said after a while. "I mean, it's obviously important and you seemed to be wasted in the office."

"It's good to see someone with faith in me."

"Oh. Oh yes. Well–I've always thought that you deserved … well, you know …" He looked away down at the stream.

They walked on in silence and Eberlin pointed up toward a scarred dead tree on the brow of the hill beyond.

"Shall we make our way up there?" "Good idea."

It was a short but steep climb, over longer grass now and along by a broken fence and up past a deserted dried cattle font and over to a tree. They rested under its bleached, split branches, breathing heavily and gazing down at the patchwork of fields below them and the clear blue sky.

"It always reminds me of Rupert Bear land," Heston-Stevas commented with a smile. "I've always felt that the artist who drew the pictures must have lived near here."

"Rupert Bear?"

"Yes. You must have read the comic annuals as a child. One

always suspects that a white bear with a red sweater and yellow scarf will appear over a brow of a hill shouting out to some Chinese pixie or something. Awfully silly...."

Eberlin smiled. He rather liked Heston-Stevas. A little harmless, but sympathetic and with a great deal of charm like most shy people.

"Could I possibly steal a cigarette off you, Eberlin? I never seem to have any...."

"Of course," and he handed him one and took another himself.

"Have you made up your mind yet? About taking the job,"

asked Heston-Stevas, lighting the cigarettes.

Eberlin glanced at him, puzzled.

"How do you know I haven't told them already?"

"Oh, well, they always make their victims walk around for half an hour to decide. It's part of their routine."

"I see."

"Yes...."

Another man had appeared on the opposite hill and was standing stock-still, staring in Eberlin's direction. They were directly in line with each other, face to face, though three hundred yards of sky separated them. The sun high-lighted the onlooker's blond hair, and even without that Eberlin knew him to be Gatiss, watching him. Heston-Stevas appeared not to notice.

"What will you do, then?" he asked.

Do? He had to accept, of course. How could he risk another man looking for him, someone like Gatiss perhaps. It was so damn ironic and in such bad taste. And yet Eberlin found that he felt remarkably calm despite it all. Incredibly in control of himself. Gatiss was still standing opposite, dark glasses covering his eyes, arms folded.

"I don't know yet. Accept probably," replied Eberlin. "I think I ought to return to the keepers."

And he moved quickly away and down the slope with HestonStevas hurrying to catch up and saying:

"I wish you luck."

And then Eberlin glanced across at the opposite hill to find it empty. A tranquil slope.

In ten minutes he was back in the quadrangle, his mind made up.

5

Billet-Doux

If the rich could hire other people to die for them, the poor could make a wonderful living.
–YIDDISH PROVERB

In civilization, anyone can be king. But it takes a rare man to be king on a desert island.
–ALEXANDER EBERLIN

THE room was empty when Eberlin returned, and he looked around at the uncleared assortment of blotters, pencils and ashtrays on the table. Chairs scattered back. He turned to leave and almost collided with Lake.

"The gentlemen are outside, Mr. Eberlin. They requested that you meet them on the terrace."

* * *

The terrace was more an open yard than patio, a concrete floor under the sky overlooking the lower trees of a wood. Lunch had been served, had been eaten, and was now a pile of dirty plates and scraps on two small tables. Eberlin noticed that it had been some form of salad and was angry for not being invited. He picked up a spare chicken leg from a tray and stood chewing it, ignoring the others. They were all there, smoking cigars and drinking brandy, laughing and chatting among themselves. Gatiss, sitting alone, smiled at Eberlin and threw some untouched slices of ham to a hungry dog at his feet.

"Ah, Eberlin, didn't see you there." Frazer smiled, beckoning him over to the table and gesturing to the other men. Eberlin crossed to the table, nodded and was offered a seat.

"Have a good walk?" asked Frazer. "Yes."

"Lovely around here, isn't it?"

The terrace had grown quiet and all concentrated on minute matters, stubbing cigarettes, sipping coffee or brandy, wiping brows, straightening ties. Brogue, Copperfield, Heston-Stevas, Ridley, Moon and Lake stood up, made their apologies and left quickly, not into the house but down toward the wood, not talking but walking with deliberate casualness, not looking back and hovering in a small group beneath a large beech. The Negro, Brogue, was walking farther away, cigar holder clenched in teeth, farther toward a white cattle fence. Eberlin continued picking at the chicken leg.

"Were you hungry, Eberlin?" inquired Quince. "Had you not eaten?"

"Yes I am, and no I hadn't."

"Oh dear. Well, we won't keep you long."

He rubbed the side of his nose vigorously and made patterns in the ashtray with his index finger. "Oh dear," he repeated.

"If I may come to the point," said Frazer quietly, keeping

his voice out of earshot of the house and of Copperfield who had approached conspicuously near the terrace. "What is your answer, Eberlin? Do you agree?"

"Yes," replied Eberlin. "Yes I do."

There were immediate smiles on the faces and Frazer nodded twice, saying "Good. Good," and "Good," and Gatiss himself gave a brief smile, then walked to the edge of the terrace and glared at Copperfield who moved away, saying, "Hot isn't it?" and stumbling over the root of a tree.

"May I ask one thing?" inquired Eberlin, glancing across at Frazer.

"Oh, do. Do. By all means."

"Why haven't you chosen Gatiss rather than me? Surely this is more his line, sir."

"Well, it is and it isn't. We had considered him, of course, but he has other business to deal with first. Of a more direct nature. Believe me, he won't be neglected."

"I see."

"Good. How's the brandy? Oh, you didn't have any. Well ... let's get down to details shall we? We suspect that Krasnevin, our man, *your* man, was in London but we believe that now he has left and is in Germany. Probably in West Berlin, but we can't be sure. Anyway, that would be your first base, and since you know it well and can speak German, an ideal base." "Why do you think he's in Berlin, sir?"

"Good question. Well, as I said, we can't be sure, but we're anticipating his movements. We're assuming that he hasn't just stopped his plans, but is waiting for his next victim. That man would be Gatiss."

"Gatiss?"

"Why so surprised? I would have thought that was obvious. He is involved in *Hesperides* too, and not only that, he is known to the Russians–on unfavorable terms of course. Gatiss has been in Munich and Berlin for the past months, and will be returning there. Our Krasnevin, if he is as clever as we think he is, will surely be there too. Do you not think so?"

"I'm prepared to accept your theory, sir." "Not blindly, I hope."

Frazer smiled and lit his pipe. Flowers was drawing a deformed squirrel on the table napkin. It was holding a nut in its paws and had ears like a horse. The feet were badly conceived.

Quince said suddenly, "See that rabbit? Running across the field there. Did you see it? Large one with brown fur. It just ran across the field."

Eberlin walked slowly across the concrete and stood five yards from Gatiss, and stared like him at the wood. Neither said anything for a moment, then Gatiss without turning his head, asked "Confident, Eberlin?"

Eberlin looked down the terrace edge and across at the speaker, standing arms behind his back, dark glasses pushed forward down the nose, the sun-tanned jaw pointed up arrogantly.

"I haven't thought about it. Perhaps after dinner." Gatiss smiled to himself.

"I recommend oysters for thought. Try Wheeler's. They're rather pleasant there." He stepped off the concrete onto the grass, and walked down and around the corner of the house and out of sight.

"Eberlin?"

It was Frazer's voice.

"Follow us downstairs. I want you to see something." Eberlin turned and joined the group.

"It's a photo," Frazer said, "a photo of Krasnevin."

Eberlin stopped deadstill and turned his back on the men and went cold. It suddenly struck him with awesome simplicity. They know. It's all a gigantic trap. They know he's Krasnevin. They've known all the time. The invitation to Selvers, all the people here, the scrutiny. It's all a ridiculous trap, a macabre game. They don't want him to do anything at all, not to go to Berlin, not to find Krasnevin. Because they've found him. He's standing on the terrace with them, smoking their cigarettes. My God, they *know.*

"Come along, Eberlin, there's a good chap," said Quince sweetly. "It's only downstairs." And Quince put his hand on his shoulder and led Eberlin into the house.

He walked dumbly, his mind filled with a thousand things, a mad desire to run away and be caught in five minutes by the others or by the dogs. He had been so innocent, so unsuspecting, so damn innocent. Gatiss himself had told him not to trust anyone, no one at all, and here he was, being led by this grinning, ridiculous clown on his right, into the web, ready to be eaten.

"Mind how you go, because there are a few steps. That's it."

His footsteps resounded loudly in the narrow corridor, down steep stone steps toward an open door at the bottom.

"Just in here. There we are. Just here."

He was in a low cellar, lit only by three angle-poise lamps on small tables, and empty except for a screen and half a dozen folding chairs. Frazer was standing by the screen, talking quietly to Flowers, ignoring Eberlin. They didn't even look at him; they were that sure.

The door was closed behind him. This was it.

"Take a seat. We won't be a minute," Quince said and hurried over to Frazer and whispered something to him. Eberlin, perched on the hard narrow chair, studied the three faces before the screen for any sign of their intentions. There were none. Flowers said something and the other two men glanced over at Eberlin, then looked away. Finally Flowers and Quince sat one on each side of him, Quince offering him a chocolate which he refused, and Fraser said:

"The film of Krasnevin reached our files only recently. I think you might find it very interesting, Eberlin."

He nodded to a projectionist hidden in the darkness. There was a whirr of machinery, and the six-by-four screen was suddenly filled with white light, and then reversed numbers, and then, the film shaking as if taken by a hand-held camera, a zoom shot of the London Transport bus terminal at Victoria. The screen was blotted out momentarily by a bus passing across it, and then the camera, shooting wild and low, was focusing across the rows of people queueing at respective stops, into the taxi rank, and attempting to pick out a man emerging from the depths of the railway station itself. Eberlin's heart raced. The lighting had been bad and the figure was blurred and hazy, then suddenly it came into the light and the camera cut in closer and onto the face and the picture froze. The man's head turned, one hand a streak of gray as if he had been hailing a taxi, and Eberlin stared at the enlarged, black and white, still face before him on the screen and his heart sank, and he wanted to rip the film from the wall and attack the men in the room and rush out. He was sweating profusely under his clothes and he was angry and hemmed in and frightened. He ought to have shouted out but he didn't. He sat there and said nothing. He couldn't speak. He had to keep quiet. For he had underestimated them. All the careful planning and cover was breaking apart. The face before him, unmistakable, terrifyingly clear, belonged to Pavel.

6

Pavel

Could the carpenter who constructed Christ's cross
have conceivably been called Joseph?
–ALEXANDER EBERLIN

"WHAT about the one with that squiggle on top?" "Oh. Let me see.... Coffee I think. Yes, coffee." "No.... What about this one?"

"Diamond?"

"Yes. I suppose so." "That's nougat, sir."

"Oh. Well, I'll try it then."

"Yes. It's nougat. There's another underneath."

Half an hour had passed and they were sitting in the long room again, curtains drawn around the table once more. The Four Musketeers. Eberlin was asked if he wanted another chocolate and he said he didn't and then he said he really didn't. The chocolates lay in their box in the center of the table, the only occupant, discussed, revered, elevated like a host. Quince, nose shining, bounced his exclamations from one to another, the inside of his fingers deep brown from chocolate tasting. Suddenly Frazer looked across at Eberlin, seeing him sitting there, quiet, a reluctant onlooker to the feast.

"Not a great sweet eater, I see."

"Not a great sweet eater," replied Eberlin.

"Well, it's just a small break after talking for half an hour. I hope you feel more confident about tackling Krasnevin. Do you think you can handle it?"

"I think I might surprise you."

"Good. Good. Well, we ought to go through your cover now." Frazer crossed the room to a chair and brought over a thin black briefcase with the initials R.R.F. embossed on the front, and set it down on the table, pushing the chocolates aside. Unlocking it, he pulled out a sheaf of neatly typed papers, classified SEC.55F and carboned twice. The words CONFIDENTIAL and TOP PRIORITY were stamped on each page, which were forty-three in number. He handed a carbon copy to Eberlin and set one before himself.

"All you will need to know is there, but I'll run over the salient points now in case there are any questions. As you see from the first page, you will be traveling under the name of 'George Dancer' and your occupation is Agency Supervisor for National Oil. You are in Berlin on your three-week holiday, and since you are interested in cars, are going to make a special point of watching the Berlin Grand Prix which takes place on the Avus on Saturday the twenty-ninth of August. Two weeks' time. You are unmarried and will be staying at the Kliest Hotel in Leitzenburgerstrasse. Modest room. I'd like to put you in the Kempinski, but neither we nor Dancer could afford it. All right so far?"

"What exactly does an agency supervisor do?"

"Nothing much really as I understand. The Agency works on this principle: an oil firm will control a number of garages throughout England, say, and any commercial company whose lorries obtain petrol from these particular garages can have a contract with the oil firm concerned. This means that the drivers do not pay for their petrol in cash but sign an invoice, which is then sent to the Agency. The Agency then reimburses the garage and charges the company. Pure paper work done by a lot of wretched clerks. The supervisor therefore looks after the clerks, answers the phone and answers queries, bad debts, etc. It's all there. Page five, I think. No, page six. Beginning second paragraph. By the way, there is a *real* George Dancer, who is an agency supervisor, but he's happily in Majorca now on our money. So no trouble there."

"How much does he get paid?"

"Ten fifty a year thereabouts. Clerks get seven fifty. That's there too. Of course the difficulty of this cover is that you have only three weeks, but I want that to be sufficient. If there's no joy after that time, you come back to England and we think again. Here is your passport. It's seven years old and your occupation is listed as *Accountant* since you were promoted only five years ago. As you see, you've been to France twice, in '59 and '60, and Berlin once in '61, but only for one week.

Eberlin flicked over the pages of the passport, then put it aside and lit a cigarette. He now had *three* names. The permutations were infinite. The maze terrifyingly committing. The Eberlin Trinity. "How much do you pay for your suits, sir?"

It was Flowers' voice once more, scrutinizing him.

Eberlin raised his eyebrows and turned toward him. Flowers continued:

"How much, sir? A man like Dancer couldn't afford clothes like that. You will have to wear something cheaper and not so well cut."

"I do not possess a suit that is cheaper or not so well cut, Colonel," Eberlin replied. Frazer smiled. "But I appreciate your questions. I am less of a fool than you think and will dress the part, however demoralizing."

There was a brief pause, then Eberlin turned back to Frazer. "How do I contact you, sir?"

"Simply by writing letters, airmail, to a girl friend. We've chosen Vogler and you will write love letters, New Code D5, to her at her private address. The first one, of course, should be harmless so that we can see if it has been tampered with on its way over. Sorry about the love letter bit, but Dancer would do it. Anyway, Vogler will write back. Here's a snapshot of her for you to keep in your wallet."

He passed over a small photograph of Heather Vogler, standing in a bikini on a beach–Eberlin recognized it as Brighton–smiling into the camera shyly, one hand posed on her left hip. It was gauche and self-conscious, but Eberlin liked it. She was really rather a sweet girl and he suddenly remembered her standing naked in his room, hopping on one leg and pulling off a pair of white nylon pants, two nights before. He wondered if he had dreamed it. He had been drunk. What a *hell* of a weekend.

"Here are a couple of old letters we asked Vogler to write to you, and in one she talks about your first night together–her idea–so assume you are lovers. The letters are dated six months and four months ago when you went north to Glasgow on business."

The letters were passed across the table, and Eberlin tried to envisage Vogler sitting down at a desk trying to make up billets-doux to nobody. He wondered who she had in mind when she wrote them. As a model. Gatiss? Good God, he hoped not.

"If we are lovers, I mean Dancer and Vogler," Eberlin inquired, "Why isn't she in Berlin with me?"

"Impossible. You both had a row about it but she is an actress and is committed to finishing a film. Of course there's always a chance she could join you for the last couple of days. That's up to you."

"Yes."

"Now. Company-stamped ball pen, two old theatre tickets and a few visiting cards. Couple of other character pieces and a check-book. By the way, we're going to allow you an emergency fund of six thousand dollars but don't touch it unless you really have to. Are you happy so far?"

Eberlin nodded. He was stalling his plans, for he had none. He had decided for the present to wait till Berlin before he made a move in whatever direction seemed more favorable. The Wall seemed a perfect symbol for his state of mind.

"Any more questions?" asked Frazer.

They talked there for another two hours until it began to get cold and Eberlin's stomach begged to be fed. And then, eyes pained by the concentration and the smoke, he said good-bye to the others and went downstairs and outside to the quadrangle for the last time. The chauffeur was waiting by the Zodiac, leaning against the hood, legs crossed, smoking. He jumped up as he saw Eberlin and hurried to open the rear door.

"I've been asked to drive you the whole way, sir."

Eberlin paused, one hand on the roof, the other on the side of the door and looked at the chauffeur.

"You mean all the way to London?" "Yes, sir. If that suits you, sir." "Well it'll save me ten shillings."

He glanced back at the building around him and saw that Gatiss's Jensen was still there, but the trunk was closed and the wheels straight. He had driven somewhere and returned during the last two hours. That reminded him.

"Oh," smiled Eberlin, holding the door, "I'd better see your papers."

"Oh, yes, sir."

The chauffeur took out a wallet from his inside pocket and held it in front of him. Eberlin checked the photo with the face and nodded, smiling.

"You'd better see mine as well. For the record," and he showed his own identity card and then sat back in the seat and the door was closed.

The chauffeur turned the car smartly into the center of the gravel square and then headed it out through the arch and on, fast, toward London. The whole journey took place in silence and Eberlin spent it in going over the events of the day in his head, and planning his own moves and counter-moves. If any. Only once was his thinking disturbed. And that was when, just north of Frant on the A267, a steel-blue Jensen with a dented fender roared past, cutting in fine in front of the Zodiac, then roaring on ahead, the blond-haired driver impassive behind the wheel, roaring away up the road and disappearing, a blue speck, into the distance.

* * *

Arriving in London, Eberlin told the driver to drop him at Grumble's Restaurant in Churton Street–he almost said Wheeler's–where, like a just-released convict, he ordered too much, left half of it, and finished it off with a cup of coffee that nearly decoated the lining of his stomach. He had never cared much for the High Mass of coffee, preferring the instant cares of Maxwell House to anything else. Once he had been invited to dinner by a young high-liver in Security called Palmer, and suffered the full ritual of grinding, pouring, repouring, settling, percolating and stirring in varying degrees, until he was allowed to participate in the Communion of it all, a penitent at the rail, parched, self-conscious and unconvinced. Gathered in his rapidly overflowing file of public bores, a file that included such stalwarts as *The Young Banner-Thumping Socialist* (*plus Partner*), cheek to cheek with *The Earnest Pop-Art Intellectual, The Turnip-head Bigot* and that classic *The Proud Husband*, he had allotted a prominent niche for *The Self-Confessed Connoisseur*. It was all too much.

Sitting, satiated and despairing, in the small half-lit restaurant, he considered his role as Dancer. He would have to get in touch with Pavel that night. That, at least, was on the cards, pontooned by *The Circean Pig*, the chosen code name of his operation. For fifteen minutes they had sat in the cellar of Selvers trying to think of a name for the project. It was a customary procedure and the company, all excepting Eberlin, had gone about it like prospective parents with a Name Book. They must have suggested a hundred names, beginning with childish glee, then moving to individual possessiveness over words like *Falcon* and *Hereward* and *Valiant* and other words advertising their military and public school upbringing. Flowers had suggested a whole range of battle names but had been squashed as the discussion turned into a row about military tactics. To Eberlin it had all seemed absurd and he had said that he would prefer it if the operation were anonymous. Hot cries of indignation smattered the air and phrases like "unethical" and "unprecedented" and "traditional" were hurled at him, and he realized once again that he was not of British stock. Finally they gave up and had to resort to the Greek Myths, the eternal source-book for Code Classification. Just as they were frantically searching their memories for an unused god or hero, Gatiss had entered like the leading actor on his cue and had said, "There were some voyagers, employees of Odysseus, who visited a foreign island and were turned into swine. Call it the Circean Pig," and had left, closing the door–and striding upstairs. A blue pencil was found and the phrase was scrawled in capitals on page one of Eberlin's file. It was *Operation Circean Pig*. All were content. Eberlin paid the bill, left the restaurant quickly, took a taxi straight home to South Street, and in ten minutes discovered that his rooms had been searched.

* * *

At 8:17 P.M., just as Eberlin was deliberating whether to contact Pavel forcibly, the phone rang. He took it in the bedroom, closed the door, sat on the bed.

"Hello?"

There was a brief pause, then the voice, faint and slightly blurred, drunk or perhaps disguised, asked:

"Kidner?"

"Who?" replied Eberlin. "Who's that? Is that Kidner?"

"I'm afraid there's no one called Kidner here."

A silence and Eberlin could hear contemplative breathing.

"I want to speak to Kidner." "I'm sorry you must have–" "Is that not Mayfair 1128?"

"No. This is not Mayfair 1128. You have the wrong number, it seems."

"Oh, that's constantly occurring. Sorry to have bothered you." "That's all right."

Eberlin put down the receiver, lit a cigarette, walked out of the bedroom, poured a drink and picked up the TV papers, turning to the day's viewing. Outside it had begun to rain. Kidner, he thought.

* * *

Later, Eberlin was sitting sprawled in an armchair, slightly drunk now, staring at the television screen on a small table in one corner of the room. His feet were crossed, slippered, and resting on a small paisley-covered footstool, while one hand clutched a glass of warm Pernod and the other hovered over the RECORD button of a small tape recorder. Benign, powdered by makeup girls, cleancollared and self-conscious, the Reverend A. J. Kidner, all black and white and rehearsed, stared out into the room through the nineteeninch screen, declaiming the Epilogue, tempered and fashioned by a dozen hands of dubious beliefs.

At eleven twenty-eight precisely, the program having begun on time, Eberlin started the tape recorder.

And if Christ returned to earth today, would He be surprised at what He saw around Him? The incredible progress of man in the fields of science and technology, and in the fields of the arts, of architecture, of fashion? Would He, this first-century son of a carpenter, be surprised? Of course He would not. For being the Son of God, man is predictable to Him and He, brethren, should be predictable to us. There are no secrets about His love for us. It–

A click and the Reverend A. J. Kidner was reduced to a dot. Eberlin then rewound the tape and played it back at a slower speed in order to decode the words more easily. In three minutes, he had written in pencil on a piece of paper:

STAY ALONE DO NOT CONTACT REPEAT SEVER LINK TEMPORARILY DORMOUSE

The paper was destroyed and the tape wiped clean and then Eberlin, insolently defiant, put on his shoes and overcoat and left the flat and ran out into the rain, surprised by it. He found he had to walk to the Hilton Hotel in order to get a taxi, and only then by tipping a florin to the commissionaire, who said "Thank you, sir" and offered the shelter of an umbrella large enough to contain a circus.

Eberlin sprawled in the back of the taxi, wet and breathless, and noticed for the first time that he was drunk, and the driver, an elderly man with the eyes of a marionette, was saying:

"Where to, sir?"

* * *

The small white card pinned inelegantly to the board read in petite lettering of no great charm:

EXPERT: ERECTION AND DEMOLITION PHONE MISS SHARON. PARK 4169

Eberlin, standing in the pouring August rain of Queensway, regretting the absence of his hat, collar turned up, took mental note of the number, turned quickly away and hurried through the babel of strangers constantly stirring in this cockpit of mannered sordidity, past the late night steak houses and tasteless coffee bars, on until he reached a phone booth, solitary in a side street, the permanent light inside proclaiming it like an altar lamp. He entered and dialed the number. The dialing tone rang on seemingly for an eternity, then a sharp, bored female voice answered with all the femininity of a battery hen.

"Park 4169. Hang on a minute."

Eberlin did for two minutes and then the voice returned with: "Yes?"

"Is that Miss Sharon?"

"What did you want, dear?"

"I gather oilskin is still fashionable, is it not?" There was a fractional hesitation.

"It depends if you're regular." "As a dormouse."

"Did you want to see me tonight, love?" "Now."

"Anything particular you had in mind?" "I'll see you in five minutes."

Pause.

"You are a regular, aren't you, dear?" "Yes."

"All right. Oh–if you pass a milk machine can you bring some milk for me. I haven't had much chance–"

"I'll be there."

There was a milk machine on the corner by the Underground station, and Eberlin lost two sixpences in it because it had been broken earlier by vandals who made a habit of it. He arrived at the house in Cornwall Crescent twenty minutes later, having walked all the way, and pressing the fourth bell, walked up the staircase slowly to the third floor. A sliver of light shone out from under a door and he knocked twice. The door was opened six inches by a young girl of about twenty, blond dry hair piled up over her head, charcoal-sketch eyes, a small mouth but attractive, and a thin, bone-protruding body wrapped in a pink and yellow housecoat. She squinted out into the hallway, seeing only the shape of Eberlin in the shadow.

"Did you bring the milk?" she asked, unsure of herself, trying to see the face. There was a smell of joss sticks from the room and Eberlin could see a framed photo of Michelangelo's David (of all things), on a far wall, with a faded charity poppy stuck in the corner of the glass.

"The machine was empty," he said quickly and pushed his way into the room and locked the door. Ignoring the girl, clutching the housecoat around her as if her immodesty was at stake, he glanced around the room, peered through a hanging curtain divide into a small kitchen, and said quietly:

"I want to contact Pavel. Where is he?"

It was a small room, ten by ten at the most, and unusually clean despite the horror of the décor. It contained only a bed and a sink and a chair, two chairs, and a small gas fire. A wardrobe and a table piled with papers, cheap makeup, old copies of *True Romances* and cans of soup. Two cups. On the back of the door was tacked a magazine photo of Marilyn Monroe in a white shirt, a picture postcard of some abysmal ruin in Italy, and a girl's telephone number followed by a question mark. There was an attempt at creative invention in the lampshade which was white and round and had been made by the tenant, squat-legged on the floor one Sunday afternoon, tongue between teeth, as she pasted squares of tissue paper onto a greased balloon. Then laboriously, hurrying to complete it before dark, she pasted more squares till the balloon had a skin of paper and her bottom, sitting naked as she did, since it was hot and she possessed few casual clothes, was patterned red with the rush matting and her neck ached. But the shade was completed and in two days, dry and free from its foundation like a sucked eggshell, was hung around the light bulb, dispersing the light, and became a cynosure for the girl as she lay on her back, drawn to it like a moth, and a source of part-time work as other girls, calling in to borrow stockings and sugar, said, "What's that?" and asked for one for themselves. It was a pleasant way to spend the leisure hours.

The girl's eyebrows were drawn tightly together in a W of bewilderment and she didn't reply.

"I haven't much time," said Eberlin. "Where's Pavel?" "I don't know."

Eberlin leaned over the bed and looked out of the small white-painted, uncleaned window at the gray yard and empty washing lines outside.

"They broke contact with me two days ago," he said quietly, running his finger across the moist inside of the glass. "Do you know why?"

There was still no answer. He turned and looked at her, standing body hunched, arms clutched to her, a smear of faded pink, eyes wide, her shape seeminly disproportioned under the light, like a neglected puppet.

"Do you want a cigarette?" Eberlin asked. She shook her head and walked to the table and took the phone off the hook.

"They're angry with you for giving them orders," she said, not looking at him.

"Damn children," he said and lit a cigarette. "When did you last hear?"

"Not for a week." "From Pavel?"

"No, from Rotopkin. I've never met Pavel." "Do you know where he is?"

"Rotopkin?" "No. Pavel."

"No."

"What about Rotopkin? Where is he?" "I don't know."

Eberlin sighed and stood up and stared at the *David*. What a sordid little room, all broken and overcharged and pathetic. A baby crying upstairs suddenly. A toilet flushing.

"Where's Rotopkin?" "I don't know. I–"

Eberlin grabbed her arm tightly and pulled her around toward him.

"I don't know what is happening here but I've got to see Pavel.

They know about him. They have his picture."

Her eyes opened wider for a second, then she tugged at her arm. "I'm not sure where Rotopkin is."

"Where was he last?"

"I'm not sure. My contact hasn't–" "In London?"

"Yes."

"Where? The Gallery?" "No."

"Where then?" "I don't know."

"If Pavel doesn't leave London, they'll kill him."

The rain had stopped. Eberlin released the girl, hesitated, then turned away toward the door, buttoning up his coat.

"I could try to phone Rotopkin," she said, her voice nervous and breathy.

"Now?"

"Yes."

"Well, do it. Find out where Pavel is." "He might not tell me."

"Pick up the phone."

"I'm not really supposed–"

"For Godsakes pick up the phone."

The girl, frightened now, moved back to the table and picked up the phone, the housecoat falling aside like a theatre curtain to reveal a gray scrawny stomach and chocolate-button nipples. Eberlin stared at her cold, ribby body and said, quietly, pointing at the lampshade:

"Did you make that yourself?"

* * *

Pavel was in bed but not asleep when Eberlin arrived two hours later, creeping up the emergency stairs of the council apartments like a prospective burglar. The back-street, hushed-voice, nightprowling codified pantomime of undercover contact always irritated Eberlin's sense of style. To him, it was all unnaturally vulgar and clichéic, and it was for that reason he preferred his own role as assassin, independent of the groups and the intermediae, living a life of his own choosing for most of the time, and only going to ground on those rare occasions of accidental mismanagement.

The thirteenth floor of the Estate was predictably deserted at this time of the night. Nevertheless, Eberlin paused on the concrete passage, listening for any sound, then walked quietly to 137. He had known plebeian associates of the K.G.B., like Rotopkin, to revel in the pseudo-glamour of back-street rendezvous, exultant in the whole façade of counter-espionage–a word he never used–and then reaching retirement age, dream of beach cottages and fat wives. Eberlin rarely concerned himself with the inherent politics involved in his profession, though he respected the motives of his own side, and was rarely asked to pass information to Moscow, though he had done so once or twice with obvious disdain. That was not his job. He left that to the unfortunate majority and was intensely disliked by them. Working alone, in solitude, was his preference, at least until recently when he desired nothing more but to get out, give it up, return to Russia, anywhere for Godsakes, and live in ease with his personality intact. The only thing he feared, a recurrent nagging, was that the character of Eberlin, not the ministerial and social environment of the man, but the essence of Eberlin himself, had slowly along the way become much, much more attractive. He had to get out

The lock of the door was a standard Yale fixture and consequently easily opened, and Eberlin stepped into the dark stillness of the flat, listening cautiously to discover if Pavel was alone. There was no sound. Pausing only to adjust his eyes to the gloom, he noticed a faint haze of light under the door on his left and crossed the thick pile carpet to it moving silently and reaching for the handle of the door with both hands. Holding his breath he turned the handle and found the door moving inward noiselessly on its hinges, and he stepped into the blue painted bedroom as a Browning .38 automatic was rammed under his jaw, knocking his head back, and Pavel said quietly:

"Stand just exactly as you are."

Eberlin did. Pavel's arm was straight as a ramrod holding the gun, as he glanced out into the hallway and then with a forceful jab in the jaw, he gestured Eberlin into the center of the room and closed the door behind him. There was a momentary pause and the sound of heavy breathing as Pavel moved behind him, ran his hand quickly over Eberlin's clothes and then said:

"Are you alone?" "Yes."

"Then perhaps you'd like some coffee."

With a soft thud the Browning dropped onto the clean linen, pink-white-and-blue-striped pillow on the bed.

"Let me take your coat."

"I can't stay," replied Eberlin and perched on the edge of the bed and looked up at the thin, balding Pavel standing in white pajamas near the door, his face flushed and his eyes seemingly myopic.

Eberlin noticed that the room was as hot as hell, though without the charm, and yet its occupant seemed disturbingly unaware of it.

"Do you mind if I open the window?" He smiled. "Yes I do mind," was Pavel's curt reply.

"Well, may I turn off the fire?"

"No."

"Hot for this time of the year isn't it?" "You're not supposed to be here." "Understatement of the year."

But Eberlin didn't grin. He sat and gazed at a copy of *Pnin* lying without its jacket (damn the heat) on the bedside table. He had read the book himself with quiet enthusiasm a year ago. Eberlin picked it up, measured its weight in his hand and then said:

"How are you?"

Pavel didn't answer but crouched before the fire chewing a large piece of chocolate.

"I find electricity dearer than gas," he said finally. "So I understand."

"I'm thinking of getting rid of it and buying a gas fire but there isn't a point."

"To the decision?" "No, to the gas." "Too high up?"

"You mean the apartment?" "Yes."

"Could be. Never thought about it."

"I'm being sent to Berlin to kill Krasnevin."

"I know. Did you say you wanted some coffee?"

Eberlin looked up startled at Pavel, but the other man had his back to him and was lighting a cigarette.

"How did you know?" "How did I know what?"

"That I was going to Berlin?"

"Why? Is it supposed to be a secret?" He turned and smiled back at Eberlin. "What are you going to do about it?"

"There is a solution."

"Good. But if you go to Berlin, you'll stay in the West, won't you?"

"Why do you say that?"

"They don't want you in the East. Remember that. Even the boys in St. Antonius know about you."

Eberlin shrugged and stood up. He glanced at Pavel puzzled. The man looked ill, sick. What did he need the bloody fire on for? It was already stifling with central heating. "Are you all right?" he asked.

"Of course."

"You don't look well, Pavel."

"I think you'd better get out of here." "Don't you care what I do?"

"Not particularly. I'm sure your plans are perfectly adequate as always."

"Don't be so damned supercilious. They want me to kill myself."

"How amusing. I must get some sleep, so do you mind–" "Oh go to hell."

Eberlin crossed to the door. He was about to shout something, then changed his mind and said, "Did you search my rooms tonight?"

There was no answer. Pavel had lain down on the bed, facing away from the door, and was humming to himself, one arm hanging over the edge of the bed. Fingers hovering over the carpet. A cigarette lying neglected in an ashtray.

"Did you have my rooms searched?" repeated Eberlin, controlling his voice.

"No," was the answer. "Are you sure?"

"Yes, dear boy."

"Then it must have been the British."

"Of course it must have been the British by the simple reason that you discovered that fact."

Eberlin gave a cynical grunt and moved nearer to the bed.

"Oh really? I suppose if you had searched the rooms, I would never have noticed?"

"That's right." "So positive?"

"Well, we searched your rooms three days ago while you were at the V and A. But perhaps you were too drunk to notice."

"Good God."

"Oh dear, Eberlin, you're getting awfully irritating. Are we about to have a brawl or something? A pathetic duel at dawn on Wimbledon Common. You and your histrionics. You're nothing more than a stand-up tragedian."

And Pavel laughed, Eberlin swore to himself and picked up the Browning automatic from the pillow by Pavel's feet. He held it in his hand and pointed it toward its owner, squinting up at him and humming to himself some unrecognizable tune.

"It's loaded, dear boy."

"You amaze me," remarked Eberlin disdainfully, and thrust the gun under the pillow out of sight. There was a light chink of metal against metal. Puzzled, Eberlin moved aside the pillow and revealed the long, disturbing shape of a hypodermic needle pushed hastily in this cache, resting next to the gun. Eberlin glanced at Pavel with contempt and walked away from the bed. There was a gurgling laugh from behind him and Pavel said:

"Well now you know the reason for my odd manner. It ought to teach you not to go bursting in everywhere unannounced."

"They have a film of the man they think is Krasnevin," Eberlin said quietly.

"Obviously not of you." "No."

"Why that's excellent," cried Pavel, sitting up. "I never knew that. All you have to do now is find the man in the film and kill him, then announce him to the British as Krasnevin. Couldn't be better."

Eberlin didn't reply. Pavel smiled broadly and added:

"Did you know the man in the film at all? Recognize his face?" There was a pause, then: "Yes. It was you."

Pavel's jaw dropped in cold parody of Marley's ghost, then he gave a machine-gun burst of laughter and said: "You're not serious?"

"Perfectly. They think *you're* Krasnevin. It was you in the film." "But–oh, God!"

A frightening stillness entered the room and observed the two men frozen like waxworks in a pageant, and then Pavel looked unsteadily at Eberlin and asked quietly:

"What–what are you going to do about it?" "What would *you* do, Pavel?"

"I'd kill you." "You'd have to."

"Yes. Yes I would, I'd have to kill you. After all, it's your life or mine."

"Something like that."

"That's why you came here. To …" "Yes."

"Funny. I was going to go away for a couple of days as well." "Oh really?" asked Eberlin. "Where exactly?"

"A little place I know in the Cotswolds." "It's very pretty around there."

"Yes I think so. The hills. Oh God!" Pavel suddenly began to shake as if in a fever.

"You are ill, aren't you?" said Eberlin.

"Yes. For the last three days. That's why I–" "Didn't go away."

"Yes…."

Eberlin picked up the Browning and held it in his hand.

"I wouldn't use that," said Pavel. "The man upstairs complains bitterly if you make a noise after midnight."

For a full minute Eberlin stood there, holding the gun, and then suddenly he threw it on the bed, turned on his heel and walked to the door.

"Get out," he snapped to Pavel. "Get out of the country. Do it now."

"You're a fool," said Pavel.

"I'll find another way, but you've got to get out of sight."

He opened the door, glancing back at the other man for a moment.

"Thanks," said Pavel self-consciously.

"Don't be so damn melodramatic," shouted Eberlin, and added, "You make me sick."

He closed the door behind him and was hurrying silently down the stone corridor and darkened stone stairs of the building, down to the courtyard below. He walked rapidly toward the dimly lit street by the railway line, almost colliding into a black Buick that emerged suddenly from the depths of the bridge, lights out, and turned into the Estate car park.

* * *

Eberlin had just reached the corner of the street when he suddenly stopped in cold realization and turned and began to run, run back up the road, under the bridge and back toward the darkened hulk of the apartments. He was committing suicide by walking away and he knew it. He had to kill Pavel, no matter who he was, and he had to do it now. Breathing hard, his coat flapping around him and catching on the cars in the park, he ran to the entrance and saw gratefully that the lift was waiting for him. He slammed the gates and pressed the thirteenth button and the small, room-forfour lift was surging upward, breaking the silence of the building with the sound of its motor and the rattle of its cables. Eberlin no longer cared about caution or secrecy as he threw open the lift gates on the thirteenth floor and hurried to Pavel's apartment. The door was closed but unlocked and he burst into the bedroom, but it was empty, deserted, without Pavel, without anyone. A chair had been knocked over and the bed blankets dragged to the floor. Anxiously Eberlin threw aside the pillow but the gun had gone and the hypodermic was smashed and the mattress ripped. He moved to the window in the darkness and looked down toward the car park, screwing up his eyes to put the shape of it in perspective with his limited knowledge of the area. Then he saw it. The Buick. It was still there.

In no time, he was in the corridor again and into the lift and sweating as the enormity of time seemed endless before he arrived on ground level. And then he was running out into the dark yard and across the concrete toward the Buick, now turning and gathering up speed, heavily and slowly like a giant airliner on a narrow strip. But the engine was already warming to a speed as Eberlin reached it, his hand groping for the handle. For a brief instant he caught a glimpse of two men in the front, and the car was away and Eberlin knew it was too late. He had hesitated and he had lost. It was as simple as that By telling the girl he had told the Russians, and Rotopkin no doubt, that Pavel was known, revealed, no longer under plain cover. It mattered little in any degree, for he had seen Pavel lying crumpled in the thin pajamas, one arm tucked under his chest, and his face distorted and dead above the bruised gape of the throat. Kuzmich's hoods had been unusually final this time.

Eberlin walked back toward the bridge, noting that it was of rather interesting design and finer in its curve than the majority of Victorian counterparts. They would take Pavel's body away so that it would never be found and there would be a reshuffling in the hierarchy that Eberlin always found rather dull. His own particular problem wasn't eliminated but all he wished now was to sleep. In his own bed preferably.

He arrived at his apartment and was horrified to discover that it was three twenty-five, but the rain had stopped and by all favorable signs, it would be a pleasant day in the morning. Eberlin made himself some hot chocolate, undressed and folded his clothes, then slid into bed and fell asleep immediately, neither dreaming of anything whatsoever nor even waking up once during the night. As he remarked to himself a few days later, it was the finest night's sleep he had had for weeks.

7

Metamorphosis

West Berliners who will not in future be able to visit their gardens or other property in East Berlin and the DDR can complain to the guilty party–the city council of West Berlin–and ask them for compensation.
–THE SOVIET ZONE MINISTRY OF INTERNAL AFFAIRS
Berliner Zeitung, June 26, 1952

"That's true enough," said Candide, "but we must go and work in the garden."
–VOLTAIRE

Common sense isn't.
–ALEXANDER EBERLIN

AS expected, the favorable portents of weather were deceptive, and the next morning was recorded as one of the wettest August days for seventeen years. The rain flooded southeast England continuously for eleven hours, and in Kent nineteen people were rendered homeless and half a village sank slowly under a burst bank of fresh water. To Eberlin, it was all a fitting *valete* to his stay in London, for on the Wednesday, the day after the flood, he was to fly by BEA Viscount to Berlin as George Dancer, baggily trousered, narrow-minded and distasteful.

He spent most of the day at Chesterfield Street conferring with Frazer and Flowers, retracing moves of the operation with admirably concealed apathy, and collecting last-minute necessities. It was suggested at one point, at a lull in the conversation, that he go to Wilkinson's in Pall Mall and ask Mr. Barrett for a titanium waistcoat. Eberlin laughed and refused on the grounds that titanium was hardly a fashionable material that year, and he would feel, by wearing it, conscious that he could be shot at. The others had laughed in descending order of status and passed it off as a joke–which it was–and the waistcoat idea was dropped. However, they insisted that Eberlin take a gun, and led him to the Armory to select one. He chose a Browning Model 1922 caliber .32 ACP, a Belgian gun manufactured by Fabrique Nationale of Herstal, and signed for it, though he stated quite categorically that firearms disturbed him. He was reassured that he would probably never need to use it.

Later he took Heather Vogler out to dinner and they sat in a quiet corner of Terrazza Trattoria and talked about themselves and about their respective roles in the next three weeks, and then Eberlin took her home and kissed her good night like an acned schoolboy, and then returned to South Street to reread the Dancer file and pack his valise. He knew now exactly what he would do in Berlin. Pavel's unfortunate death had given him little option. He was entirely on his own, utterly without any being he could turn to. The ball, the gigantic, precarious detonated ball, was in his lap. Eberlin began to run with it next morning, quite early, by taking the Underground to Gloucester Road and waiting for his flight bus at the Terminal, sitting in the restaurant with a warm cup of tea, a copy of the *Daily Mail*, a shiny-seated suit and a self-conscious leer at the breasts of a friendly but hideous waitress of dubious age.

"Call me George," said Eberlin, helping himself to sugar.

* * *

He had always considered Berlin a rather unattractive city on the surface. It had neither the architectural pedigree of Munich nor the intense, strident redevelopment of Cologne or Frankfurt. Instead this apathetic whore of a capital, oblivious to its national allegiance, was a potpourri of styles, moods and ideas that were neither uniform nor, in the long run, appealing. West Berlin jarred his sense of finesse, and to him, ironically, the only aesthetic construction since the war was the beige ribbon of the Wall. That at least had a form. And so Eberlin barely glanced at the city as he emerged from the long hall of Tempelhof Airport, but hailed a waiting taxi, slumped next to the driver and stared, for most of the journey, at the encircled triangle on the hood of the car. The immense sculpture to the Air Lift in the forecourt of the airport, stuck like a concrete mantilla in the earth, reassured him that he was finally at his destination and that was all he wished to know.

The Kliest Hotel was just off the Kurfürstendamm, tucked

behind the barrage of glossy restaurants and shops. It was brown and old, having survived two world wars intact, adequately furnished inside in the traditional green, and competently suitable as a hotel except that the service was bad and the plumbing worse. Eberlin was shown up to his small room on the second floor, told in no self-conscious way of the unfortunate failings of the building, and then left alone with the striped wallpaper, a print of the Kaiser-Wilhelm Church in its original state, and an uncommanding view from the window of the top of the Ka Da We. Disturbed in not the slightest degree by this, Eberlin unpacked and spent the following four days fulfilling his role as George Dancer, visiting with overt enthusiasm, for fear of being watched, all the few tourist attractions in the city.

On the first day, he had sent a picture postcard of the Radio Tower to Vogler with the words:

Having a wonderful time. Just arrived. Wish you were here. Love and Kisses, George

P.S. How's filming?

The next day he received a long, passionate letter from Vogler that overpowered him, and he read it three times until he realized it was a vacuous impersonal message and so threw it away in disgust, and wrote an even more passionate letter in reply, pouring out ridiculous statements of desire and ignoring completely New Code D5. In the four days he wrote five such letters in similar vein for the sheer fun of it and as a release from the tension and boredom of the situation. On the Saturday a coded telegram arrived from the Ministry that read simply: WHAT CODE ARE YOU USING? CANNOT COMPREHEND MESSAGES.

By this time, Eberlin didn't care, for he had decided that by Monday he had given himself a long enough safety margin, and would quit the West. It was a simple solution to it all. He would just get on a train and return East and damn them all. He owed them nothing and was big enough to look after himself. Let's face it, he repeated to himself, all he wanted to do was retire to his own small corner and let the rest of the world fend for itself. What could be wrong in that? He considered. And then he saw Rotopkin.

Or at least he thought he saw Rotopkin. It had all happened so quickly that Eberlin was unsure of the true facts. He had waked up unusually nervous on the eve of his departure day, the Sunday, partly due to the heat and partly due to a nightmare. He had decided to visit the lakes on this day, and had walked the few hundred yards to the Zoo station, his hands in his pockets, attempting to enjoy the sun and the prospects of a lazy day away from the crowds. It was about eleven in the morning when he entered the cool, dark hallway of the station and paused at the kiosk to buy a copy of *Newsweek*, and then crossed to the counter to buy a ticket for the S-Bahn. Moving away from the circular window, the ticket clutched in his hand, Eberlin happened by chance to glance back toward the newsstand, twenty yards or so away near the entrance, and he stopped suddenly so that a woman holding a small child bumped into him and swore. The man in the Madras jacket at the kiosk turned away quickly and studied some books in a far window, but Eberlin had seen his face. It was Rotopkin. Here in Berlin. Following him. He tried to catch sight of the man again, but his line of vision was obliterated by a crowd of visiting schoolchildren and a woman was shouting in his ear. When he moved away, farther down the hallway, the man had gone. The chances that it was Rotopkin trailing him were strong for the KGB were hardly likely to allow him to wander around Berlin unobserved. He knew they were suspicious of him. But was it Rotopkin? He would probably never know for sure. He hurried upstairs to the platform and in three minutes was sitting on one of the wooden seats of the S-Bahn on the way to Wannsee.

The long, rattling red and yellow train ran overland all the way and was now out of the residential part of the city, and was running parallel to the Avus, that arrow-straight autobahn built by Hitler as a racing circuit, to the west of the city. Eberlin had put the magazine away and was sitting smoking a Rothandel cigarette, his chin on his hand, staring out at the road and the thick forest behind. Now and again he caught sight of a U.S. Army truck or a jeep resting in the trees, and at one point passed a clearing which he knew to be the American firing range. When he had been in Berlin before, he had lived on this side of the lake and had been constantly deafened by the sound of practice mortars. Windows had been shattered. The occupying soldiers here, he reflected, went about the business of peace in such a clumsy, demonstrative way. He was prepared to guess quite confidently that there were more Sherman tanks than squirrels tucked away in the neighboring woods, obvious to all but the men inside. Ah well, he was here on holiday, and absurd trivialities concerned him no more for the present.

Though the train traveled farther than Wannsee, Eberlin had to get out whether he liked it or not, for it was the last stop in West Berlin–the S-Bahn belonged to the East. He strolled leisurely out of the station and across the road and into the forest and down to the small jetty on the lake. The Havel was populated now by only a few boats and a dozen or so small dinghies, and the queue for the translake steamer was small for such a fine day. Eberlin was one of the first on board and he chose a bench at the bow of the ship with his back to the others and an uncluttered view of the beautiful expanse of water and the villas surrounding it. The boat went nowhere in particular, just back and forth over the Havel, which suited him since he just wanted to sit and think, smoke perhaps, and idle away his last day.

The steamer eased away from the small jetty and manoeuvred into position and set off toward the far corner, cutting straight across the water in a direct line. Eberlin had found this a pleasant journey before, in his earlier stay in Berlin, since there were no irritating guides directing one's attention away from one's own choosing, and the beauty of this part of the city reminded the visitor more of the Riviera or Switzerland, never of an occupied city surrounded by alien fencing. And so Eberlin sat quietly engrossed in his own thoughts, smoking a cigarette, until halfway across the lake he was disturbed by the disquieting sound of English voices coming from behind him. High-pitched feminine giggles and chatter breaking the peaceful quiet of the scene. Two dreadful English schoolgirls on holiday, Eberlin thought without turning around to look. He quickly hid the copy of *Newsweek* for fear of being dragged into a conversation, and slumped farther down into the seat. The voices stopped suddenly and he assumed the girls had gone to the other end of the boat. He was mistaken. A pair of sun-tanned and not unattractive legs appeared beside him, and he saw out of the corner of his eye the white triangle of a bikini bottom delicately covering softly curved hips, and heard a voice saying, "Hello."

Too late to pretend to be asleep, he thought. And he assumed the wretched tweed jacket and the cravat had betrayed his supposed nationality. Heart sinking, he looked up at the smiling face of the girl. "Fancy seeing you here," said Caroline, smiling down at him through enormous sunglasses, "I could hardly believe it when I saw you getting on the boat. I knew we'd meet again. Isn't it super? Just bumping into each other like this. Miles from anywhere."

A yacht, struck by a freak wind, suddenly sailed too close to the bows of the boat and a man on the bridge shouted a warning. Eberlin stared up at the face of Caroline, tilted on an angle, framed by a translucent halo of sun-bleached hair, and then glanced behind him into the stern of the steamer at the other girl, a stranger, who was hovering self-consciously a few feet away toying with an Air France carryall.

"You're wondering where we've met before, aren't you?" asked Caroline, taking off her sunglasses and crouching down before him. "What?" Eberlin replied, then looking down at her into those violet eyes, added, "Did you bring any of your Amontillado sherry with you? I suddenly feel like a drink."

She gave a low chuckle and tugged up the bra of her bikini. "Holiday?"

"Yes," Eberlin said.

"Us too. Tour of the Continent and all that. Isn't it super weather?"

What the hell is she doing here? he thought. This ingenuous seductive little creature, kneeling before him on the deck of the boat in the middle of Berlin. She'd been in Tripoli too. And London. This persistently engaging little debutante was to be watched. God! First Rotopkin. Now her. With an omen like this, fat Copperfield was probably steering the bloody boat.

"Are you slumming or something?" she asked. "Pardon?"

Caroline pointed at the baggy trousers and the heavy shoes. "Oh?" said Eberlin with a smile. "Oh yes. In a way."

"Look, I must introduce you to Susan. You'll like her. She's

awfully sweet and horsey. Daddy's a big thing in the City and an MFH. Pots of money. Just a minute, I'll call her."

She stood up and moved to turn away when Eberlin grabbed her arm and pulled her down to him.

"Look, Caroline, don't ask questions but my name is George Dancer and I work in an oil company. All right?"

She pulled back slightly and stared wide-eyed at Eberlin's face. He could see flickers of indecision and puzzlement in her eyes and then she bit her lip. The other girl was approaching now. Eberlin released Caroline's arm and with a smile nodded to her. Then the bewildered expression vanished and Caroline straightened up with a laugh and plonked the sunglasses back on her nose.

"Fancy, and fancy," she said, and then, taking hold of the other girl's hand, added, "Susan, I want to you to meet an old friend. He looks awfully stuffy and square but he's not like that at all. In fact I've been nursing a secret crush on him for months," and she laughed again and touched Eberlin's shoulder. "George, I want you to meet Susan. Susan, this is George Dancer. He's in oil."

* * *

The beach at Nikolasse was crowded, as was to be expected. It was a hot Sunday and this was the only sensible stretch of sand in the city. Looking around him and seeing the colored basket chairs and the hundreds or so stripped-down sun worshippers in varying costumes lying on the sand or swimming in the warm water of the lake, little children losing parents, stubbing toes, standing ankle deep in the unnatural swell of the no-tide, tugging at father's hand, and bronze girls in briefest bikinis flirting with heavyset young men, Eberlin felt much too overdressed in his heavy trousers and shirt and so buried himself deeper in the obscurity of the basket chair. Near him lay half a dozen American soldiers drinking beer, listening to AFN and whistling at girls running by. Caroline and Susan were in the water, out of sight, somewhere near the diving pier. They had left the boat together, the three of them, and had driven around to the beach in Caroline's MGB, Eberlin suffering the overweight of Susan's fat rump on his lap and the mischievous glances of Caroline as she smiled at him over the girl's shoulder.

Now he had been sitting on the beach for an hour drinking a bottle of wine bought on the way over and getting quietly plastered. He raised the bottle in a dumb toast to himself and said, "Bon voyage." Then he put the wine to his mouth and swallowed nothing. The bottle was empty.

"Wooooeee!"

There was a shriek and Eberlin saw Caroline running out of the water, legs splayed clownishly as she jumped over recumbent sunbathers, then hurrying up toward him smiling and waving like a jazzed-up emerging Venus. All eyes turned toward her and Eberlin felt smugly possessive of her and found himself smiling back at her stupidly. One of the soldiers made a grab for Caroline's ankle, but she leapt nimbly away and stuck her tongue out at him, then collapsed in a wet huddle in the basket chair.

"Wow! Getting through that lecherous crowd is a horror," she gasped in Eberlin's ear. "Are all Germans as randy as they are here?

Some dirty old Fritz kept grabbing at my pants while I was swimming."

"I'm in full sympathy with him," replied Eberlin and pulled a wisp of wet hair from her forehead.

She poked him in the ribs with her finger and laughed and said, "Got a fag, George?"

Eberlin gave her one and they sat smoking quietly, staring at the water, Caroline put her arm on his shoulder and scratched her nose. "It's just dawned on me. My clothes are in the trunk of the car.

I'll have to stay in this wet bikini till we go. Hate that. We never intended going in the water. Not getting wet, I mean."

"You'll soon dry off." "Horrid."

"Where's Susan?"

"Oh, I don't know. Floating around somewhere," she said unconcerned, then added, "Fat thing."

Eberlin moved away from her and took her arm from his shoulder.

"Caroline," he said quietly.

"Why are you wearing those dreary clothes? You were always such a super dresser–"

"Caroline, listen to me," he repeated and she clenched her hands between her knees like a schoolgirl about to be scolded. Eberlin glanced at the soldiers but they had drifted away and were talking to two girls by the ice-cream stall.

"Look–I don't expect you to understand," he continued, "but don't go acting all dramatic and thinking ridiculous things. I want you to forget my name is Eberlin. At least for the moment. You see I'm here–"

He stopped to look at her but she was sitting frowning at her feet. He put a hand on her leg for a moment, then took it away and folded his arms.

"Well anyway," he said, "it's all rather confidential, but you've got to trust me. I mean, telling you this is in confidence, you understand?"

Caroline sighed and without looking up said in an irritated tone, "Oh dear, I don't know why you're getting all spooky about going around under another name. Mummy does it all the time when she goes away on a dirty weekend. She's done it hundreds of times. But I think you're sweet anyway for telling me.

Eberlin smiled. "Well, it's a bit different from that."

"God, I hope so, George. I'd hate to think that you're shacked up with some rotten old fräulein in some hotel or something. Let's have a swim and forget about it."

"I haven't got a swimsuit."

"Oh yes. I forgot. Never mind. We'll sneak back at midnight and do it in the nude."

He laughed and picked up the bottle to drink, realizing it was empty, and threw it away.

"Let's go, shall we?" "Where?" she asked.

"I want to talk to you. Let's go somewhere quiet."

"Oh lovely. Let's have it in those woods and ruin all those silly army manoeuvers."

Eberlin turned her face toward him with his finger under her chin and shook his head in mock disapproval.

"I think you ought to join your friend Susan, don't you?" he said.

Thrusting the last stub of the cigarette defiantly into her mouth,

Caroline dropped back down into the basket seat so that her stomach stuck up in the air and her feet hung six inches from the churned-up sand. She tugged childishly at the loose straps of the bikini top and sunk into a pouting sulk. Eberlin waited.

"I suppose you think I'm just a silly little child," she said finally.

"Yes," he answered blandly.

"Well I'm not," she said and kicked him, hurting her toe. Eberlin smiled and offered to buy her ice cream.

"Oh shut up," she said and pulled her legs under, sitting up and pushing out her jaw and staring at the American soldiers nearby. "I know you think you're so mature and superior and all that, but at least I don't go around in silly clothes like some kind of spy or something."

"Oh I agree. The clothes you're wearing now are nothing less than delightful."

"Well then …" "Well then what?"

"Well, it's just that I've been so bored tramping around Germany with Fat Susan, and then all of a sudden I meet someone nice like you and I suppose I behave a bit silly … oh dear, I'm not really so bad, am I?"

She pulled a face at an American sergeant who had wandered near to where they were sitting, and was standing half-dressed, drinking beer from a can. The sergeant smiled and proffered a cigar. Caroline shook her head. The cigar was held out toward Eberlin, who, surprising himself, accepted. The sergeant approached the seat and put one muscled arm on the top and stood negligently looking down at Caroline's breasts. Eberlin took the cigar with a "*Danke schon*" and lit it. The sergeant scratched his chin, keeping his eyes fixed steadily on Caroline's body despite her angry glares, and spoke out of the corner of his mouth to Eberlin, under the impression they were both German:

"*Sie ist ein süsses Mädchen.*"

Eberlin agreed and Caroline turned her back on the American and busied herself with combing her hair now that it was drying out. The sergeant, watched by an amused Eberlin, made another attempt to attract her attention, but she yawned openly and ignored him. Then with calculated effrontery, he slowly poured the half-full can of cold beer over Caroline's head. Eberlin moved aside, waiting for the onslaught, but there was no immediate reaction. Instead, with superb aplomb, she turned her face up slowly toward the American, her eyelashes flickering, and said in the sweetest possible way:

"Fuck off."

There was an immediate stunned surprise from the sergeant, then he burst out laughing, and grinning over his face, held out his hand and shook Caroline's hand, seized Eberlin's hand and shook that, then walked away back to the others laughing loudly. Caroline continued calmly combing her hair.

"I must congratulate you," said Eberlin, "on a game played and won."

"Well, now you see what a girl like me has to put up with." Eberlin smiled and touched her arm.

"Come on. Let's go back to the car."

They both got up and collected the few belongings. Then they crossed to the stone path and made their way up the three flights of steep steps to the lawns above. As they reached the top, a short bald-headed man emerged from the shadow of a beer stand and hurried quickly away.

At the car park, Caroline took a sweater and a pair of jeans from the back of the car and was about to put them on, when Eberlin stopped her, calling over the hood of the car:

"You're not going to put those on over your wet things, are you?"

"Why not? I can't drive through town in a bikini."

"You'll catch cold. Now put them back and you can wear my shirt. I've got a T-shirt underneath."

"No, don't bother–" "Do as I say."

She pulled a face, then smiled and said quietly, "Keeping me in place, George?"

"Yes."

"Thank you." And she buttoned up Eberlin's gray cotton shirt over the wet bikini.

"I'll drive," he said and sat behind the wheel. "You just sit there and shut up till I find my bearings."

She pulled her mouth shut till her lips disappeared from sight, and sat straight-backed staring out of the windshield. Eberlin reversed the car, drove slowly down a maze of lanes till he found the Avus, then headed fast toward the center. As they were passing the Radio Tower, Caroline said suddenly:

"Can I speak now?" "Depends."

"Just wanted to say that there's been a car following us since the beach."

"Which one?–No, don't turn around. Describe it to me," said Eberlin.

"Gray car. One of those funny German ones everybody has." "Volkswagen?"

"Is that what it's called? Well, one of those." "I know."

"Oh. Is it following us?"

"Shouldn't think so. This is the main route back to town, so it's not surprising other cars are going our way."

"Oh," Caroline said, disappointed. "Well, just thought I'd say it."

Nevertheless Eberlin was concerned. It was almost certainly a coincidence that the Volkswagen was following them but it made him jumpy. He turned sharply off the autobahn and cut down a side street leading to his hotel.

"I'm going back to my hotel. You can change there."

He parked the car in the next street to Leitzenburger-strasse, and they hurried quickly to the hotel. Eberlin ignored the stares of the receptionist glaring at Caroline, and casually took the key to his room. Once inside the room, he locked the door and, on the pretense of opening the window, glanced out into the street, just in time to see the gray Volkswagen disappear around the corner. He turned back, lit a cigarette and sat on the bed and caught sight of Caroline on tiptoes gazing at the wall prints.

"Room's a bit dreary, George. Is this all it is?" "Yes."

"Just one room?" "I'm afraid so." "Oh well."

Eberlin lay down on the bed and rested his head on his arms, the cigarette sticking in his mouth. Unbuttoning the shirt, Caroline took it off, folded it and put it on the chair. "Towel?"

"In the drawer. Bottom one."

His eyes strayed to her as she bent over and fumbled in the drawer for a towel and pulled out a white-and-blue-striped one. Then, standing in the middle of the room, she took off the bikini.

"What on earth are you doing?" said Eberlin realizing suddenly that she was naked.

"Pardon?" she replied casually, peering intently at a graze she had just noticed on her left elbow.

"Do you always strip before strange men?"

"The bikini's wet and there's no other room, and anyway you're not so strange." She smiled and looked at him, then at herself in the wardrobe mirror. "I think I look rather smashing except for a little weight on my turn. What are you making such a fuss about? I don't mind you looking at me."

"That's hardly the point."

"Stop moaning," she replied, drying herself, "I'm an existentialist."

"A what?"

"Isn't that the right word?" "Exhibitionist is more to the point."
"What's existentialist then?"

"Well, it's a little more complex than romping around naked."
"Oh, well–I must be the other thing then. What you said."

Eberlin watched her as she finished drying herself, then she took a cigarette from the side table and sat by him on the bed, toes turned in, arms to her side.

"Won't you catch cold?" "Immune to them."

She turned and smiled at him, then leaned down and kissed him on the cheek. He could see the reflection of them both in the wardrobe mirror opposite the bed. He lying there in those ridiculous clothes, and Caroline with her small naked body balanced precariously on the edge of the bed. He ran his hand over her stomach so that she gave a shuddering sigh until he brought his other hand back and slapped her hard on the bottom.

"Ow!"

"Get up and put some clothes on. It's late and I've got things to do. Go on."

She got up and stood up rubbing the sore part of her body and pouting at the floor. Eberlin sat on the edge of the bed and handed her a cigarette, but she ignored him and slunk over to the window and stared out at the street. Throwing the cigarette on the bed, Eberlin walked over to her took hold of her shoulders and pulled her away from the window.

"Look, Caroline, it's no use going into one of your debby sulks. I'd be delighted to seduce you right now but I'm here on business and I've only got a few hours left. So take your thumb out of your mouth and make it easier for both of us by putting on these clothes." He scooped up her trousers and sweater and dumped them in her hand. Keeping deliberately quiet, Caroline pulled on the jeans, zipped them up carefully, and slipped on the V-neck cashmere sweater.

"It tickles without a bra," she mumbled.

"Lucky thing," Eberlin replied. "Anyway, you look infinitely more seductive with your clothes on."

She gave a quick scowl and searched for the cigarette on the bed, found it and lit it.

"What made you come to Berlin?" Eberlin asked her, leaning casually against the mantelpiece.

"Just wanted to see it." "Is that all?"

"Yes. Why?"

"What were you doing in Tripoli?"

"I went there with Mummy. I told you. Why?" "Where are you staying in Berlin?"

"At the Bristol. Why all these questions?" "How long are you staying here?"

"I don't know. Look, I'm not following you if *that's* what you think."

Rain clouds had suddenly sprung up from the west and darkened the sky, so that Eberlin, becoming conscious of the gloom, switched on the light even though it was still only afternoon. Caroline didn't move but remained sitting on the bed smoking the cigarette. The wet bikini was lying in a damp heap on the carpet. Eberlin picked it up and laid the parts over the windowsill.

"You can collect these later if you wish. When they've dried out.

Any questions?"

With a shrug, Caroline looked up at him, looking through the straggles of blond hair over her forehead and then she smiled and said:

"Yes. Where's the john? I'm dying for a pee."

* * *

Eberlin moved rapidly as soon as Caroline had returned to her hotel. He wrote two letters, one signed Dancer and the other Eberlin, then gathered all his belongings together and sorted out only essential objects he wished to take. He intended to leave his suitcase in the room in the morning, and create the impression that he had just left for the day. Satisfying himself that all was prepared as far as the hotel was concerned, he left his room, locked it, and took a slow walk back to the Zoo station. After eating a leisurely steak meal in the restaurant above the station, he collected his gun from the luggage locker on the ground floor. It was hidden in a camera case which he hung over his shoulder. Then he made three phone calls from the public call box near the booking office.

At six o'clock he bought a copy of *Der Tagespiegel* and checked the details of cinema showings and times, deciding to see the revival of *The Scarlet Pimpernel* at Steinplatz. He had seen it three times before, during his first stay in Berlin; it was one of the rare films to be shown undubbed and seemed to have a curious attraction for the Berliners. Something to do with the similarity to the contemporary escapes over the Wall, Eberlin decided, but that didn't mar his enjoyment of the film, sitting hunched up in the tiny cinema waching Leslie Howard with rapt attention as the Pimpernel saw home again, returned again to his native country after the regretted espionage was over.

When Eberlin returned to the hotel, it was late and so he showered as best he could in the communal bathroom, and then got into bed and read till there was a knock on the door. He opened it cautiously to see Caroline standing outside, wrapped in an immense fur coat, and holding up a tooth-brush.

"For an awful moment I thought you were askeep." She smiled and then came into the room. He locked the door, and was about to switch on the main light when Caroline held his hand.

"Don't put it on, George. I'm not really such an exhibitionist as I made out."

And she turned away and stood facing the wall.

"It's late," Eberlin said quietly and touched her arm. She turned back and hugged him tightly.

"Let's get into bed," he said quietly. Caroline sniffed and nodded and he took off her coat and dropped in on the chair.

Staring into the darkness an hour later, he lay in the bed, his arms around the thin warm body of Caroline curled up almost like a cat on his chest. Listening to her breathing as she slept, he felt a tender protectiveness for her. He bent his head and lightly kissed her breast, and heard her murmur contentedly in her sleep. Women were so fragile, so incredibly fragile.

He was about to fall asleep himself, when he thought he heard a sound in the corridor outside his door. He held his breath and listened, and there was a faint but distinct knock on the door. Eberlin glanced at his watch. It was fifteen minutes after midnight. The knock was repeated and then a voice:

"Herr Dancer?"

Eberlin was silent for a moment listening, then gently eased Caroline away from him, sliding his arm under body for fear of waking her, tiptoed from the bed across the room to a drawer and took out the gun. Checking it, he slipped on a dressing gown, unlocked the door and opened it a few inches. A small, bald-headed man was staring up at him. Eberlin, keeping the gun out of sight behind the door, said quietly:

"Was wollen Sie?"

"Herr Dancer, I am sorry to bother you," the man replied in German, rubbing the side of his head nervously with his hand, "but I understand you were the last to use the shower."

"What about it?"

The man attempted to peer into the room but Eberlin moved in front of him.

"Well, apparently, the plumbing isn't very good, for Herr Elsner below complained of water seeping through his ceiling. Perhaps you could come and see." "At this time of night?"

"I'm sorry to disturb you like this but … well the water is …" His voice trailed away and he rubbed the side of his head again. "Is the water still leaking?"

"Well it is a little, Herr Dancer. We're terribly sorry to bother you but … perhaps you could help me fix it before it …. floods everything."

Eberlin stared at him, then along the dimly lit corridor and then back to the nervous face of the man.

"Just a minute," he said brusquely and closed the door. Caroline was still sleeping soundly as he put on slippers and tucked the gun into the sleeve of the dressing gown. Glancing out of the window, he saw that the street was empty, then he opened the door and joined the little man in the corridor.

"It shouldn't be a big job," the man said and hurried down the corridor toward the bathroom, with Eberlin following warily.

The bathroom was at the end of the corridor on the right, and on reaching it, the bald-headed man stood aside for Eberlin to enter. It was empty inside, and there was no sound except for the dripping of the shower. The floor was as dry as a bone.

"What exactly was it–" Eberlin began, when he heard the snap of the lock. He turned around in time to see his caller lean against the door and stand looking up at him. There was a pause and then Eberlin quickly backed away and pushed open the doors of the two cubicles.

"It's all right–we're quite alone," the man said in perfect English, lighting a pipe.

"You're a funny little man, aren't you?" Eberlin replied. "Who the hell are you?"

"My name is Henderson actually."

"How nice for you. Would you unlock the door now so that I can leave?"

"In a minute. I must confess I don't actually work for the hotel.

"You surprise me," Eberlin snorted and sat perched on the edge of the towel rack and folded his arms.

"Look, Eberlin, I'm sorry to have had to go through all this silly subterfuge, but if you insist on picking up stray tarts, how on earth can we get in touch with you?"

"Oh, I'm sorry, Henderson. She's got a friend though that might be your type. I'll see if we can arrange a double date." Then he added, "Who's *we*?"

"Frazer." "Oh really?"

Henderson smiled and strolled up and down the tiled floor, puffing at the pipe.

"What exactly does he want?" Eberlin asked.

"Well," said Henderson, turning and giving a quick smile, "well, you must realize that he is getting a bit worried about you. I mean, you don't seem to be doing anything."

"So he sent you here?"

"More or less. Do you want a cigarette? I have those as well."

"No thank you. He never told me you were coming."

"No, well, it was a spur-of-the-moment thing. You know how things are at home. I was in Munich actually when I got the wire."

"Oh yes? You must have been with Gatiss."

"Yes. Poor old Gatiss. Hates the place, but no one will give him a transfer. I left him drowning his sorrows in a bar."

"That's Gatiss for you," said Eberlin deadpan.

"Yes," said Henderson with a smile and repeated, "Poor old Gatiss ..."

"Drive up this morning?" Eberlin said suddenly, startling the other man.

"What–oh yes. Straight route."

"That must have been you in the gray Volkswagen following me then."

"What? Well ... yes it was actually. Awfully careless of me to let you notice–"

"Why?"

Henderson gave a quick laugh and rubbed the side of his face. A door banged in the corridor outside and they both waited in silence until someone tried the bathroom door, swore, then returned to his room.

"It's getting cold in here," said Eberlin after a while, straightening up and moving toward the mirror. He stood so that he could see Henderson's nervous face in the reflection beside him.

"Just met that girl today, did you?" inquired Henderson with a nervous laugh.

"Why?"

"Oh–nothing. English, isn't she?"

"She was driving an English car and wearing English clothes and her name is Anne, so work it out for yourself."

"Oh yes. Yes. English then. Rather attractive though." "Look, Henderson–what exactly do you want?"

"Well I was–that is, Frazer was just wondering what actually were your plans. For the rest of your stay here."

"Oh–is that all? Well, I'll tell you, shall I?" "If you could. We'd be awfully grateful."

Moving casually away from the mirror, Eberlin seemed to turn his back on Henderson, but, in one sudden action, had swung around and grabbed hold of his lapels, pushing him backward into the shower and ramming the muzzle of the gun deep into the man's paunch. Mouth open in stunned surprise. Henderson tried at first to struggle, then glanced down and saw the butt of the Browning seemingly disappearing into his navel.

"All right–who sent you here?" Eberlin snapped.

Henderson's cheeks sagged and he seemed to be thinking once more about struggling, until Eberlin quickly searched his pockets and threw an automatic onto the beveled floor of the shower. The gun spun around noisily on the tiles and slowly slid to rest over the disposal grille.

"What are you doing–Frazer sent me–"

"No, he didn't," said Eberlin, pushing the gun farther into the man's stomach. "There's no one called Henderson in the files and furthermore I would have been notified if there was or if you were arriving. And for your information, Gatiss left Munich ten days ago. Now tell me who you are. And that gun's a Tokarev."

Immediately Henderson's face froze into a defiant dumbness. Eberlin knew the expression well. Still keeping the gun in the man's stomach, Eberlin pulled Henderson's wallet out of his pocket and shook its contents onto the floor. One glance revealed the man's identity. What an incompetent fool, he thought, and reached over and turned on the hot tap of the shower. The nozzle bubbled, then burst into life and flooded Henderson with hot water. Eberlin stood

back, still pointing the gun, and said:

"Was this Rotopkin's idea, to send a clown like you?" No answer.

"What did you hope to achieve by this pathetic attempt at subterfuge?" Eberlin continued. "Tell Kuzmich that if he hadn't been so eager to kill Pavel I wouldn't be in this damn mess."

"You're under a gross misunderstanding," the man said in Russian but Eberlin cut him off.

"I think they ought to send you back to Oktyabr," he said. "You need a rest."

He leaned forward abruptly and thrust the small soaked man sharply upward so that his head hit the nozzle of the shower with a sharp crack. The Russian collapsed in a heap at the bottom of the cubicle.

Eberlin quickly bent down and searched the pockets of the unconscious man, pocketing the Tokarev, and then, leaving the shower running, unlocked the bathroom door, glanced out into the corridor and returned to his room. What does one make of that incident? he thought. And what misunderstanding? The only misunderstanding was that Kuzmich was treating him like an enemy not as a friend. Damn them all.

Caroline was still asleep, but in her slumber had spread-eagled herself across the sheets so that the covers lay crumpled on the floor, and she was occupying the whole bed. Stealthily, Eberlin locked the door and hid the two guns. He took off his dressing gown, then stood staring down at the small, childlike figure below him, her right leg draped over the side of the bed. For a moment he was reluctant to disturb this innocent repose, but craving sleep and, more urgently, comfort, he carefully slid his right arm under her back and then, cradling her with his other arm under her bottom, he picked her up and kissed her on the mouth. Still half-asleep, she murmured contentedly and let her hand stray softly over his body. He lay down on the bed, still clutching her, and she stretched out drowsily on top of him, moving her body against his and hooking her arms under his shoulders.

"Little sad creature," he whispered in her ear, "little, sad, sad, creature."

PERIGEE

8

Friedrichstrasse Nein

There have to be some obstacles to heaven,
otherwise the dog could get in.
–ALEXANDER EBERLIN

THERE was a resounding slam and a crack as the metal doors of the S-Bahn slammed shut, and the train slid out of the overhead station at Zoologischer Garten. Eberlin felt nervous. There were three stations before the S-Bahn crossed the Wall and entered Friedrichstrasse. Crossing overland, over the Tiergarten and the long, wide, ten-lane Strasse des 17 Juni that once cruised through the Brandenberg Gate but was now crippled by a barbed-wire and sandbag dam; past the tall golden Victory pillar and, away to the right, the ostentation of the Berlin Hilton and the precociousness of the Concert Hall, and then rattling in a curve over neglected tracks across the Wall itself–remarkably small and tame at first glance, but nonetheless unnerving–and the train decelerating and stopping in the immense glass arch of the Friedrichstrasse station itself.

Eberlin got out with the other few tourists and curiosity seekers, and stood on the platform a moment taking stock. The blue-coated railway guards checked the compartments, and glancing up Eberlin could see, framed high on the metal catwalks of the roof, the silhouettes of two Vopos, immobile, machine guns resting on their hips. He had known of an East German youth who had tried to escape by clutching onto the roof of a train, and of another who had hid in the engine of a locomotive. Both had died on the journey. One shot from above, here, the other, untouched, unnoticed by the Vopos, entering the safety of the West as a charred, burnt-out body. But that was of no consequence to Eberlin. His journey was the other way, crossing the Wall as a mere tourist. A simple procedure.

Reaching the bottom of the gray stone steps from the platform, Eberlin was guided by signs along a narrow corridor until he reached the Passport Control. There were about two dozen people waiting there in the hot, uncomfortable tunnel, standing quietly, awkwardly, hardly looking at each other. After half an hour, Eberlin had reached the counter, handed over his passport, given particulars of the money he carried, and been told to wait till his number was called. He moved away to a corner and stood smoking, avoiding the glances of the armed soldiers lounging by the door to the street. He waited a further half hour, then an hour until all other passengers had been cleared and others had taken their place, and still he waited anxiously, eyes aching from the strain. Only one other person besides himself had endured the long wait without being called. This was a tall man with round shoulders and prominent teeth which hovered on the front of his mouth as if he were about to spit them out in disgust. He was still standing a few yards from Eberlin, apparently unconcerned. Once the stranger smiled at him, but Eberlin, not caring to enter into pass-the-time banalities, turned away. Finally a door opened near him and a young private in the Volkspolizei approached him.

"Herr Dancer?" Eberlin nodded.

"*Wollen Sie ins Zimmer gehen*?" smiled the private and gestured toward a door in the corner of the tunnel. Eberlin frowned.

"*Was ist los*?"

"*Bitte*," said the soldier and walked toward the door and waited. Eberlin walked slowly to join him and was led into a small office adjacent to the Passport Control, fitted out only with a desk and three chairs, a telephone and the inevitable framed photo of Ulbricht. The soldier closed the door.

'Bitte, nehmen Sie platz."

Eberlin did and lit another cigarette and was left alone. He glanced around the room, but it was impersonal and betrayed nothing of its nature. Crossing to a second door, he tried to overhear conversation from the next room but it was just a murmur. He looked out of the window at a restaurant opposite and a park, and the wide entrance to Friedrichstrasse itself. Fifteen minutes later he heard the door open and turned to find that the young soldier had returned, together with a second soldier who introduced himself with a bow as Stein. He was a tall man with mousy cropped hair and a strong, thin, almost Semitic face. He smiled pleasantly at Eberlin as he sat down at the desk and gestured to him to sit opposite. The passport was placed between them. A cigarette was offered, which Eberlin accepted, noticing that it was American. He remarked on this but received only a brief smile in reply. He felt himself being studied as he lit the cigarette, and wondered if this was mere routine. "Your passport states that you are an accountant, Herr Dancer?"

"That is right. Actually I've been promoted since." "How so?"

"I'm a supervisor." "Ah."

Stein was turning the pages of the passport carefully, snapping each page with his thumb. At last he closed it and placed it neatly back in the center of the desk.

"Ah," he repeated. "Why exactly are you visiting East Berlin?" "Just sightseeing."

"Sightseeing?"

"Yes. Looking around." "Looking around?"

"Well–yes, you see I would like to see the town and ... while I am in Berlin I thought I might as well take the opportunity–"

"To visit the Eastern Sector." "Yes."

"For how long?"

"I beg your pardon?"

"How long do you intend to stay here?" "Oh–just for the day."

"Just for the day?" "Yes."

"I see."

Stein smiled and stared at the ceiling for a moment, then: "Perhaps you wish to see the Pergamum Museum. Things like that?"

"Yes. Things like that...."

"The museum is closed on Mondays." "Pity."

"Yes. What is your name again?" "Dancer. George Dancer."

"Ah yes. Dancer. You work in an oil company–is that not right?"

"How did you know that?" "It's in your passport." "No, it's not."

"Is that so?" Stein said blandly.

"Look," said Eberlin, irritated now, "what is this all about?" "Just routine matters...."

"Yes–but I notice nobody else has been dragged in here. I've been waiting now for two hours–"

"Yes, we apologize about that. But you must realize, Herr–?"
"Dancer."

"You must realize, Herr Dancer, that we have an immense problem here checking all incoming visitors."

"I thought it was outgoing visitors you were concerned about."
Stein gave a brief smile and said quietly, "Not always, Herr

Dancer. Not quite always."

Eberlin turned his head and saw that the private was still there, leaning against the wall, staring at the floor.

"Is that how he's supposed to stand in front of an officer?" said Eberlin, gesturing toward the soldier, who took no notice.

"It's not *his* position we are concerned about, Herr Dancer. It is Dancer, isn't it?"

"Yes. How many times–"

"Quite. How much money are you carrying on you?" "I've reported that."

"Tell me again."

"455DM and six pounds sterling approximately." "Rather a lot for a day's visit."

"I don't intend to spend much. In fact, if you keep me here much longer, I won't have time to spend any."

"How do you mean?" "How do I mean what?"

"How do you mean–spend any?" "I don't follow you."

"But you speak excellent German for–what is it–an accountant?"

"We English are not all illiterates."

"Ah. So I've been told. I too have read Shakespeare. Schlegel and

Thieck translation of course."

"Of course. Look, I–"

"Boses Werk muss unterhegen, Rache folgt der Freveltat. Do you know what that means? Evil deeds have got to end in ruin because vengeance follows hard on crime."

Eberlin shrugged impassively and said: "Schiller also said, *Rache tragt keine Frucht."*

"What an intelligent accountant. You amaze me, Herr Dancer–"

"Why am I being delayed here?" "You will soon know. I am waiting–"

The phone on the desk rang suddenly. A jarring *Hey*! that startled Eberlin.

"–for that," said Stein, and picked up the phone.

Eberlin watched him as the officer listened on the telephone, then finally glanced up at him and put down the receiver. Scooping up the passport, Stein stood up, turned slightly away as if deliberating on something, then stepped forward and dropped the passport carefully in Eberlin's lap.

"We're sorry to have kept you so long, and apologize. One passport returned to owner."

Eberlin looked up puzzled, glanced back at the soldier, then, with a dissatisfied grunt, stuffed the passport into his pocket and stood up.

"Well," he said, somewhat relieved, "choose someone else next time for your little conversations. Your damned city isn't that bloody marvelous."

And staggering under his attempted pose and blandness he strode to the door. Stein's voice stopped him in his tracks.

"Not that one, Herr Dancer. The other one."

Eberlin turned and looked back into the room. Impassively, Stein continued:

"There's a train to West Berlin in about three minutes. If you take the other door, it will lead you straight to the platform."

Eberlin hesitated, not quite understanding at first, incapable for a moment of saying anything. Then:

"What the hell do you mean? I wish to go into East Berlin." "I'm afraid not," Stein said. "Permission has been refused." "Refused? But I thought you–by whom? Why?"

"That is beside the point. We cannot allow you to enter the DDR. Not now or at any time. If you try to enter illegally, you will be arrested immediately."

Eberlin swore and shouted back at Stein, but to no avail. The officer calmly collected some papers from the desk and prepared to leave. Suddenly Eberlin grabbed his arm, turning him around.

"Who said I couldn't enter? You haven't given me any reason for refusing me permission. You allow hundreds of British tourists through each week. Why not me?"

"Please let go of me, Herr Dancer. I cannot do anything about it."

Stein called to the guard over Eberlin's shoulder, and he was pulled roughly away and pushed aside.

"You really are rather silly," Stein muttered, straightening his jacket. He opened the door and entered the next office.

"Is that all you have to say?" said Eberlin approaching Stein again. "Just like that?"

Stein stopped and sighed.

"Herr Dancer, you are being abnormally insistent. May I suggest you leave now before I begin to make further inquiries about you. We are a very tolerant state but do not pressure us."

Eberlin hesitated, studied Stein's face for a moment, then moved away.

"If you wish to lodge a complaint, why not try your Consul? In West Berlin, that is. Unfortunately, by some oversight, there isn't a British Consulate in the East. Good day, Herr Dancer."

And Eberlin left the room.

* * *

He sat in the train carrying him back to the center of West Berlin feeling like a master thief caught stealing apples by a farmer. It had the painful idiocy of that. In an oblique way, he had been chastised by Kuzmich, and sent away–told to be careful in future, warned of his position. And that, Eberlin knew too well, was dangerous. It soon became worse. The two opposing walls of his nightmare suddenly closed around him as if released by the same lever. For, leaving the train and returning solemnly to his hotel, he entered

Lietzenburger-strasse and saw, double-parked outside the small Berliner-Kindl bar opposite his window, the familiar steel-blue Jensen with a dented fender. Two minutes later, he entered the room and saw Emmanuel Gatiss standing by the window, one hand clutching a half-eaten apple, the other holding the top of Caroline's forgotten bikini. It was all Eberlin needed–this sudden concern by the British over his welfare. He closed the door slowly behind him.

9

Winterhilfe Whore

Der Mensch ist frei der Vogel in Käfig; er kann sich innerhalb gewisser Grenzen bewegen.
–LAVATER

EBERLIN glanced at the cheap alarm clock on the mantelpiece and discovered that he had been sitting in silence, sitting on the bed dumbly, for almost half an hour. His body had grown stiff and one leg was almost asleep. Gatiss had said not a word since Eberlin's return, but remained quietly, irritatingly relaxed, reading Goethe's *Young Werther* in German. The situation was unbearable. What the hell was Gatiss doing here? Did they know after all? It was becoming a stupid farce. Eberlin suddenly got up, almost collapsing on one leg, and reached for the door.

"Going out?" Gatiss said quietly, barely raising his eyes. Eberlin hesitated, then said, "I'm getting hungry."

"Good idea," replied Gatiss. "Let's ask them to send something up."

"I don't think they do things like that at this hotel. It's rather doit-yourself."

"Is it really?"

Gatiss smiled and continued reading. Eberlin stood at the door for a moment, then sat back down on the bed. There was no point in avoiding the issue. If the worst had happened, he at least ought to know the odds. He lit a cigarette.

"Fly?" he said.

"Car," was the answer. "Good journey?" "No."

"Why did you come then?"

"This really is the most absurdly sentimental book. Have you read it?"

"Yes, I have."

"I suppose he commits suicide in the end?"

"Werther?" "Yes."

"Yes," replied Eberlin.

Gatiss glanced across the room at Eberlin, then nodded and threw the book into the corner.

"You're an absolute failure, aren't you?" he said, folding his arms.

The question threw Eberlin for a moment and Gatiss smiled.

"I mean," he continued, "you've done nothing since you've been in Berlin, have you?"

"Well, I–"

"Have you found Krasnevin?" "No–"

"Have you any idea where he is?" "No–"

"What have you done then?"

"It's just not as straightforward as you think." "How straightforward is it then?" said Gatiss. "Well, I didn't have much of a lead, did I?" "Didn't you?"

"Well, to begin with–we don't even know if he's bloody well in Berlin."

"Oh he is, Eberlin. He is. You can be sure of that." "You seem very confident about it."

"Well, I take my work seriously and never approach any aspect of it without being absolutely sure. Today, I was followed from the border, which encouraged me greatly. You may rest assured that I will find Krasnevin before the month is out. I will do it for two reasons: one, because the odds are in my favor, and two, because I hate this city and I hate all the people in it. The sooner I get out of this Auschwitz of a country the better, so the impetus is there. What was she like?"

"Who?"

Gatiss held up the bikini. "All right. She's just–"

"You're a fool, Eberlin. Did you have to pick an English girl?" "What makes you think that?"

"It's written on the backside of this. I suppose you told her your name was Dancer." "Yes."

"And when she bumps into you in London and calls you George before a host of puzzled intimates, you'll wonder why you were demoted."

"Don't be ridiculous." "Was she a whore?" "No."

"Why not?"

"Look, Gatiss–who the hell asked you to burst in here? For Godsakes, it is quite obvious there is no love lost between us, so let's avoid any vulgar bitching, shall we?"

Throwing his head back, Gatiss suddenly burst into laughter. Eberlin stared at him, irritated for a moment, then got up and strode to the window. After a moment, Gatiss stood up and joined him and stared out at the street.

"Tell me about the man in the shower."

Eberlin sat down and lit another cigarette, and gave a detailed account of the meeting with the Russian the night before, omitting his own remarks to Henderson but giving Gatiss an accurate description of the man. Gatiss listened without comment, then said:

"Well, they know you're here, which is interesting. But I'm surprised they would reveal themselves like that. Very amateurish. I don't understand it. Did he say anything else?"

"No, I'm afraid I didn't give him much of a chance."

"It doesn't matter. But it doesn't make sense. The whole naïve approach of this man who calls himself Henderson. It's almost as if he knew you."

"Why do you say that?" Eberlin said quickly.

"Well, he obviously didn't expect you to attack him, that's for sure. When did you first suspect he wasn't from us?"

"Well, I didn't exactly. It was a guess. I don't know. I panicked." Then Eberlin added suddenly: "He wasn't from Frazer, was he?"

"Good God, I hope not," Gatiss laughed. "Well, that's a relief."

"Where were you this morning?" "Oh, nowhere in particular." "How do you mean?"

"I just went for a walk." "Picking flowers?"

Eberlin turned quickly toward Gatiss, was about to shout something but changed his mind. Gatiss coolly walked past him and took the Tokarev from his pocket and dropped it on the chair.

"Get rid of that. Don't leave it lying around." And then:

"I don't like you, Eberlin. I don't like you personally because you are weak and dishonest and pathetic and I deplore that. But more than that–I don't like you because I don't trust you. You're frightened of me and that disturbs me. I want to know why. Frazer must have had some valid reason for putting you on this job, but I'm going out now to begin the work you should have finished. Don't leave the hotel till I return. You take orders from me from now on. Understand?"

Gatiss opened the door, went out, returned and said, "Oh by the way, you received a call in London that your car was ready. Prentiss is driving it up. He'll be here tomorrow probably. *Guten Tag.*"

He closed the door again, leaving Eberlin standing tense and white-faced, in the pale gray light of the wretched, fading afternoon.

* * *

The third whore who approached him looked like Jean Harlow but was probably not. She was distinguishable by her bottle-blond hair that hung like washing around her head, and a magnificent pair of cabbage-white breasts, barely covered, which she exhibited to the world as if they were first prize in a raffle. Eberlin ignored her.

It had taken him ten minutes of lethargic thought after Gatiss' departure, and forty minutes of decisive action to arrive at this squalid tenement block in Kohlhaasstrasse. Above him, on the fourth floor, lay the offices (as he knew from the past) of *Breysach*, a minor and yet potent rival to the mercenary Gehlen organization. The building shuddered under its pressure of corrosive silence. Broken plaster hung everywhere and the floor was littered with discarded milk bottles. Eberlin had been told of the place many years ago by a stalwart bore, as the notorious but clandestine headquarters of an illegal smuggling company. It had been checked and dismissed. Three fatalities in a row on the Wall (one wretched creature having to submit to the indignity of a street dedicated to his dead name) had registered the organization as *active yet harmless* in the FJ files. This absurd irony was sufficient to allow *Breysach* to enlarge and become the second most profitable defection racket in West Berlin. Only Gehlen was superior, but with them even Faustus had a better deal.

Eberlin lit a cigarette and attempted the second flight. "Hello, thugar," Harlow lisped. (Camera-shutter wink.) Eberlin continued walking.

"Buy me a drink?" she asked. (Linguaphone voice plus pout.)

Eberlin made the question rhetorical and wondered if Greiser would still be there. He had played dominoes with him once and had lost. It was an amusing pastime.

"I'm the betht in the houth."

God help the others. Eberlin turned, glared at her, muttered some veiled obscenity and moved toward the next flight.

The girl, defeated, retired. (Plate-balancing nose.)

By the fourth floor, Eberlin was breathing hard. He put it down to lack of exercise for convenience and walked to a corner door marked, in small faded capitals, WINTERHILFE. Nothing ever changed. He knocked twice and waited. After two minutes, more or less, the door was opened by a myopic spinster in a quandary and bun who stared blandly at him and said:

"*Ja?*"

A slight smile and a bow from Eberlin. "*Guten Tag. Herr Greiser?*"

"Who?"

"Herr Greiser? I have come to the right place I presume."

The woman blinked in reply and hurried back to the apron strings of her office. Undeterred, Eberlin walked to the edge of the landing and stared down into the well of the tenement, spiraling below into a darkness of mundanity. He could see the platinum-blond whore still there, talking to a co-worker and gesturing like a semaphore instructor. She really had remarkable breasts seen from this angle, and yet painfully bracketed and laced under the thin dress. Eberlin in a fit of conscious reverie imagined her in a cot, naked and plaster-white, lisping into his ear the plagiarized *suadela* of the hack.

"Would you come this way please?" came a diminished-seventh voice from the door and he was led into a green and white, cell-like room filled with nothing.

"Wait here please. Your name?" "Dancer. Herr Dancer, but he–" "Do you have an appointment?" "No. But I–"

"I see."

"We are old friends. If you could just persuade him to appear." "Herr Greiser is very busy."

"No doubt. But I can wait."

The woman glared at him with overt resentment. Then: "One moment. I will see."

She left via a door next to an immense filing cabinet that dominated the room like a Buddha. Eberlin walked slowly up and down, glancing out of the window briefly at a tasteless vista of slums, and lit yet a further cigarette. Finally, after five more minutes, a small blue-chinned man in a suit that obviously belonged to his tailor, entered the room and stared in abject puzzlement at his visitor. Behind him, like altar boys, hovered three other people, including the secretary, their faces aping Greiser's expression.

"You wanted to see me?"

The answer had to be negative. Negative, at least, because this wasn't Greiser. At least not the Greiser Eberlin knew. No feasible metamorphosis could resolve such an appearance. The hostile old man before him was a stranger.

"*You* are Herr Greiser?" Eberlin asked, stubbing out his cigarette on the carpet.

"That is correct. Who are you?" "Herr Josef Geiser?" Eberlin insisted.

"No. My name is Oskar Greiser. What is it you want?"

All eyes turned toward Eberlin and the room went cold. A door opened miles away, two floors down, and he heard a man laugh and a snatch of English pop music and then silence.

"Perhaps," he offered defensively, "Herr Josef Greiser is a relation. A ... brother?"

"There is no Josef in my family. Good day."

And, Mass over, Greiser scuttled back into the next room and left Eberlin alone and resentful with the secretary. He attempted a smile of apology but it died in embryo.

"I must have made a mistake. But you must have heard of Josef Greiser?"

"Never."

"But he was in this building as little as four years ago."

"There is no Josef Greiser here," the woman snapped and strode to the landing door. "Please leave quietly. This is a private establishment."

Eberlin frowned, confused, and then reluctantly ambled to the door. He glanced at the secretary coldly and then said with all the enthusiasm of a eunuch:

"Tell me when you're on duty and perhaps we could make a night of it."

He didn't wait for an answer. Instead he pushed past her and was on the second flight before he heard the door bang behind him and realized the full impact of the scene. Greiser, *his* Greiser, had left and he had no knowledge where he had gone. Times had changed and his best and, more important, most secure inlet into the East had been smashed. There was little room for frivolity.

"Help,
I need t homebody"

trilled the whore on the flight below and Eberlin groaned. He hunched his shoulders and plunged down toward the ground floor

"Not jutht anybody, Help ..."

The whore was standing in the middle of the broken staircase staring up at him with the smile of an executioner. Eberlin made no attempt to relax his speed but shouldered past her, one elbow sinking momentarily into fleshy bosom, and hurried out, deaf to the cries, into the dim deserted street. He covered two blocks before he slowed his pace, and took stock of his environment. Kohlhaasstrasse is a walk-on as far as credits in the street maps are concerned, and so rarely mentioned. Consequently, it was difficult to find a taxi in that quarter, save in the early hours when uniformed drunks and faithful husbands disgorged themselves into the loins of the numerous brothels recommended to them by no one.

Eberlin paused halfway down the street, numbed by the experience, and regretted the absence of a coat. He tried vaguely to remember another contact, but the name–if there ever was one–did not occur. He sighed reluctantly and began to walk, hands in pockets, toward Mehringdamm, quickening his step after a hundred yards as if to shrug off his disappointment. "Hello, thugar," he muttered to himself for no apparent reason and cursed audibly. And then, to his horror, found he was shaking like a dog.

* * *

'Eine grosses bier, bitte, und ein Korn," he muttered to the owner of a nearby bar.

The drinks were served and he drank them thirstily and ordered another round. And then another six rounds in succession. And then a seventh for a drunk who bored but distracted him, and whom he found, on the eighth round, was himself. Finally, feeling as sober as a judge, Eberlin paid the bill, turned, collapsed into a door marked PULL and vomited absurdly all over the newly scrubbed easy-to-lay, black and white tiles on the beer-room floor. It was all, he thought, staring up at a print of the Rokeby Venus, such a pathetic failure. He made a dignified attempt to rise but vomited again onto the shoes of the barman and wanted to die. It was only the utter tastelessness of the decor, and that bunch of plastic roses (pink and yellow) over his head that changed his mind. Anyone, he thought before he passed out, *anyone* is worthy of more than that.

* * *

He awoke one hour later to find himself lying on the pavement and without his wallet. He lay there, feeling like death, for a full minute before he realized where he was. Around him the street was empty and alien to him. Yet, by the dismal architecture of the houses and the scattered squalor, he assumed himself to be in the same quarter as the whore-house The whorehouse! What a farce that was. And yet …

He stood up cautiously and discovered that he was pleasantly alert, despite the acrid stink of vomit on his trousers. Twenty past eight. Or had his watch stopped? No, twenty past eight. Why did his watch always read twenty minutes past the hour? Eberlin peered around him and then, anxious to reach the hotel before Gatiss returned, set off at a steady stride in what he hoped was the direction of Schöneberg, He had barely walked a quarter of a mile when the Porsche drew up beside him.

At first Eberlin ignored it, thinking it belonged to a resident. But when the car emphasized its presence by crawling parallel to him, he hurried faster until he was ahead of it. Before him he could see the lights of a busy street which encouraged him greatly, and the Porsche was momentarily forgotten. Then suddenly he was aware of footsteps hurrying after him, and of his name being called:

"Herr Dancer? Herr Dancer, *bitte*?"

Eberlin turned and saw a tall man, built like a boxer and yet with an almost girlishly pretty face, running toward him with a large smile and one hand raised as if in a primitive gesture of peace. Eberlin recognised him immediately as belonging to the Herr Greiser he had just met. He had hovered elegantly in the background, like a figure in *Primavera*, during that cryptic but brief interview two hours before.

"Herr Dancer," the man was saying, "I've been looking for you everywhere. I'm so glad I finally caught you."

And he exhibited a broad grin of immaculate teeth and such a flurry of relief that he could hardly contain himself. Eberlin didn't stop but merely walked slower. Unconcerned, the Adonis fell into step with him, almost dancing, and then strutting backwards improvising his choreography, to face him.

"My name is Uwe Greff and you don't know how I've been looking for you. I almost gave up hope. Then I saw you just as you were–"

"What do you want?"

The question was snapped out and stunned Greff immediately. He emitted an embarrassed laugh, scratched a side-boarded cheek, and then adopted a confiding manner that troubled Eberlin.

"Perhaps if we got in my car?"

He put his hand out to touch Eberlin's arm but stopped as Eberlin stepped back and moved to a wall.

"What do you want?" he repeated.

A gesture of childish dismay from Greff and a delicate replacing of tie into jacket. The clothes were in exquisite taste, as Eberlin noticed, and mostly of English cut, though slightly effeminate for his own preference. The shirt however was remarkably tailored in a pale, yet superb, shade of yellow. Greff, Eberlin decided, whoever he was, had *ton* and that, ridiculously, was in his favor. He waited.

"Herr Dancer–perhaps I should explain. I saw you tonight at the office ask for Josef Greiser."

"Oh yes?"

"Well, it's obvious that you have been out of touch. Josef, unfortunately, well–he was arrested."

"Arrested?" asked Eberlin surprised. "When? Where?" "Last

year. By the Vopos."

"How did it happen?" "You knew him?" "We met."

"Well–let me say it was no accident. Someone informed on him," said Greff quietly, lowering his eyes suitably, "and it wasn't someone from Breysach."

"Gehlen?"

Greff shrugged and said nothing.

"I see," murmured Eberlin after a moment.

"Yes. Well, Oskar–that's the present Herr Greiser, the one you saw tonight–very confusing–knows nothing about Josef's"–and here he sought a word and attempted–"activities? It's pure coincidence."

A long pause. Eberlin gazed at Greff's face steadily, glanced at the Porsche, standing as conspicuous as a beacon against the dank backdrop, and then turned back to Greff.

"But it still exists? Breysach I mean?" "Oh, most certainly."

"And you?"

Greff gave his first genuine smile and braved a pat on Eberlin's shoulder.

"Shall we go to the car?"

"One moment," said Eberlin blandly, lighting a cigarette, "What about Kasperl? Does he still supervise the section?"

Greff's sudden burst of laughter startled him by its robustness. "Herr Dancer–we have now proved that neither of us are fools.

Kasperl does not, never was and never will supervise the section. In fact it would be truly remarkable if he did, considering he is secondin-command of the HVA. Games, Herr Dancer, forget about games. Come on. I have some coffee in the car which I'm sure you will like. It's Blue Mountain. *And* in a flask."

"I am unimpressed," replied Eberlin with a smile, "but will drink it nevertheless."

He followed Greff, still wary but more relaxed, to the Porsche.

* * *

"What did you think of our whorehouse?" said Greff as he eased the car into Gneisenaustrasse. "Rather distasteful, didn't you think?"

"Aren't they all?" asked Eberlin as he sat in the passenger seat sipping coffee from the flask.

"Well I suppose so. Are they? I never go to them myself. Do you?"

"What?"

"Sleep with whores?"

"No. I try to avoid off-the-peg goods." "Oh, I suppose you go for virgins?" "No, I dislike virgins."

"Why?"

"I always suspect someone has been there before."

Greff laughed at this and congratulated Eberlin on his German. "Where did you learn it?"

"Oh, I picked it up here and there, you know," said Eberlin deadpan, "Belsen, Auschwitz, Buchenwald ..."

Greff's smile faded and he bit his lip and then said, "Well first-hand knowledge of a language is always the best."

He smiled self-consciously and was obviously relieved by Eberlin asking, "Where are we going?"

"Oh. Oh, just driving around. Give us time to talk."

Greff gave him a quick smile, and then after a moment's introspection, ventured rather self-consciously:

"I wouldn't have thought you were ..."

"I'm not," replied Eberlin and opened his window slightly, conscious of the smell of vomit in the car. Greff, however, seemed unaware of it and switched on the car radio with his right hand as he drove. The soothing upsurge of Rodrigo's *Guitar Concerto* filled the Porsche, cleared the air and silenced the two men.

At Yorckstrasse, Greff turned right and right again into the slum quarter, and began humming the music to himself as if they were both suddenly on their way to a picnic or returning from a concert.

"Look," said Eberlin, irritated by Greff's reluctance to talk, "I can't drive around all–"

"Sssh!" admonished the other, with a raised index finger and a gesture to the music.

"Damn the music," Eberlin said and switched it off. For a moment, Greff tensed and then he gave a brief smile and said quickly:

"Forgive me, Herr Dancer. I was being selfish." Eberlin grunted.

"Why were you looking for me?" he asked. "You were inquiring about Josef, were you not?" "Yes."

"For some–reason I presume." "Perhaps."

"Then perhaps I can help." "Who is Oskar Greiser?"

"Oh no one. Nothing to do with Breysach at least. He runs some small private … concern."

"In a brothel?"

"Well … it's rather … 'undemocratic,' shall we say." "You mean he's a Nazi?"

"Herr Dancer–try not to jump to conclusions. The word 'Nazi' is a very broad term, and every foreigner who enters Germany has it on his lips, is itching to voice it."

"But you work for him?"

"In a sense. Look, my private life should not concern you. I myself have not the slightest interest in your political sexual, or, God help us, religious bias. So let us forget about Oskar, shall we? He is of no use to you."

Eberlin was silent for a moment as he sipped at the coffee. "Well at least," he said finally, "your office is close to Love and

Kitheth. If you desire it."

There was a hearty laugh from Greff and he slapped Eberlin's knee.

"Oh, you noticed her? She's really rather sweet. And with those enormous tits. I can't bear to think of them released from their silk hammock." He laughed again and said, "Her name's Hedwig something or other. Comes from Bavaria. She told me she was an actress or wanted to be one. I can't remember. Anyway she apparently took the part of a nun in some minor film."

"Who did she play? Mother Inferior?"

"God–I wouldn't be surprised," said Greff, and he smiled to himself and scratched his nose.

The Porsche was cruising continually in a circle of about a quarter-mile radius and Eberlin was relieved to notice that Greff kept to the quietest streets. He was offered a Kent cigarette and refused it.

"Actually the one you should have met," mused Greff after a moment, "is Malesuada Gage. Incredible creature. She must be six feet in height, blond with a magnificent body. Very popular of course and very expensive but I hear well worth it. Malesuada Gage. Remember the name. I prefer boys myself. You?"

"No."

"Well, never mind. You're British, aren't you?" "Yes," Eberlin replied automatically.

"Yes.... I've been to London many times myself. Adore it. Do you know–No, of course you wouldn't. Not your scene. I fly there to see my tailor."

"Jackson and Wavell."

Greff's mouth opened in a gasp of astonishment and he almost lost control of the car.

"Good heavens. How did you know that?"

"I guessed," Eberlin replied, "from the cut of your suit. Especially the lapels."

"But that's fantastic. Do you go there yourself?"

"No. Schwitzer and Davidson. Cork Street." "Well, I would never–"

Eberlin suddenly raised his voice.

"Greff, I haven't much time. Can we drop the pleasantries now?"

With a pursed-mouth reply, Greff nodded. "There's an alley up ahead. I'll park there."

"No. Keep driving. But get out of this district. Your car is too conspicuous. Drive toward the center."

"As you wish."

The car accelerated back toward the Anhalter Banhof, skirted the Wall and headed north in the direction of the Tiergarten. It had just entered the dark lanes of the park, when Eberlin said suddenly:

"Stop the car here."

"What?" asked Greff in surprise. "Why–" "Stop it. Park it just in that shadow."

With a frown, Greff slid the car into a deserted alcove of trees and switched off the lights. Opening both doors, Eberlin bade Greff get out. There was a moment's hesitation, then Greff obeyed and watched in amused interest as Eberlin quickly searched the car–under the dashboard, behind the seats, even the flask–until he was content.

"All right. Let us go," he said and casually poured himself another cup of coffee.

"The car isn't bugged, Dancer," Greff commented matter-offactly as he slid the car back into the road. "And the reason is that we are much more vulnerable than you. For all I know you could be a damned Vopo in mufti."

"I could be, yes," replied Eberlin. "But you're not."

"Now, how can you be so sure?" Greff smiled.

"May I have a sip of coffee? No, it's all right. I'll use the same cup."

Eberlin handed over the coffee and studied the bronzed, straight-nosed profile of the man as he drank. The blond hair, grown long and curled over the nape of the neck and over the forehead, together with the deep, clear eyes reminded one of Michelangelo's *David*, and Eberlin saw for a brief second, almost subliminally, the wretched little girl in Bayswater whose soul had miscarried before she could even walk. Greff, drinking and driving at the same time, glanced at Eberlin for a second, conscious of the scrutiny, and then looked away. There was no doubt in Eberlin's mind that Greff was probably very successful as a queer, and even perhaps as a petty, Nazi, if his suspicions about Oskar Greiser were correct. But as an operator, he was unsure. He lit a cigarette.

'*Un ange se passe*," smiled Greff and handed the cup back. "What are you thinking?"

"You were going to prove that I wasn't a spy from the Vopos."
"Was I? Oh yes. Well, I'll tell you who you are."

"Please do." Eberlin attempted a passive interest like a party guest cornered by an amateur palmist.

"Your name is indeed Dancer. George Dancer in fact. And you work in an oil company."

Eberlin sat up straight.

"All right so far?" said Greff with a laugh, but didn't wait for an affirmative. "You are a supervisor in the Accounts department and are thirty-six years old and live in London. This is your second visit to Berlin and you would like to get into the East but, for certain reasons, permission has been refused. As you discovered this morning."

Silence. Eberlin stared out at the dark streets passing by and the constellations of insects caught in the headlights. And then he nodded and said quietly:

"I think we're in business. Who tipped you off? Stein?" "No. Too high up for us. It was the private."

"Oh yes." Eberlin nodded and added, "There was someone else watching me. A civilian."

"Him?"

Greff handed over a photo of an unsmiling man with freakishly prominent teeth. Eberlin said "Yes" and put the photo in the glove compartment.

"He's a failure. Too conspicuous and too memorable. I'd keep him behind the counter," he said.

"You're right," replied Greff. "Do you think you can do it?"

The Porsche cornered sharply into Beusselstrasse and Greff switched on the radio again, found a music program and turned it low.

"When do you want to go over?"

"Within the next twenty-four hours," replied Eberlin, not looking at the other man.

Greff hesitated for almost a decade, then said, "Tomorrow morning. I'm sure it can be fixed for then. It'll mean more pressure but it can be arranged."

"I'm known. I can't afford to be seen by anyone–East or West." "That'll be taken into account. We can perhaps take you right across the Eastern Sector to the edge of the city, but it will cost more."

"Can you do that?"

"Yes. We are very–let us say–influential. Don't ask questions now on the mechanics of the operation because I won't answer you. After all, you might still be a plant. It's happened before."

Greff smiled with nauseating sweetness and ran the small finger of his right hand along one eyebrow.

"Driving the car like this is incredibly monotonous, George. I may call you George, may I not?"

"How much do you want?"

"Well it's a rushed job and your face is known. And as you well know we avoid all the pathetic kamikaze devices such as tunnels, coffins, after-dark dashes and other such trivia. One is likely to get killed that way. No, our methods are neat, open and safe."

"Not quite all the time. There was–"

"Mere teething troubles. We've learnt from them." "How much do you want?"

"For a daylight crossing, with papers–" "How much?"

Greff suddenly put on the brakes and brought the Porsche to a halt at the curb. Swiveling around toward Eberlin he took a notebook from a pocket and glanced at it. Three or four more pages were flickered over before he returned the book to his pocket.

"Six thousand dollars or two thousand pounds sterling." Eberlin gasped in unconscious reaction.

"Half in advance," added Greff toying with the radio.

"Too much," replied Eberlin. "I'll give you three thousand." "I'm not a fool, George," said Greff, placing a peppermint in his

mouth and resting the dial of the radio on Vaughan Williams' *Thomas Tallis*. "Don't you think this is divine?" he added. "So English. It must make you feel very nostalgic."

"I can give you fifteen hundred pounds in advance and that is the most I can raise."

Greff hesitated. "In cash?"

"I'll get it first thing in the morning."

"Make it five thousand dollars in cash and we've got a deal." "All right. Half on this side of the Wall and half on the other." "Agreed."

Two intakes of breath and Greff started the car. "Where shall I drop you?"

"Better make it Steinplatz. I can walk from there." "All right."

They drove in silence now till they reached Spandauerdamm, and then Greff said:

"The main bank in Hardenbergstrasse?" "Yes."

"Be there at eleven. When you leave, wait on the corner where I drop you tonight. A black Mercedes taxi number B 4485A, will appear on your side traveling south. Hail it and it will stop and leave it to us from there."

"I might be followed."

"Don't worry. We can take care of that. Have you got the number?"

"B 4485A?"

"Good. Don't bring any luggage of course, but bring your passport."

"Passport? Why?"

"It will be exchanged for another one. We will use yours as a base for someone else. You're not going to need it after tomorrow, are you?"

"Is that all?"

"That's all for now–oh, there is something. What's your collar size?"

"My what?"

"Collar size. You know–on your shirts." "Fifteen," Eberlin replied, puzzled.

Greff wrote *Fifteen* down in the notebook as the car halted at some lights, then said:

"I'm sorry I can't make it more cloak-and-dagger for you, but it's just routine for us. Skilled routine but routine nevertheless." He grinned and added as an afterthought, "Oh, and don't worry about being seen leaving this car. I only bought it this morning. I gather Willi Brandt has an identical model, so don't be nervous."

"I'll get off the next corner."

The car stopped in the small Steinplatz park. Eberlin was about to open his door when Greff leaned across and held his arm.

"Don't underestimate us, George. You have more to lose than us." He patted the arm and said, "Well, it was nice meeting you. If I can suggest a way to spend your evening–find a nice, sensual tart and take her to bed as quick as possible. You'll find the girls in the East are either catatonic beauties or rapacious monsters. Get it while you can. Malesuada Gage if you're lucky–incredible name–but even thexy Hedwig would be profitable."

"No thank you," snapped Eberlin and opened the door sharply.

Outside it was cold.

"*Gute Nacht,*" smiled Greff and shut the door. But not before mouthing silently "Till tomorrow" at the back of Eberlin's head. Then the Porsche, with a violent roar, was into Hardenbergergstrasse and gone.

Eberlin hurried away toward the Ku-Damm. *Iacta alea est*–or is it? He wondered how much he could trust Greff or even if at all. God, it was so absurd to have to sneak into one's own country through the parlor window. If Rotopkin hadn't been so eager to kill Pavel, all this wouldn't have happened. Damn Kuzmich! Eberlin was well aware that his welcome in Moscow wouldn't be favorable–if he got there–but at least it would be safer than the West. Three more days with Gatiss and his cover might as well be made out of polythene.

He stopped at a stand-up soup kitchen on the corner of Joachimstalerstrasse, and drank a bowl of thick lentil soup in order to silence his stomach. What he failed to understand even now was why Kuzmich was so reluctant to help him. They must realize that his value to them was in being alive and above suspicion. He bought another bowl of soup and spilled half of it over his shoes. If Emmanuel Gatiss discovered his mask first, he could only be of harm to the KGB. If he was kept alive.

Through the window of the café, he could see the gaudy façade of the Zoo Palatz, illuminated like a barrage balloon. A phalanx of people were queueing up to see the film starring Brigette Bardot. She herself lay, in one dimension, boy-legs apart, snapdragon mouth open, across twenty square foot of the cinema outside, and spoke in ventriloquized yet fluent German in the cinema inside. Eberlin thought about Caroline. Was she as innocent as she professed? And Oskar Greiser. What of him? And Caroline's obese friend Susan? And the man in the cap standing next to him. Or the soup cook? Who was *he* spying for? Or the four-year-old child in the Opel Caravan that just passed? Even Brigitte Bardot over there was to be watched. But not at those prices.

Eberlin suddenly caught his reflection in the window smiling stupidly back at him, and so he drained the last of the soup and hurried away into the night.

At nine fifty, he arrived at his hotel and was relieved to discover that Gatiss was still absent. He inquired at the desk whether he had returned and left again, but Gatiss' key had remained untouched all day. Eberlin nodded thank you and went upstairs to his room, closed the door and sat on the edge of his bed. He felt suddenly very lonely and, for the first time for years, frightened.

Not bothering to put on the light, he sat in the gloom and stared at a discarded piece of paper on the floor for what seemed an eternity. His mind remained a complete blank, almost trancelike, except for a brief vision of his son which sadistically dried his mouth, then vanished. After half an hour, the paper on the floor was only a blur and then he noticed its presence for the first time. Picking it up, he realized that it was a note, dated that day and presumably pushed under the door within the last couple of hours. The reality of it brought him to his senses since no one in Berlin (except Gatiss) knew of his presence, and even Caroline believed him to have left twelve hours ago. Puzzled, he opened it up and glanced down to the bottom where the signature was scrawled. It was there, very legible in black Pentel: *Caroline*.

10

Melpomene AWOL

A woman should open everything to a man except her mouth.
–ALEXANDER EBERLIN

GATISS was bored. He had sat in the Stygian darkness of the club, waiting for Melpomene, for over an hour. Before him was an untouched glass of Berliner Weisse which he'd ordered on arrival, and, as on every other table, a red telephone. Beyond the self-conscious rows of male faces was a long counter where eight girls, in various stages of pulchritude and undress, sat and waited for their number to be called. They perched like budgerigars on high barstools, skirts squeezed up to reveal suspended thighs, and gaped in cold expectancy at the ceiling. Every now and then, one would answer a phone at her elbow, murmur into the receiver, then assume an Identidikit smile and join a grinning customer at his table. It was a dreary preamble to the norm and Gatiss was bored.

From the guide list on his table, he noticed that the hostesses had been named after the nine Muses, by some rare intellect who must have stumbled into the club one night by mistake. Terpsichore, a sailor's daughter from Hamburg with tomato-red hair and eyes that had been lent to her by a basset hound, was, as Gatiss observed, very popular. Wretched Clio however was obviously on the way down, for she hadn't had a call all night and was becoming noticeably anxious. Her neighboring Muse was Erato, an obese harpy, whose only link with poetry was in a calendar for which she had posed naked, except for a red carnation in the navel and which was still hanging in innumerable garages five years after publication. Her only rival in body-art was Melpomene herself who, much to Gatiss's relief had just arrived.

As soon as she had sat down, patted her blond hair and ordered a drink, Gatiss dialed her number. He saw her swear audibly and hesitate, before picking up the phone. Then, peering into the darkness, she raised the receiver to her ear and listened.

"This is Gatiss," he said. "Come to Table Y."

The blond Melpomene, taking her time, finished the drink, then stood up and pushed her way past the groping hands and sniggered innuendos toward Gatiss's table in the far corner. He moved aside as she sat down, plonked her small cheap bag before her and gave a breast-shuddering sigh.

"You're late," Gatiss said, signaling to a deaf waiter.

The blonde pulled a face and shrugged her bare shoulders.

"I'm thorry, thugar," she replied quietly. "I had to wait for Othkar."

* * *

Dear George,

Extraordinary thing, George. Fat Susan who is a horror and smells said she saw you this afternoon. Course I said you had gone but she says she saw you lying in the street!

What a horrid liar she is. Anyway I came around just in case cos you know I think you're super and fab (ugh!) but you were out. Have you gone? Or are you still here? You needn't bother to tell me if you are, if you don't want to see me. But please, George, would love to see you if you are and reading this. How do you spell 'passionately'?

lots of kisses,

Caroline

PS. Am at Bristol. Room 141. And alone!!

PPS. Bought super hat. xxxxx

PPPS. If you are here and you do come, you don't have to say anything. I won't ask. Miss you awfully. I wish, darling, I wasn't such a child. C.

Eberlin read the note twice, then tore it up. He had not the slightest desire to see Caroline, and yet wishing to avoid Gatiss till the morning, found her invitation not unwelcome.

One hour later, he put his passport, checkbook and gun in his pocket and left the hotel. No one saw him leave. Walking west along dark side streets, Eberlin reached Uhlandstrasse and saw the back of the Bristol Hotel one hundred yards away. He stood and stared at it for a moment, then turned and walked away.

At ten fifty he returned to the very same spot, crossed toward the side of the building and then entered quickly into the sumptuous foyer. Avoiding the eyes of the reception staff, Eberlin crossed to the stairs and walked, almost stumbling on the third step, to the first floor. 141 was mercifully at the end of a quiet corridor.

There was no answer when he knocked. Instead the door, unlocked, swung open under the pressure of his knuckles. Eberlin hesitated and involuntarily touched the butt of the Browning under his coat, before slowly entering the apartment. Shutting the door, he switched on the light and glanced around. It was a typical expensive hotel room–small, cluttered and in extreme bad taste. On the floor was a discarded copy of *The Sunday Times* and an ashtray full of cigarette ends. A cardboard box lay on the table next to a ridiculously ugly hat about the size of a cartwheel. Eberlin sighed and crossed the carpeted floor, past a large Chesterfield upholstered in purple velvet, and toward a door leading to the next room. Pausing, he listened for any sound but there was none. Slowly he opened the door and saw, the light still being on, that Caroline was in bed and asleep, one arm around a crippled teddy bear and the other curled up, under her, inside the sheets. On the floor near her lay a discarded copy of *The Last Tycoon*, page-marked by a Kleenex tissue.

Eberlin stared at her for a moment, then closed the door and returned to the sitting room and lay down on the couch. He remained there for an hour, smoking cigarettes and staring into space, until, exhausted by the long day, he fell asleep, to be awakened ten minutes later by Caroline.

"I thought you were a burglar," she said, standing over him in a long, opaque nightgown covered in bows and Victorian lace. "Fancy sleeping out here, George."

Eberlin attempted to answer, but changed his mind and submitted reluctantly to Caroline's invitation to sleep in her bed, which he did, but without making love to her despite her relentless encouragement. Pleading a dire and truthful necessity to sleep he turned his back on her and slid gratefully once more into unconsciousness. Realizing finally that he was irretrievable, Caroline put on her nightgown again and fell asleep herself, her head against Eberlin's shoulders, her knees against his back and her left arm curled comfortingly around the teddy bear.

In the morning, Eberlin awoke puffy-faced and dry-mouthed and saw a cup of coffee hovering, out of focus, three inches before his face. He took it without comment, spilling some of it on the bed as he sat up, and saw Caroline, still in her nightgown and wearing the absurd hat, standing smiling at him.

"What's the time?" he asked anxiously. "Ten past nine."

"Ten past nine," he echoed and realized he was early.

A bath was run for him which he refused and showered instead, while he watched Caroline take the bath herself, her small suntanned body, with its white negatives on the breasts and thighs, ridiculously out of proportion in the giant tub. Then, after two further cigarettes and the remains of the cold coffee, Eberlin left the apartment with a muttered "Good-bye" to Caroline, who, still in the bath, gaped with surprise and began:

"When will I–"

She didn't finish it, for the door closed and she was alone, staring at the taps and her distorted reflection in the chromium. Oh hell, she thought, moist-eyed, and lay back in the water, her small stomach floating to the surface. She squinted down the front of her body toward her toes and thought about Eberlin and knew, finally, that she would never see him again. She would leave now, for there was no more reason for her to stay, and anyway, she realized, the water was cold.

11

Breysach

V. relinquish, give up, abandon, desert, defect, forsake, leave in the lurch; depart –, secede–withdrawfrom; back out of, back down from; leave, go back on one's word, quit, take leave of vacate &c. 757.
–ROGET'S THESAURUS
(The Voluntary Powers)

No comment.
–ALEXANDER EBERLIN

AT the bank in Hardenbergstrasse, Eberlin drew six thousand dollars from the emergency fund he had been granted by Frazer, and walked out into the street. It was a fine day and rather pleasant if one wanted to take a stroll or visit the nearby Zoo to listen to Wagnerian tenors tremoloing all over the beer tables. Berlin indeed could, like the hausfrau it was, startle one suddenly by assuming forgotten makeup and jewelry in order to rekindle one's initial attraction. Today was such a day. Girls were dressed in bright fashionable cottons, and tourists in open cars cruised lazily along its immense highways listening to rock and roll from transistor radios. And yet, to Eberlin, as he crossed the street toward Steinplatz, it was still an electric chair. Ornately covered in the finest silks, padded with goose feathers and designed by a Chippendale, but an electric chair nevertheless. And the switch was set.

He stood on the corner attempting to be casual about the whole affair, and was relieved to find that the taxi approached him almost immediately. He double-checked the number, then hailed it with a slight gesture of his arm. The Mercedes drew up at his feet and he noticed the driver was the man in the photo, teeth jutting out like an eave to his chin.

"I'm Dancer," Eberlin said quickly, reaching for the back door.

The man didn't speak until Eberlin was settled in the car and the taxi was heading west toward Grunewald.

"Drop your passport on the front seat."

"I'll drop it nowhere," snapped Eberlin. "If you want to check my references, stop the car and turn around."

The man frowned, hesitated, then parked the car, engine running, at the curb. Attempting a vain assumption of authority, he turned around slowly and peered into the back of the car. Eberlin held up the passport and showed the photograph.

"All right?" "Let me–"

"Is it all right? If I have to endure an endless parade of petty inquisitors from now on, I'll get out of the car now."

He snapped the passport shut and reached for the door. The driver nodded reluctantly and apologized.

"We have to be careful."

"Give me a light," Eberlin replied and reached over for some matches. Lighting a cigarette he said, 'What's your name?"

"Schmidt," the man said.

"Let me keep the matches, Schmidt. I need them more than you."

The driver grunted and put the car forward. They drove in dead silence till they reached Grunewald twenty minutes later.

Eberlin was surprised when the taxi parked outside a large, spacious mansion. The neatly cut lawn, the privet hedge and the diligently cultivated garden seemed an odd setting for such an illicit organization. But on reflection, he realized that it was, on the contrary, perfectly apt. Ugliness is often disguised by extravagant ostentation, if funds are high. Rather like the parade of elderly dowagers he had witnessed once at Ascot, who had worn enormous flower and lace hats in a vain attempt to distract the onlooker from the sagging wrinkles and the collapsing body. And so he refrained from comment, and stepped slowly out of the car, burning his hand momentarily on the hot steel of the roof, and was led by Schmidt into the house.

At first, no one rushed to meet him and shake his hand, and he began to notice his nervousness. Then finally, after he had exhausted his perusal of the tapestries and vulgar furniture in the hall, a butler appeared from nowhere.

"Would you come this way?" he said, and then abandoned him.

The cordiality reminded him of Selvers.

At the back of the house, carefully hidden by a high wall and a semicircle of poplars, was a kidney-shaped swimming pool, where a dozen male guests swam or lazed idly on the blush-red tiles drinking whisky sours. Eberlin stood at the edge of the pool, deserted both by the butler and Schmidt, and looked curiously around for Greff. He was nowhere to be seen. Then suddenly, with a bellowing laugh, he emerged like Poseidon from the depths of the pool and swam toward a yellow raft, floating nearby, which contained a dry towel, a pair of sunglasses, and a young black-haired boy, with enormous eyes, wearing nothing but a pair of denim briefs. Clambering onto the raft, Greff whispered something to the boy, then noticed Eberlin a few yards away, standing staring at him. He raised his hand in a gesture of recognition but Eberlin had turned and was walking back to the house, flicking his cigarette into the clear blue water.

"*Ich sehe Sie später*," Greff said quietly to the boy and then was swimming strongly toward the side of the pool. In a few strides he had reached Eberlin and caught his arm.

"Where are you going?" he said. "Sit down and have a drink." Eberlin pulled his arm away.

"Is this a farce, Greff?"

"A farce? My dear George, I don't understand–"

"You know exactly what I mean. As far as I am concerned, the deal is off."

He began to stride angrily toward the rear door of the house. Greff glanced back at the guests who were attempting to ignore the situation, then he ran after Eberlin again.

"Please, George," he gasped breathlessly, "don't get annoyed. Everything is arranged as planned. Just because you don't like the décor, don't run off in a temper. I'm sorry I can't supply some secret passwords or mysterious dungeons, but you really have a romantic impression of Breysach. And indeed of Berlin."

Eberlin hesitated slightly and Greff, seeing an opening, plunged on.

"This is just a business, George," he said, putting his arm on his shoulder, "and happens every day. These men you see around you are businessmen working for Breysach. You will see this scene around a million pools in a million business hotels. You know something–I sometimes think we employ more people than Krupp."

He laughed and turned to a silver-haired man nearby who giggled and repeated, "More than Krupp."

Eberlin turned and looked coldly at the guests around the pool. "What happens now?" he said.

* * *

They were below him now, the people at the pool. He could see the men clustered in small groups at the edge of the azure water, talking intimately to each other and now and again throwing up manicured hands at visual jokes. The young boy was still on the raft, lying quite still as if he had died suddenly, unknown to the others, and was merely waiting to be discovered. He sat up suddenly as if to disprove Eberlin's thoughts, glanced around, then turned over and settled himself back on the raft, one hand trailing in the water.

"Pretty, isn't he?"

Eberlin turned from the bedroom window and glanced at Greff. The German was standing behind a giant screen soaking his body in Arpège after showering. Eberlin ignored the question and sat down in a bentwood rocking chair and studied the room. It was large, grotesque and decorated solely in blue. The bed, carpet, walls, even ceiling, were in a deep shade of ultramarine, and when Greff dressed, his clothes too were of the same color. Anticipating the question, Greff said with a smile:

"Actually my favorite color is red–magenta–but like all precious things, one must preserve them not exploit them. Blue means nothing to me."

"How long have we got?" Eberlin said suddenly.

"Plenty of time, George," Greff replied, selecting a tie from a wardrobe. He made his choice because of the material rather than the color, since all his ties, like Eberlin's, were black. "Would you like to listen to some music? Calm your nerves."

He crossed to a transparent-topped Braun record player and switched it on. Eberlin didn't recognize the voice nor did he care. With the slightest prompting he would have got up, strode to the

door, left the room, and washed his hands of the whole affair. He would gladly write it off as a failure but it was too late. The decision had to be followed through for his own sake. He returned to the window and stared out at the garden. The landscaping was below par.

"Jacques Brel," Greff said, gesturing to the music. "He's telling his friend Jef not to get upset over a woman. You speak French?"

Eberlin didn't reply. Combing his hair, Greff glanced at him and then, sensing the other man's mood, said quietly:

"I apologize if the setting is alien to how you imagined Breysach should be. But you must admit it is much less suspicious and anyway, I like it. Believe me, George–"

"Don't call me George," snapped Eberlin and Greff gave a short embarrassed laugh and replied:

"As you wish." A pause, then:

"Have you got the money?" "Yes."

"May I see?"

"When you tell me how it will be used." "I see. Well, all right."

A further pause. One of the men outside suddenly giggled outrageously and echoed the punch line of someone else's joke and laughed again.

"As I said yesterday," Greff began, walking up and down, "you will go over openly and without any silly histrionics. And may I add, in comfort."

"You're sending me through in a Rolls Royce?" commented Eberlin sarcastically.

"No," replied Greff blandly, "it's a Mercedes Benz actually." Eberlin stifled a laugh but Greff was playing it straight.

"Not an ordinary Mercedes, of course. This one will be a military vehicle. A staff car."

"You can't be serious?" exploded Eberlin.

"Perfectly. It has been done successfully many times. Military personnel as you know are allowed to travel back and forth between sectors without interference. They are neither searched nor questioned. It's part of the Charter–didn't you know?"

"Yes, but–I can't–"

"Can't what? My dear George, let me tell you that all the forces in Berlin have recruits, even officers, who are quite prepared to take an unauthorized person through the Wall for a small consideration, without batting an eyelid. The Americans do it, the British do it. Some diplomatic cars make a small fortune from rich defectors alone."

"And that's how you intend to take me across?"

"There's an officer's car leaving for the Checkpoint in fiftyfive minutes. There is nothing to worry about–they are expecting you. You sit comfortably in the back seat and let yourself be driven across. Simple, isn't it?"

"The Vopos may recognize my face. I can't just sit in the car while they stare at me–"

"You will wear a uniform, of course, and some glasses if you wish. They will never suspect because they will not be looking for you."

Eberlin was unsure. It was *too* absurdly simple and Greff was much too blasé about it. After a moment he stood up.

"I'm sorry. I don't like it. It's unrealistic." He walked toward the door.

"Don't be a fool, Dancer," Greff called after him coldly. "You haven't much of an option, have you?"

There was a fleeting shudder in Eberlin's body and he stopped and looked back at the other man.

"How do you mean?" he asked.

"Well," replied Greff, "you are rather desperate, aren't you?

And with a great deal to hide." Eberlin didn't move.

"What are you trying to say, Greff?"

"Only this," the other replied, adjusting the curtains around the window. "I know almost nothing about you but I suspect a lot. This, as I said, doesn't concern me one bit. But I say I suspect. Let me tell you something. I'm not a very intelligent person, hardly well read. Not even talented in any way. But I have always had one attribute I pride myself on. I have a very good ear." He tapped his ear as if to emphasize the point. "I can pick out a wrong note played in an orchestra of fifty as if it were written on the conductor's back. When I was a child, elders pressured me to take up music but ironically, I was a failure. They expected nothing less than another Mozart and got me. It was tragic. I could hardly master *Für Elise.*"

"What has this to do with me?"

"One moment. Despite my inability to become an infant prodigy, I still retained my ear. My instinct for sounds. Not only with music but also with language. Now it's a strange thing about accents and perhaps you don't realize this. When someone speaks a foreign language, he naturally speaks it with an accent, which generally is very noticeable depending on his fluency. But more than this: a Frenchman, say, no matter how long he has been out of his own country, still speaks a foreign language with a French accent. My aunt is a good case in point. She is Italian. She left Italy at eleven–*eleven*–and moved to Germany. She is now forty-eight and has spoken German every day for thirty-seven years. Recently she learned to speak English. Of course she speaks it with an accent, but *not*, Herr Dancer, a German accent. But an Italian one. Odd, isn't it, this lingual atavism?"

Eberlin didn't reply.

"You're still wondering what this has to do with you? Well, George, you tell me you're English. You have an English name and an English passport. But when you speak German, it is not with an English accent, though you speak German very well."

"Oh really?" said Eberlin dispassionately. "And what accent do I have?"

"This I'm not sure. It's very difficult. Hungarian? Rumanian? Or perhaps"–and Greff smiled slightly–"perhaps a little farther north. Whatever it is, I know you are not telling me the truth."

"You're way off your mark, Greff," Eberlin said steadily. "I'm afraid you've let your imagination run away with you. Anyway I could be an immigrant, couldn't I? Like your damned aunt."

"Yes, you could," replied Greff, with a slight bow, "and now you want to emigrate again. Don't you, Ge-org-e?"

Eberlin stiffened for a moment. Greff had pronounced his name as if it were Russian–hardening the *g* and lengthening the *e.* There was a knock on the door and the butler entered with an anemic expression of apology.

"Eleven forty, sir. You asked–"

"Yes. Thank you, Kreide," Greff said quickly and ushered the butler out of the room. "We have thirty minutes," he said to Eberlin, "so you'd better make up your mind. I repeat, I don't care what you are, but the scheme will work. I assure you."

Eberlin said nothing. The record had stopped but not clicked off and was spinning around noisily under the pickup. Greff switched it off.

"Where is the uniform?" Eberlin asked finally.

"In the taxi. Schmidt is meeting us outside. He'll take us to another rendezvous where you can change and pick up the staff car. All right?"

Eberlin was worried, but he couldn't think clearly enough to rationalize the plan. On the surface it was feasible. He shrugged and replied, "All right."

There was a mercenary smile from the German and he patted Eberlin's arm.

"Relax, George. In one hour you will be on the other side–though I can't see why anyone would go to all the trouble for such a dreary little place. By the way, did you pick up a nice tart last night as I suggested?"

Eberlin didn't reply but lit another cigarette and felt sweat beginning to trickle under his arms.

"Well, never mind," continued Greff. "I was going to send round Hedwig but I didn't know your hotel. Anyway she was out all evening. Where's the money?"

"Now?"

"Half of it, yes."

A package of dollars was taken from Eberlin's pocket and handed over to Greff, who counted it slowly then placed it in his wallet.

"You'll deliver the rest to a contact in the East. He'll meet you.

Shall we go?"

This was it. Eberlin nodded and followed the German out of the bedroom to the top of the stairs. Both men descended the stairs in silence, like pallbearers, then at the bottom, Greff stopped.

"One moment. I ought to say good bye to my …" He gestured toward the rear of the house and the pool. "He's a very–jealous–boy."

Eberlin nodded politely, but his face was strained.

"Perhaps there's time for a drink before I leave?" he asked. Greff gave a brief smile.

"French courage?" "Dutch."

"Ah yes. The Dutch get blamed for everything. I'll call Kreide." He walked to a large oaken door.

"Kreide!"

No answer. Greff rubbed his eye. "Kreide!"

Still no answer. Greff swore. "Where the hell is that man?

Kreide!"

"Perhaps he's in the garden."

"He has no right in the garden. We have another–Kreide!"

Complete silence. Both men suddenly became aware that no sounds came from the garden, even though both doors were open. At first, Eberlin dismissed it, then noticing a puzzled anxiety on Greff's face which rapidly turned to concern, he glanced around him uneasily and walked over to the other man.

"Something is wrong," muttered Greff and turned away. Then, as if struck by a sudden thought, he ran quickly to the back of the house and Eberlin heard his footsteps breaking clear of the house and running onto the tiled patio outside. Then suddenly they stopped abruptly.

Eberlin hesitated and followed, moving faster as the light from the garden came in sight, and then he saw him. He was standing stockstill staring out across the lawn, one hand frozen in the air as if he were posing for a statue. He was looking at something, or someone, hidden from Eberlin's view by the heavy doorframe. But with a few steps, he saw the reason for Greff's odd behaviour. Around the pool and under the trees were seven men. They were not guests nor were they casual visitors. They were policemen. And in the pool the raft was empty.

Immediately an explosion of sound and action erupted. Greff broke out of his paralysis and turned and ran back into the house, pushing past Eberlin and shouting at him:

"You bastard! You bastard!"

Then he was running across the hall and collapsing under the blows of other men, and a kick on the nose from one of the police as he fell, spread-eagled, onto the floor. And then Eberlin was being pushed aside and the whole house seemed crowded with policemen who glanced briefly at Eberlin then dismissed him, as if he were a stray glove someone had picked up and placed on a gatepost, and then he heard a voice nearby and he turned and saw Emmanuel Gatiss.

"Wait there and don't move," he was saying and then he too was gone. More faces peered at Eberlin out of this sudden nightmare, until finally Gatiss returned alone and led Eberlin dumbly into the garden toward the pool.

"What on earth were you up to?" he said.

Eberlin blinked and for a brief second felt some vomit rising in his gullet for an unknown reason, and then he peered at Gatiss as if he were in fine print and blabbered, "What you say?"

"Fine bloody goose chase you led us. You didn't expect to find Krasnevin here, did you?"

"Krasnevin?" Eberlin repeated, barely conscious of any reality. "If it wasn't for me you'd probably be halfway to some bloody Russian prison by now. You are a damn fool and God knows why Frazer put you on this. If I have to go around dragging you out of every ditch you fall into, I might as well be back in London. What

in hell gave you the idea that Krasnevin was in the East?" "The East ..."

"Well, that's where Greff was taking you, wasn't it?" "Yes," said Eberlin. "Yes he was...."

He walked over to the pool and stared down at his reflection. A million things whirled around in Eberlin's mind. What is he talking about? he thought. And then suddenly, incredibly, he realized.

"Stare at your reflection much longer, Dancer, and you'll be turned into a flower."

Eberlin gazed at the yellow raft as it bobbed slightly against the side of the pool, and was momentarily puzzled by a dark object lying at the bottom of the water until he recognized it as a pair of sunglasses. Then he turned and without looking at Gatiss, walked back across the lawn toward the melee of policemen and stood among them, hands in pockets. No one approached him or spoke to him or even acknowledged his presence. A wagon had arrived and the guests were being loaded like squealing pigs into the dark interior, sitting on wooden benches in their pastel swimsuits, and clutching oddly snatched objects like a bottle of Ambre Solaire, or a single sandal or a glass of whisky. At one point, the young boy saw Eberlin and ran toward him, his face contorted in anger, and attempted to claw Eberlin's face. But he was seized by two policemen who sadistically ripped off the boy's trunks and threw him stark naked and struggling into the laps of the other prisoners, and then shut the door, sealing him in like an atheistic Daniel in the lions' den. And then, sirens two-toning to the sky, the cars spun around on the gravel, lurching over newly planted flower beds, and drove out fast into the main street and roared away, leaving Eberlin standing alone in the middle of the drive, long after the sound of the departing cars had disappeared.

"Get in the taxi," said Gatiss touching Eberlin's shoulder.

Eberlin did, sitting in the back seat of the Mercedes. Gatiss sat behind the wheel, started the car and eased it slowly out of the lane and toward the center of the city. He didn't speak for a full five minutes and then said, without turning around:

"How much did you give him?" "Two thousand five hundred dollars."

"His price has gone up." Then he added, "Did you seriously think that Greff could lead you to Krasnevin?"

"Yes," replied Eberlin immediately. "Greff has contacts in the East–" "But Krasnevin is not in the East." "You can't be sure."

"Can't I?" said Gatiss. "Prentiss arrived this morning. He's waiting to speak to you–about Krasnevin. He will show you that Breysach was a mistake for you."

Silence. Eberlin put his hand on the door handle and then took it away.

"Military car?" Gatiss asked suddenly.

"What has Prentiss to say?" said Eberlin, ignoring the question. "You'll see. Was it military car method?"

"Yes. I was going to pose as an American colonel." "American?"

"Well, American or British. One or the other." "Didn't you ask Greff which army it was?"

"No, why?"

Then Gatiss began to laugh. Eberlin felt sick again, claustrophobic in the oppressive atmosphere of the car. They were traveling at well over eighty miles an hour now down the central autobahn of Berlin, and Gatiss was still laughing.

"Look in the box next to you," he called to Eberlin. Look inside."

Lifting up the lid of the box, Eberlin saw a military uniform, neatly folded and pressed. He looked away, then glanced back in horror. The uniform was that of a colonel in the Red Army.

"Don't you see?" continued Gatiss, his voice rising. "You were being asked to pose as a Russian!"

* * *

There was a silence in the car. Neither men had said a word for quite a time now. Then just as the Kurfürstendamm came in sight, Gatiss, framing his eyes in the driving mirror, said quietly:

"You know, if I hadn't been informed, you'd probably be in the East by now, wouldn't you?"

* * *

The Mercedes was abandoned, and Gatiss and Eberlin walked the remaining three hundred yards toward the Jensen.

As they reached it, Gatiss said, "You meet Prentiss for late lunch in there. Give me your gun."

"Gun?"

"Give it to me. I'll put it in your room."

Eberlin handed over the Browning and turned to go, then stopped.

"Who's Oskar Greiser?" he said.

"Never heard of him," replied Gatiss vaguely, staring at an American tourist nearby who was clutching a recent copy of *Playboy*. Then he glanced back at Eberlin and said:

"Oskar Greiser? Oh –he's a Communist, isn't he?"

He walked to the Jensen without looking back. Eberlin frowned and turned away and was almost knocked down by a heavyset German. He was becoming paranoic. There was no doubt about it. Greiser a *Communist*? Greff did say that his activities were "undemocratic" but he never thought....

"Come back to the hotel immediately you've eaten," Gatiss called to him and then drove away.

Eberlin didn't go to meet Prentiss for about an hour. In fact it was more like an hour and a half, and when he did, he was drunk.

"I'm still sober," he protested to the barman, "I'm still bloody sober," and then left quickly, knocking over someone's glass, and ran out into the street. I'm going mad, he said to himself as he leaned against an alley wall, shaking all over. Then he realized he was making a fool of himself, and consequently straightened up and walked quite calmly and sensibly, back to the rendezvous building. "I'm still sober," he said to a small girl in a green dress at the entrance, and gave her ten pfennigs as a keepsake.

12

Didactic Nude

Life has nothing to offer anymore but me.
–ALEXANDER EBERLIN

AT the west end of the Kurfürstendamm there is a small restaurant specializing in *Wurst* of varying degrees of edibility, which had often been a rendezvous for Eberlin in his earlier stays in the city. It was perched on the seventh floor of one of those new classless buildings erected since the war, and stuck in the back of the building unheralded and out of the way, in the vain hope of collecting a chichi clientele who favored such mysterious and hard-to-find venues. Consequently, the restaurant was packed daily with multitudes of tourists, recommended to it by an aunt in Maine or a campus cousin from UCLA as a "quiet little place away from the beaten track," who, after standing in line for half an hour, sat exuberant and smug over a chipped plate containing two nauseous sausages and a fistful of sauerkraut which they wouldn't, on any other occasion, have offered to their dog. It was here Prentiss was waiting.

Eberlin reached the ground floor of the building, crossed the buff-painted lobby and took the lift up. It appeared to be a rare moment of quiet, for no one else entered the lift with him except a small man with a crew cut, a Pentax camera and a recent copy of *Playboy* bought illegally from a back-street shop specializing in eighteenth-century Japanese prints.

The two men stood silently side by side staring at the floor indicator as the lift heaved itself sluggishly upward. Eberlin, his hands in his pockets and still feeling deathly sober, glanced out of the corner of his eye at the other man, who was carefully flicking through the magazine, dismissing the wads of words and stopping only at the photos of the retouched, paintbox-colored nudes from Little Nowhere, Wisconsin. The charmless array of backsides and bosoms seemed endless and Eberlin looked away and was about to light a cigarette when he was thrown forward and back as the lift panicked to a halt halfway between the third and fourth stories, and the magazine was flung to the floor throwing open its triple-fold Playmate of the Month who pouted demurely up at Eberlin's astonished face. The other man, his right index finger jammed into the red STOP button of the lift panel, spoke in Russian with a slight trace of a Ukraine accent.

"Your reflexes are incredibly lax lately, Krasnevin. You really must ask your doctor for a tonic or something."

Eberlin stared across at the man and said nothing.

"Look, we haven't much time since there's a limit to how long one can jam a lift. Do light a cigarette and offer me one. My name's Sobakevich. How do you do?"

Eberlin didn't move. The name Sobakevich was very familiar to him.

"Well," Sobakevich continued unperturbed, "we'd just like to say how sorry we are that we had to treat you so badly at Friedrichstrasse yesterday. But don't you realize that we cannot afford to lose you from your present position? In Russia you are worthless to us." "I'll be worthless to you here if you don't do something quickly," replied Eberlin vehemently. "Aren't you supposed to protect me?"

"You refer of course to Gatiss?" "And others."

A buzzer from the seventh floor rang. Sobakevich ignored it. "Can you contact us tonight?" he said. "We might have an answer."

"I can't. Gatiss is watching me all the time." "Yes, I saw him. Why were you at Greiser's?" The buzzer sounded again impatiently.

"Look, we'd better get this lift moving before they haul us up.

We'll get in touch with you." "Soon."

"We'll do our best. But relax."

Eberlin swore. Sobakevich transferred his finger to the 6 button and the lift shuddered for a moment, hesitated, then churned upward.

"Is Rotopkin here?" Sobakevich looked up, irritated.

"This is no place to talk. Haven't you got any sense of timing?"

He smiled as the doors opened on the sixth floor and walked away, turning only to say, in German:

"Don't forget your magazine. Read it in private."

He disappeared around a corner as the doors closed, leaving Eberlin angrily lighting a cigarette and stooping to pick up the *Playboy* as the lift reached its delayed destination.

He pushed his way through the puzzled, complaining faces of the half-dozen people on the seventh floor and hurried into the restaurant. Prentiss was sitting at a small table before three empty coffee cups and staring anxiously at the entrance. They saw each other immediately, and Eberlin gave a quick smile and pointed to a door marked HERREN. Prentiss nodded with a grin, and Eberlin hurried across the room toward the door and entered.

Sitting on the toilet, trousers still belted around his waist, Eberlin flicked through the magazine, then held it up by the spine, shaking it. No stray piece of paper appeared. Eberlin sighed and turned to page one. It was all so bloody childish. Fortunately he found what he was looking for after a few pages. On a page headed PARTY JOKES and decorated with pen drawings of overdeveloped prepubescent girls, Eberlin found the message. Drawn in ink over the left breast of one of the nudes was a clumsy piece of graffiti. It was badly presented and with a poor sense of perspective, but the point was to Eberlin unerringly clear. There, over the black and white heart of the girl, was etched a miniscule Star of David.

Eberlin ripped the center pages out and flushed them down the toilet. Then he unlocked the door, thrusting the magazine into his pocket, and throwing the cigarette into the urinal, left the toilet; left the white-tiled toilet and walked over toward Prentiss.

* * *

"We're all back to square one," said Prentiss ordering two more coffees. "All the way back to square one."

He was a large man, six foot one or so, with dark hair, a remote Welsh origin, and utterly likable. He was one of those uncomplicated people who appear to treat everyone they meet as if they were the most precious thing on earth, and consequently women adored him. In this latter respect, however, he adhered rigidly to a penchant for young, pretty girls in their late teens, who fell in love with him after a week, and remained loyal to him months after he had moved on, sending him passionate letters from Torremelinos or their country house in Oxfordshire, with poetic comments on the heat of the sun or the state of their pregnancy. All this Prentiss took in his stride with a wry smile and a bashful grin when close friends discussed his pedigree of prettily rich ex-lovers, and would repeat over pints of beer at his Chelsea pub, when others admired his latest girl-child: "I would give her to you but she's part of a set," and she invariably was.

He seemed to care deeply about only two things: his work and his religion. He worried about the former because it constantly involved him, and about the latter because it didn't. "He is what you call a *lapsed Catholic*," Eberlin had re-remarked once of him, "that is, he still accepts Jesus Christ rising from the dead and walking on the water, but thinks the bit about Him riding on the back of a donkey is a little far-fetched."

"It's a bit of blow I must admit. Coming like that," Prentiss said gloomily, staring at the remains of Eberlin's lunch.

"How do you mean?"

"Well, did Gatiss tell you I received a PB message from Frazer to contact Loomis in Düsseldorf?"

"No."

"Well I did. Incredible panic about it." "What did Loomis want?" Eberlin asked.

"They found the man whom we thought was Krasnevin. He was dead."

Eberlin stared at Prentiss for a second, then looked away. A man at the next table leaned over and asked to borrow the menu. When no one answered him, he snatched it.

"How do you know he wasn't Krasnevin?" Eberlin said finally, keeping his voice low.

"Well, we checked him out and found he had been living in London for four years under the name of Jeffries, and before that, when we learned that the man hadn't been out of the country at all in that time. He just hadn't moved. Which made it impossible for him to kill anyone–at least anyone we are concerned about."

"How could you be sure?"

"Well, it's rather embarrassing for all concerned. Frazer's gone off to the Scillies to recover."

Prentiss lit a cigarette and glanced out of the window at a blond fraülein selling newspapers on the pavement below.

"You know how we all feel about the CIA," he continued. "Well, it was they who proved that the dead man wasn't Krasnevin. Apparently they had a file on him all the time. The man's called Pavel. He's a Russian all right, or was, but he's no assassin. Just a contact man."

"They had a file on him all the time?"

"Yes. You can understand how Frazer felt when he found out. He had to go on his knees before Sir Hugh and explain this trivial oversight. And then telling him that they had been upstaged by the CIA–well, it was pathetic. No one spoke to each other for a week, so Loomis said. He was glad to get out. Well, anyway, Frazer refused to let the CIA be so smug about it and started shouting at them, even throwing the Bay of Pigs in as a rejoinder. He was pretty annoyed. So–back to square one."

"Does Gatiss know this?"

"Yes. He just nodded as though he knew all the time. You know how Gatiss is."

Eberlin didn't answer.

"But the most incredible thing is, who the hell is Krasnevin?

Even the CIA is wary about that." "How do you mean?"

"You wouldn't believe it," said Prentiss, sipping at the coffee, "but they hinted that this Krasnevin was actually a double. One of us. Well, you can imagine Frazer's reaction to that one."

"What was it exactly?" asked Eberlin. "Well, he–"

Prentiss stopped and laughed. "It's quite an interesting theory, you must admit. Plausible." Then he said, "Is that this month's *Playboy* in your pocket?"

Eberlin didn't answer, and allowed Prentiss to take the magazine and glanced through it.

"The Playmate's missing as usual," Prentiss muttered. "I didn't know you read stuff like this?"

He caught Eberlin's expression and put the magazine away.

"I'm sorry about that," Prentiss said quietly.

Eberlin stirred the coffee pensively and glanced across the room.

"It doesn't help you much, does it? I mean not knowing even what he looks like."

Eberlin looked up at Prentiss's face and then didn't say a word for a long time.

"Your car's outside, by the way," ventured Prentiss but Eberlin wasn't listening. Self-consciously Prentiss opened the magazine again and began to read parts of it halfheartedly, conscious of the silence, then with a shy smile said:

"What do you think of the girls in Berlin? Mmm? Not like the luncheon in München ones I bet, but casual enough I should think...."

Eberlin lit a cigarette and ignored him.

"Oh by the way," continued Prentiss gamely, "you know that Suzanne girl I was going to marry? Well, that fell through. As soon as she knew how interested I was, she changed. Everything cooled and in one second we were back to nervous introductions.... You know? I started being moody, then aggressive and all the recognized elements of the game. But I was alone. She said, 'You hate me now, don't you? People always do,' and then she went off somewhere. Spain, I think."

"Could I have the bill please?" Eberlin said suddenly to a passing waiter, and then to Prentiss: "What did you say?"

"Oh, just about Suzanne going to Spain." "Didn't you go with her?"

"Well I suggested it to her but she said 'No.' So I asked her if I would see her when she returned and she just shrugged and talked about Giacometti."

"I like his earlier sculptures best," said Eberlin without enthusiasm.

"So she went. I must have been a fool."

Prentiss stared into space, one hand clutching a cold cup of coffee, as Eberlin paid the bill.

"I think someone, sometime, must have burned out her soul," Prentiss said quietly and stood up.

Picking up the change, Eberlin hurried across the restaurant followed by Prentiss, who caught up with him and said, "Still, there's plenty more fish in the sea," and became embarrassed.

Eberlin grunted and stared straight ahead of him as the lift descended. Then, when they reached the ground floor, he turned and asked, "Where did you say the Mistrale was?"

* * *

It seemed just like new. He walked around it five times, prodding it, stroking it, standing back and looking at it from different angles, then actually sitting inside it and holding the wheel. It felt wrong but it was definitely the same car. The initials were there. As he sat numbed into a state of lethargy despite the awesome implications of the day, Prentiss knocked on the window and said:

"You know, perhaps no one burned out her soul. Perhaps she never had one. Perhaps I just tried to intellectualize her, create a positive personality for her because I wanted something to match her physical qualities."

Eberlin sighed. "Get in," he said.

Prentiss nodded and walked around the Mistrale and sat next to Eberlin, and stared at a girl standing outside the Kempinski who was wearing a white wool dress and carrying a copy of *Paris Match*. "Tourist," Prentiss commented. "By the way, what happened this afternoon?"

"Bloody Gatiss barged in again like God Almighty. It was worth trying Breysach–I mean, what else have we come up with?"

"Perhaps. But you would have been looking for someone who looked like that man Pavel, wouldn't you?"

Eberlin drove the car slowly to the hotel, conscious of the admiring faces of the pedestrians as he passed.

"He hates you, you know," Prentiss said. "Gatiss does?"

"Intensely," replied Prentiss, chewing at a fingernail. "But then he's hardly in love with me. He thinks I'm a sentimental romantic. Utterly without justification of course ..." and he smiled at a girl waiting at a crossing.

"What makes you think he hates me?"

"I don't know. I just know he does. Drop me just here." "Aren't you staying at the same hotel?"

"Yes. But I've got a couple of things to do first. Anyway, Gatiss wants to see you about something."

Prentiss got out of the car opposite the Drei Bären. As he closed the door, he glanced back at Eberlin and said:

"Be careful when you get back there. He's got some girl with him. Pretty sick."

Prentiss hurried across the street toward a small shop selling transistor radios at ridiculously low prices, which intrigued him greatly, since he'd promised a cousin in Norwich that he would buy one as a silver wedding present.

13

Au Suivant

The thought of suicide is a great consolation; with the help of it one has got through many a bad night.
–NIETZSCHE

THE name of the whore in Gatiss's room was Hedwig. When Eberlin returned to the hotel, he found it was about seven o'clock. He hesitated outside Gatiss's door, knocked and was told to enter, and was stunned to see the familiar face of the girl in the brothel. But only the face was familiar, not the expression. No wink or grin greeted him this time. Instead, the platinum-blond whore stared wide-eyed at the ceiling, clutching the sheets of the bed before her, her knuckles white as if she were in pain. Eberlin could see it in the girl's eyes. He hesitated at the door and muttered an apology, but Gatiss, who was standing dressing before the washstand, waved him in. Eberlin closed the door and hovered self-consciously in the corner of the room, attempting to avoid looking at the girl but finding himself drawn to the wretched face. He stared blankly at the bed, hating the oppressive atmosphere, and attempted to relax by offering the girl a cigarette.

"Don't give her one," Gatiss said sharply. Eberlin looked up, stung by the tone of the voice. "Don't give her a thing."

"I was just offering her a cigarette–" Eberlin began. "Nothing. She's a hun. A Nazi."

Eberlin recoiled from this, turned his back on Gatiss and held out the cigarette toward the girl, saying to Gatiss:

"Don't be so damn inhuman."

The cigarette was violently knocked out of his hand and Gatiss pushed him away against the wardrobe.

"The only inhumanity," Gatiss said coldly, "is that her and her race are still alive, and that six million of mine are dead. *That* is the only inhumanity."

He turned back to the mirror and studied a spot that had appeared on the left side of his jaw. Eberlin stood in the dead silence of the room for two minutes, staring at the floor, and then the girl began to sob. Tears ran down her pale cheeks and her body quivered under the bedclothes, and she buried her face in shame in the recesses of the grubby, coverless pillow, so that the sheet pulled away from her shoulder and revealed her back, mutilated by bruises and weals already beginning to swell. Eberlin stared at her body in horror and turned toward Gatiss.

"You bastard," he said inadequately and left the room and returned to his own and lay on the bed in the dark. In half an hour, Gatiss knocked on the door and invited him for a drink, and they both strolled to a pleasant little café nearby and ordered two Camparis with plenty of ice. It looked like rain but the weather was deceptive in these parts.

* * *

"Women, Dancer, are destructive animals. One can meet a beautiful woman one day and she will kiss your feet the next. You surrender your identity to them, allow them to share your waking moments in rapidly enlarging installments, and soon you will find they are using you. They wave their neuroses before you like a leper's bell, knowing you cannot ignore them, and you suffer them their self-pity and their pathetic bleats of negative living until one day you find yourself eaten by them, degraded, scoured out, tied to the rack of their pathetic nullity. Women use us, Eberlin, and the only way to treat them is to use *them*. Use them to sleep with, use them to cook for you, use them to run errands, but never, never allow yourself to enter that mental tic of their femininity. If you do, you are nothing. Your own laughing-stock. You yourself do and that is why you are a fool. But then you are a fool about everything."

They had been sitting in the café for an hour now and Gatiss had consumed almost half a bottle of Campari. It had grown dark, and he sat lounging in the chair staring blandly into the night, talking incessantly in that dogmatic way of his, not caring if he was heard or not. Eberlin had said almost nothing, for he was thinking of other things. He was thinking when he would kill Gatiss. That was obviously what Kuzmich wanted. Eberlin wondered how they would contact him, if indeed they were watching him now. He felt slightly more relaxed–partly due to the drink and partly due to the offer of help from Sobakevich. It was the first positive gesture he had had. But he had to kill Gatiss for them. He could do it tomorrow. In the afternoon. If it was sunny.

"I mean, people ask me why I only sleep with whores," Gatiss was saying, "but that is strictly an inaccurate statement. All women are whores, Dancer. All women are whores. The ones who do it for money just happen to be the cheapest, that's all."

Eberlin sighed and stood up, stretching his back. "Going somewhere?" asked Gatiss.

"Pardon?" replied Eberlin. "Please sit down. I'm talking." "It's late."

"Oh hardly. Anyway, you're here on business–in case you've forgotten."

Eberlin sat down again and lit another cigarette and contemplated the check tablecloth.

"I'm not the man for the job," he said finally. "I'm a desk man. I couldn't find him in a broom cupboard. You see what a fiasco happens if I try to do anything positive. Like this afternoon."

"Are you talking about Krasnevin?" "Weren't you?"

"Yes. Something like that," murmured Gatiss vaguely, gesturing to a waiter. "Have you ever killed a man? I mean killed him–purposefully?"

"Why do you ask?"

"Curiosity. You strike me as somebody who could." "What makes you say that?"

"Try to attract the waiter's attention, will you?"' "Do I look like a killer, then?"

"What?" said Gatiss, then laughed. "Perhaps." "I'm tired. I need some sleep."

Eberlin got up and walked out of the café and waited on the pavement. He found that he had broken into a cold sweat, which bothered him. For an awesome moment, he re-entertained the notion that Gatiss knew his identity all the time, but dismissed it in a panic and glanced back toward the café to see Gatiss walking toward him and touching his arm.

"Come with me," he said quietly. "I want to show you something."

"What?"

"Come on."

Eberlin hesitated, then said, "I must return to the hotel first." "Why?"

"Oh stop acting like a bloody school prefect," snapped Eberlin. "I'll be back in a minute."

He stalked off, watched by an amused Gatiss who wandered back to the café and ordered another Campari with ice.

* * *

The night porter was on duty when Eberlin arrived at the hotel. He nodded to him, muttered "*Guten Abend*" and hurried upstairs to the second floor. Pausing on the landing, Eberlin listened for a movement, but the hotel was asleep. He crept stealthily to Gatiss's room and knocked softly on the door. There was no answer. He tried the handle but the door was locked. Hesitating only a fraction of a second, Eberlin hurried downstairs to the foyer once more and casually sauntered over to the desk.

"*Guten Abend*," he said again with a professional smile. "*Guten Abend*," the night porter replied, smiling over a cold cup

of coffee, a full ashtray and a copy of the day's *Bild*.

"I keep forgetting to collect my key," Eberlin continued, offering the other man a cigarette. "I wonder if I could take it now."

The porter looked up, took the cigarette and gazed at Eberlin's beaming face.

"Looks like rain," Eberlin remarked, pressing a loose corner of the blotting paper into its frame on the desk.

"What number?" "Two four three."

The key to Gatiss's room was handed across the counter, and Eberlin nodded.

"*Danke schon.*"

He returned upstairs and in two minutes was inside Gatiss's room and face to face with the whore.

"Do you speak English?" he asked, glancing out of the window. "Nein," she replied and looked at the floor. Eberlin pulled the sheets from the girl's bruised body, and she winced and backed against the wall, covering her large breasts with her arms.

"I'm not going to hurt you," Eberlin whispered. "But you must get out before he cornes back."

The girl didn't move but stared wide-eyed at Eberlin's face. "Quickly," he said. "The door's open. Look."

He pointed to the door, demonstrating that it was open, and then handed the girl her clothes. Slowly, suspiciously, the girl took them one by one, gritting her teeth as the elastic of the underclothes bit into her flesh. Eberlin stared into the sink, hating everything, until she was ready, then he took her hand.

"I'm sorry," he said, and put two hundred Marks into it. "I'm sorry," he repeated.

They both stood there staring over each other's shoulder in embarrassed silence, as if posing for a sculpture, or caught practising a new dance. Finally Eberlin moved away, opened the door and glanced into the empty corridor. He nodded to the girl, and she shuffled out into the landing and stood there looking helplessly about.

"You'd better leave by the back stairs," Eberlin said and pointed to the corridor. He shook her hand like a guest bidding good-bye to a hostess at a party and said, "Well, good night."

Then he turned away toward his own room. The girl hesitated, suddenly kissed his sleeve, and then ran quickly down the corridor to the back stairs without glancing back. He heard her footsteps running down the stairs and disappearing into the night. Slowly, Eberlin walked to his own room which he always left open and switched on the light. Whatever Gatiss had in mind for tonight, Eberlin was determined to be prepared, so he crouched down and pulled his carryall from under the bed, assuming that this was where Gatiss would have put his gun. But he had miscalculated the time. Even as he unzipped the bag and reached for the gun hidden inside he heard the door open behind him, and glancing back saw Gatiss standing, towering over him, looking steadily into his eyes.

"What exactly are you doing?" Gatiss asked. "Mmmm?" and lifted the top of the carryall with his foot to reveal Eberlin's hand clutching the Browning.

Eberlin stood up slowly, turning to face Gatiss and shrugged vaguely.

"I just returned to collect the gun. I wondered where you had hidden it."

"So I see," the other man said, pushing the door shut behind him. "Were you planning to kill anyone, then?"

There was a moment's dead silence, then Eberlin smiled. "I thought we might need it," he said quickly.

He stood holding the gun in his right hand, the muzzle pointing at the floor. Gatiss studied Eberlin's face for a moment, then turned away and opened the door.

"Put it back under the bed. You might be dangerous waving one of those around–being a desk man as you are. Put it back."

Eberlin found himself ridiculously replacing the gun in the case and walking dumbly to the door. On the way out, Gatiss said, pointing at the *Playboy* magazine on the floor:

"Did you buy that?" "No. I found it."

"Not your kind of thing, I would have thought." He closed the door. "You can't get them in Berlin, can you?"

Eberlin shrugged. Halfway down the stairs he realized he still had Gatiss's key clutched tightly in his left hand.

They reached the foyer, and Eberlin, lagging behind, muttered, "I'll just leave my key at the desk."

He crossed quickly to the counter without looking back and was relieved to find that Gatiss didn't follow. The key was handed over, then he hurried out into the night air, into the cool wind of the night, hurried after Gatiss toward the steel-blue Jensen waiting to take him away to another destination where he knew the pillars of his temple would begin finally to crumble.

"I'd rather you didn't smoke," snapped Gatiss, closing the car door and revving the engine. "It would make it awfully stuffy in here, and we've got rather a long way to go."

The car slid out of the side street into the mainstream of the few cars in Joachimstaler Strasse, then roared fast, sometimes touching eighty, northwest along Otto-Suhr-Alee and up Tegeler-Weg and north along Kurt-Schumacher-Damm. Passing the Quartier Napoleon, Eberlin spoke for the first time. "Where are we going?" he said quickly.

Gatiss, overtaking three cars on a dangerously sharp corner, replied:

"To visit your friend in the shower."

Then he refused to say any more until they had arrived at their destination–a tall block of apartments near Wittenau, all brownstone and small-windowed and middle-class. It was ten minutes past one and beginning to rain.

* * *

Gatiss parked the car in a dark alley near a small florist shop and switched off the engine and lights. The two men sat there silently for a minute, then Eberlin, defying the other man's prejudices, lit a cigarette and inhaled deeply.

"Do we wait *here* for him?" he whispered, falling into the mood of the affair.

"No," replied Gatiss, winding down the window. "Do you have to smoke that damn thing?"

"It's a habit I've become attached to," Eberlin replied sweetly and flicked some ash on the floor.

"Henderson, or whatever his name is, lives in that block of apartments opposite. Number 25."

"How do you know?" asked Eberlin.

"He sent me a postcard," Gatiss replied curtly. "How the hell do you think I know? The bloody man is such an amateur, he's been advertising himself for the last couple of days. He even followed me."

"I don't think you ought to shout," Eberlin said. "I mean, one doesn't really, does one?"

He smiled and puffed at the cigarette. Gatiss didn't say anything for a moment, then:

"He parks his car in the special car park just behind the building.

I want you to wait for him, if he's not there already." "What about you?"

"Don't worry about me. Come on."

Gatiss got out of the car into the drizzling rain and crossed the street toward the dark recesses of the apartment building. Eberlin followed, hunching his shoulders under his jacket, until they reached the small car park, each space reserved for tenants only.

"His car is not there," Gatiss said, stopping under an arch. Eberlin peered across the yard and saw about a dozen cars parked neatly in a line in a small square, their noses pointing toward a row of badly planted mulberry bushes.

"See that space over there," Gatiss hissed in Eberlin's ear, "in between the black Mercedes and the small Renault?"

"Yes."

"That's where Henderson parks his car." "The gray Volkswagen?"

"The gray Volkswagen. Wait here out of sight until it returns." "How do you know it will?"

"I don't. But it might."

Gatiss walked away, out of the arch and into the street and the darkness, and Eberlin was left alone, feeling confused, helpless and profoundly annoyed. He edged into a dry corner under the arch, took out a cigarette, thought better of it, and prepared to spend half the night in a vertical position staring at an eight-by-six rectangle of empty concrete. Where the hell was Rotopkin?

The rain soon came down in buckets, flooding the yard and drumming incessantly on the steel roofs of the parked cars. It welled into puddles, seeped over onto the grass, stopped suddenly as if bored by it all, and then came down even heavier until Eberlin wondered if he would ever see a dry sky again. And still the gray Volkswagen did not arrive.

Eberlin's eyes ached, and once or twice he even closed them in a vain attempt to succumb to sleep. He found his mind wandering over a thousand things, thoughts popping up before him constantly like pheasants disturbed in the long grass. He thought of Caroline and that ridiculously naïve party he had attended decades ago, and of her lying beside him in his hotel sometime last century. He thought of Frazer, and his manservant, and of Pavel lying buried somewhere in an anonymous chunk of land. *The poor insist on being buried. It's usually the the only way they can insure of getting a garden of their own.* He wondered who had said that or where he had read it, and then realized he had said it himself in one of his many cynical moods, aping Wilde sitting in the Café Royal. He had been there only once–more Café than Royal now--and had seen another of his romantic illusions shattered by the boxed EXIT signs over the doors and the commercialized beer mats on the tables. He remembered going downstairs there and being confronted by a polite concentration of thought when he inquired from the toilet attendant if Bosie had arrived yet.

He thought of his son and remembered the boy's face the last time he had seen him, at a small tea party on the boy's second birthday. He had squatted on the floor with dozens of children and sung "Happy Birthday to You" with a red face, then, with a muttered apology, stumbled out drunk into the street on the pretense of buying some cigarettes and never gone back. Eberlin thought of Russia and his home which he would never see again, and of his apartment in London and the books he would never read. He thought of God and hoped that if He was everywhere, He wouldn't have to stand through this, and he giggled to himself like a child. He began to work out small problems in his mind, like the one about the Chinaman with the fox, the chicken and the bag of grain and some thing about crossing a river, and the other one about the two guards who either lied or told the truth; and moved on to amassing groups of things, making endless lists, like London telephone exchanges, or novels whose titles began with *An*, or names of girls he had known. He thought of one in particular, for some unknown reason, a girl he had met in London two years after Jesse's birth–a model or a ballerina–whom he inundated with presents like a dying millionaire, never to receive one in return. It had been a one-sided affair, yet he remembered her with fondness, though he couldn't recollect her name; it might have been Joan or Jane or June. And as the hours of the night passed, and the Volkswagen seemed destined never to return, Eberlin began to make up epigrams and to talk to himself on quite intimate terms, answering himself in Russian. Then he began to think about women again, this time more tenderly. The purgatory of watching a girl no longer desired as she lingered over her dressing and laboriously appreciated a book on the bedside table. That presented him with a moment's silence, and he lit a cigarette, throwing caution to the winds. Or to the damn rain. And finally he thought of Gatiss and how he would kill him, and this brought him back to reality. He thought of death and shuddered, for he knew that he himself was soon to die, and that whatever happened, no matter how far he ran, he would be killed in the end. It wouldn't be by God's hand, and it wouldn't be by his own, but it would be there, and all this, this pitiful travesty, was merely marking time. And so he abandoned the pretense, gave up the subterfuge and strode out of his hiding place and almost under the wheels of a small gray Volkswagen that turned sharply from nowhere into the wet yard and parked neatly between a black Mercedes and a small Renault. It was there.

Eberlin ducked back into the shadows, trusting to God he hadn't been seen and wishing he had defied Gatiss and brought the gun. If Henderson was taken alive and forced to speak, it could be too late for him to do anything. The car door opened, and the small shape of the man in the shower got out and calmly locked the door, suspecting nothing. He stood by the Volkswagen for a moment adjusting a carnation in his buttonhole, then looked up at the sky despite the rain. He was about to walk toward the apartments when Gatiss, appearing suddenly from the shadows, said quietly in Russian:

"Stay where you are."

Henderson stopped, stunned, and looked around helplessly, considering a panicked flight. Gatiss strode calmly across the flooded yard toward him, holding a small stubby Smith and Wesson in his hand and wearing preposterous dark glasses. Eberlin watched anxiously as Gatiss walked to a point ten yards from the Volkswagen and snapped out Eberlin's name. There was nothing for it but to emerge from the arch. He sensed the shock and puzzlement as Henderson recognized him. Eberlin, limbs aching, avoided the man's eye and walked to a two-tone Fairlane behind the Russian's back. The three men made no move for some twenty seconds, then Gatiss made Eberlin the present of a blessed opportunity.

"Search him," he called. "See if he carries a gun."

Holding his breath, Eberlin crossed toward Henderson, wiping the rain from his face, and stared down into his fellow Russian's frightened face. Leaning closely over him and feeling in the man's pockets, Eberlin whispered:

"Gatiss is going to kill you, but if you run when I shout out his name, I'll try to save you."

Eberlin took a small Beretta from Henderson's pocket, held it in his hand and walked away without glancing to see if the Russian had understood. He walked for about five yards, until he was masking Gatiss from the other man, then suddenly shouted:

"Gatiss!"

Henderson made his desperate move for his life by beginning to run, and Eberlin coldly shot him through the head before he had covered two paces. The Russian collapsed immediately and was dead before he hit the ground.

Anticipating Gatiss's outburst of anger, Eberlin said quietly, "He was trying to escape."

Then he walked away through the arch, not bothering anymore for explanations and not even caring if Gatiss put a bullet through his back. But Gatiss didn't. He ran after him, pushing him on the shoulder and shouting:

"Come on, you bloody reckless bastard, and get in the car before we have half the Berlin polizei around us."

They both ran to the Jensen and drove away, leaving Henderson lying where he had fallen on the wet stones with only the sound of the rain and the approaching footsteps to keep him company.

***

They drove for about fifteen minutes in no particular direction, then Gatiss said:

"What you did was your second mistake in twelve hours. That's two too many."

* * *

They decided it would be safer to separate as soon as possible, so they drove quickly for about fifteen minutes, mostly in silence, though the atmosphere in the car was heavy with distrust and anger. "That bloody Red was no use to us dead. Why on earth did you have to kill him?"

And for the tenth time Eberlin replied, "I'm sorry. I didn't think.

It was just impulsive of me."

"They'll never leave us alone now–now that we've come into the open. You can drop your Dancer role anyway, not that you ever adopted it."

"All right."

They parked near the Ka Da We, and Gatiss said, "I'm going back to search Henderson's room. You avoid the hotel for an hour in case you're followed, but meet me there at"–he glanced at his watch–"at six o'clock. In one hour."

Eberlin nodded.

"You aimed for his head, didn't you?" "What?" said Eberlin. "Oh, no Not really."

"Of course. You intrigue me, Eberlin. I want to find out more about you."

The sun appeared suddenly, dispersing the rain, and they both stared at the blue-glassed dominoes of the Kaiser Wilhelm Church. Then Eberlin opened the door of the Jensen only to be stopped by

Gatiss.

"How much did you give the whore?" Eberlin hesitated.

"Two hundred marks," he said.

"One for each of those on her back?" Gatiss smiled. "Who are you trying to convince of your saintliness, Eberlin?"

"No one." Gatiss laughed.

"You're not an English dandy, Eberlin. You're not even a loyal English gentleman. You know what you are?"

"Tell me," said Eberlin quietly.

Gatiss looked at Eberlin's face steadily. "An assassin," he said.

And then, "See me in an hour." He drove off.

Eberlin walked down the empty expanse of the Kurfürstendamm, past the boxed window displays in the center of the pavement and the hundreds of dead neon lights. The rain had stopped completely now, and a warm breeze was blowing. It was already Wednesday, the first day of the Berlin Grand Prix, and it was going to be hot. He glanced around him, but there was no one in sight, no one following him. And then, quite unexpectedly, the Russians made contact with him.

14

Hai-Wai Filter

Genghis Khan knew only how to bend his bow at the eagles,
Only today are there men of feeling.
–*MAO TSE-TUNG*

THE Zunta Restaurant has a reputation, not without foundation, for attracting the prettiest girls and the dullest conversation in Berlin. Neither facet however was immediately apparent when Eberlin arrived, since the place was closed.

He hadn't realized how early it was and found he had to walk four blocks before he found a small bar that was open, though with some of its chairs still on the table.

Eberlin entered cautiously, but finding three workmen already settled behind large beers, he walked more confidently to the bar, and, learning from past mistakes, ordered beer only, without Korn. He had come to like German beer, although the Berlin variety was far inferior to the Bavarian, and consequently drank two liters before relaxing sufficiently to smoke a cigarette. He saw Henderson's face for a moment, then he lit the cigarette.

"Herr Dancer?" the barman said suddenly, looking at him curiously.

"Ja?" said Eberlin.

"Telephone," said the barman in slight irritation, and pointed to the corner of the bar. Eberlin looked in that direction, then nodded and crossed the room.

"Dancer," he said into the phone, keeping his voice low and his eyes moving quickly around the room.

"*Die Welt is dumm, die Welt ist blind*," said the caller.

Eberlin held his breath for a second before he replied: "*Wird täglich abgeschmackter.*"

Abruptly he became conscious of the barman nearby listening openly to the conversation.

"One moment," he said into the phone and walked over to a jukebox. Dropping a mark piece into the machine, he pressed buttons at random, and as the raucous music disturbed the silence, he returned to the telephone and continued the conversation.

"What is it?" he asked.

"Don't talk now," came the reply. "Call me back from a phone booth."

"All right."

"Eight fifty-six eighty-one." The phone went dead.

"She says I can come home if I buy her a fur coat," he said to the barman with a smile.

With a professional laugh, his listener repeated this to the three workmen, who guffawed and made obscene comments. One shouted, "I'd ram the coat up her arse," and the others laughed again.

Eberlin smiled good-naturedly and shrugged.

"Trouble is," he said, "I don't think her husband would like it."

He paid the bill, said good-bye and left, leaving the men with smiles on their faces and discordant rock and roll in their ears.

In front of a cinema showing *The Ipcress File*, which he suddenly, incongruously, recalled Caroline had wanted to see because she knew the actor in it, was an empty phone booth. Eberlin entered and dialed the number. When a voice answered, he repeated the code phrase and was immediately put through to Rotopkin.

"Where's Gatiss now?" Rotopkin said.

"He's gone to search Henderson's apartment." "Whose?"

"Henderson's."

"Oh–Niagarin. Well, he'll find nothing there." There was a pause and then Eberlin said quietly: "I'm afraid Niagarin is dead. I had to shoot him." "We know," replied Rotopkin. "We saw you." "I'm sorry."

"He was a fool. He would have talked." "I think Gatiss suspects me."

"But he's not sure?" "No. But–"

"Go and see Greiser. Oskar Greiser."

"Greiser?"

"We can't afford to throw twenty years' work away if he finds out. We'll help you."

"How?" asked Eberlin, glancing out of the booth to see if anyone was nearby. No one was.

"The British want Krasnevin. So we'll give him to them." Eberlin frowned and waited.

"It's all right," continued Rotopkin. "It won't be you." "They know he's a double."

"They would. Well, they'll get him."

"You mean you know a double working for Frazer?" "Yes."

"Working for Frazer?" Eberlin repeated. "Yes. Ideal."

"Do I know who it is?"

"You ought to. It's quite a friend."

There was a sudden intake of breath, and a dozen faces flashed across Eberlin's mind. He was about to ask who it was when–

"You must allow Gatiss to find him. It would be best if Gatiss discovered the man."

"Man? For a moment I thought you were talking about Caroline."

"Who the hell is she?" "No one. Just a thought."

"When will you see Gatiss?" "In an hour."

"Make some excuse to take him to Oskar Greiser's. Take him immediately. Search the place. It's all been prepared."

"What are we looking for?" "You'll see."

And then:

"By the way, you're familiar with Hai-Wai, aren't you?" "As much as we know."

"Good. Now you can relax."

Eberlin smiled to himself. He'd have to send Rotopkin a birthday card now.

"Thanks," he said.

"We're doing it for our sakes, not yours."

"I know. Thanks anyway."

"Contact me before you leave Berlin. Tell me what happened." "Yes. Good-bye."

Eberlin put down the phone, sighed, and left the phone booth. Someone was waiting outside. Immediately Eberlin stiffened, then saw it was one of the workmen from the bar.

"Barman wouldn't let me use his."

Eberlin nodded and moved away, turning only to smile again as the man called after him.

"Women are bastards, aren't they?"

Eberlin pulled a face of acquiescence and hurried back to the hotel.

* * *

Gatiss stared at the wrinkled, dry bikini on the floor. "Nothing there," he said. "Nothing there at all."

He had been sitting there ten minutes, cleaning a gun and repeating his disappointment. Eberlin turned away from the window and offered Gatiss a cigarette, forgetting for a moment that the other man didn't smoke.

"He was like an old woman," said Gatiss. "Who was?"

"Henderson. Everything neat and tidy. He cooked for himself. Even had a pet cat that kept meowing all the time. I had to give it some milk to keep it quiet."

Eberlin smiled at the image, then caught Gatiss glaring at him and turned it into a frown of concentration.

"Who was he working for?" ventured Eberlin with overt interest.

"The Russians of course. Who else?" "Well, the HVA perhaps."

"Don't be so bloody naïve," growled Gatiss. "Just don't be so bloody naïve."

Eberlin shrugged, sat down on the bed and picked up the bikini. "Have you ever heard of Caroline Hetherington?"

"Her?" asked Gatiss, pointing at the swimsuit. "Yes."

"Had her mother once. Incredible bore but a good fuck."

"She's not working for us, is she?" asked Eberlin casually. "Caroline, I mean?"

"What the hell makes you think that?"

"Just that I always seem to be bumping into her. Is she?" "Not so far as I know. I'll check her out when I get back." "No, there's no need for that. I just wondered…."

He was silent for a while.

"I think I'll go and see Greiser," he said at last. Gatiss looked up, surprised.

"For Godsakes don't go running around again. What do you want to see *him* for?"

"Not see him. See if he's got anything to hide. You said he was a Communist, and when I met him he looked pretty shady. Even Greff–"

"Greff! The less said about him the better."

"Nevertheless," Eberlin continued doggedly, "it's worth a visit.

I could be there and back in an hour." He got up, reaching for his coat.

"Sit down," snapped Gatiss. "You're not going anywhere." Eberlin stopped. It was time, he realized, to get angry.

"Listen, Gatiss, stop putting your damn nose in everything I do. I don't give a damn who you are. Frazer selected me to find Krasnevin, not you. *Me*. So far, we've found nothing and through no help of yours. You've already ruined any chances of using Breysach, which might have led to something, and now that we have something else to go on, I'm not letting you foul it up. Stay here if you like, but I'm going."

He opened the door. With a sudden bound, Gatiss grabbed Eberlin's arm and slammed him against the door, almost dislocating his shoulder.

"You listen, you fucking fairy," Gatiss snarled in his face. "When this is over, I'm going to make it my personal business to break every bone in your fucking body. You supercilious bastard!"

He suddenly spat in Eberlin's face. Then he turned away in disgust, throwing the other onto the bed. Without thinking, Eberlin pulled out the Beretta and aimed it at Gatiss's head, but stopped himself in cold realization. The other man turned and looked down at him with utter hatred.

"You want to kill me, don't you?" he said. "You want to blow my brains out, don't you?"

Eberlin stared into the man's face, then lowered the gun. "I think," he said quietly, "we ought to get some air."

Neither man moved. The walls of the room wrapped themselves around them, cutting off the oxygen, and at last Gatiss gave a grunt and walked to the door.

"I was right, wasn't I?" he said looking down at Eberlin. "How?" Eberlin asked.

"You *have* killed before."

Eberlin didn't answer. Gatiss nodded to himself. "You know that magazine? *Playboy*?" he went on. "What of it?"

"Where did you find it?"

"In the toilet at the restaurant. Why?"

"There was a man outside carrying the same magazine. Same issue."

Eberlin gave a puzzled smile.

"So what?" he said. "I should think millions read it."

"Yes. But that man was a Russian. His name is Sobakevich." Gatiss opened the door and added:

"I'm going to kill him before I leave Berlin."

* * *

Two minutes later Gatiss returned to Eberlin's room wearing a coat.

"You really think Greiser is up to something?"

"I don't know," replied Eberlin. "But I want to find out."

"I'll come with you," Gatiss said. "I'm not leaving you alone.

Come on."

He left the room. Eberlin picked up the Beretta and put it in his pocket, then, with a smile locked the door and joined Gatiss in the foyer.

* * *

The bordello was dark. At six o'clock in the morning, only the ill-hung doors witnessed the first snores of the tired harlots as they lay in grubby sheets, dreaming of nothing. Beside them, curled in the fetus curve of their mercenary mothers, lay the whores' babies, most of them mongrels fed on bones and canned meat. Above some of the beds were childhood crucifixes, now merely part of the drab, cock-roached décor. It was a tragic existence. "Man," Eberlin had said once, "can offer nothing to a woman. Nothing at all. That is his tragedy. Woman therefore wants to be equal to man. That is hers."

Gatiss and Eberlin had driven to Kohlhasstrasse in the Mistrale and had parked it two streets away in a narrow alley. Then they had walked, not speaking to each other, to the brothel and entered the gloomy, musty interior. It was a place for rats, and for peripatetic drunks who urinated ostentatiously in the hallway, and it smelled of both.

"Is this it?" Gatiss asked quietly.

"Top floor," said Eberlin and made for the staircase.

Clinging to the balustrade, the two men climbed the creaking stairs toward the fourth floor. Halfway up they stopped and ducked into the shadows as a wretched insomniac left her bedroom and walked naked to a broken lavatory, leaving the door open. The two men listened to her rattling endlessly into the toilet, then the chain was pulled, and the woman, in her late forties, her white stomach scribbled with black hair, reappeared and returned to her bedroom. They ascended the remaining flights and paused outside the door marked WINTERHILFE.

Gatiss drew his gun, and was copied by Eberlin. The door was tried, then forced and opened under splitting timbers to reveal the darkened, empty womb of the office. Closing the door behind them, Gatiss said in a whisper:

"The damn place is empty."

"There's another office," said Eberlin. "In there."

He pointed to the adjoining room, wondering if the plan, whatever it was, would materialize.

Holding his breath, Eberlin opened the next door and the two men stepped into a small inner office, crammed with cupboards and filing cabinets, and dominated by an enormous ashtray, a pile of letters and a sign saying OSKAR GREISER.

Gatiss drew the curtains and switched on the small desk lamp, then looked around. Over an unwashed marble fire-place punctuated by a gas fire was a framed photograph of a Zeppelin. Beneath it was a year-old calendar with a color photo of Köln Cathedral seen from the Rhine, but no dates.

"Look in the desk," Gatiss said in a hushed voice.

There was nothing there but typed letters from various small holdings, and an empty Alka-Seltzer jar, complete with its foam packing wad.

"Nothing," Eberlin said reluctantly.

Gatiss grunted impatiently and tipped the wastebasket onto the floor, then kicked the pieces of paper away angrily. "You and your bright ideas!" he muttered. He pulled a set of keys from his pocket and walked toward the main filing cabinet. Eberlin sat on the edge of the desk and lit a cigarette.

"Put that out, you fool," snapped Gatiss. "And don't just sit there."

Eberlin stubbed out the cigarette and looked vaguely at the books on the mantelpiece, watching Gatiss anxiously out of the corner of his eye.

On top of the cabinet were a few old copies of *Bild* and *Pravda*.

"Bloody Communist all right," murmured Gatiss, glancing through the newspapers. "It stands out a mile."

"What about in the drawers?" asked Eberlin. "Are they locked?"

"They won't be for long," replied Gatiss, selecting a key from his chain.

He opened the four drawers in the cabinet in turn, starting with the bottom one, like a burglar, to avoid having to shut one in order to see into another. The first drawer contained nothing but the habitual contents of filing cabinet basements –an empty bottle of Old Grandad bourbon, one gray sneaker for the left foot, size 9, a handful of entangled paper clips, a duster, a cheap German paperback, now coverless and bent in half at page 67 and a discarded Christmas decoration. Gatiss snorted and opened the second drawer. It was equally dull and uninviting, being mainly filled with copies of letters sent out by Oskar Greiser regarding the renting and selling of apartments in West Berlin. All were harmless.

"He's just a bloody estate agent," snapped Gatiss and turned away.

Eberlin tightened his lips and didn't move. Finally Gatiss, with a heavy sigh, returned to the third drawer and studied its contents. Little more than a further collection of letters, März 1959–Oktober 1963, and two pages ripped from a copy of *Stern*. One contained a black and white advertisement for Telefunken radios, and an article on Mao Tse-tung. Gatiss glanced over it quickly, asked Eberlin what *Manschetten* meant, then looked at the second page. On the first side was the finale of the article. On the other side, however, was a foggy photograph of a Hollywood vedette who lay in a postcoital position on a crumpled bed, modestly attempting to shield her round, bare body from the prying reader by clutching a pocket edition of *Leaves of Grass* against her navel. Above her left buttock, her thighs being mercifully hidden by a sheet, some amateur wit had penciled in the words *Aus den Augen, aus dem Sinn*, Out of sight, out of mind. Gatiss held up the photo to Eberlin.

"Is this what you're looking for?" he said sarcastically.

Eberlin swore and peered at some shelves near the door. A mere collection of dusty books. He looked around the room in despair, anxiously seeking a clue to what he was supposed to unearth. Why couldn't Rotopkin have been more explicit? Hai-Wai, was all he had. He watched Gatiss open the top drawer in a great display of ostentation and fumble inside it, then restrain himself from slamming it shut.

"There's nothing here," Gatiss said once more. "Greiser's no use to us."

"Perhaps there's a safe somewhere," Eberlin suggested faint-heartedly.

"Some hope in that," muttered the other, but nevertheless glanced behind each of the two pictures without success.

Nothing remained in the room, except a small cupboard (three cracked cups, a tin of aspirins by Bayer of Leverkusen, a milk bottle containing an inch of sour milk, one teaspoon and a dud light bulb), a second shelf supporting the complete works of Jack London in Russian and a flower-pot, and a large box filled with air. That was all.

"Let's get out of this bloody place before Greiser returns," Gatiss growled, and then added scornfully, "Greiser!"

Reluctantly Eberlin drew back the curtains and walked heavily to the door, flicking his eyes vainly about the now overfamiliar room. Then he saw it. At first it seemed just a curious oddity, a slight deformity, until he studied it more.

"Wait a minute," he said quickly. Gatiss stopped and looked back.

"That filing cabinet," Eberlin said. "Do you notice anything odd about it?"

Gatiss glanced at it apathetically and shook his head.

"No, look at it," said Eberlin, crouching before it. "Look at the gap between the bottom drawer and the floor. It's about nine inches."

"What of it?"

"I've never seen a cabinet like that. It's as if it's been deliberately propped up."

Gatiss raised his eyes to the ceiling in despair. "It's just the design," he said. "Let's go before–"

But Eberlin was on his knees pulling at the lower drawer. "Look, six inches of metal have been bolted on," he said and heaved again at the drawer. On reaching its maximum extension, it stopped. "Help me get the drawer out," he urged Gatiss. "Take that end."

Caught by Eberlin's interest, Gatiss took one end of the drawer and began to pull.

"No," said Eberlin. "I think it's best if we lift it slightly off its runners, then pull."

"All right," Gatiss said. "Try it now."

The drawer jerked suddenly out of its moorings and crashed to the floor, throwing the whisky bottle spinning against its tin side. Both men held their breath and listened for any sound from below. None came.

Then Eberlin, pretending to concentrate on moving the drawer clear, allowed Gatiss to feel in the now exposed depths of the cabinet. He saw him freeze slightly, his eyes fixed on the floor, then his hand reappeared holding a green folder tied with string. Gatiss glanced at Eberlin.

"Draw the curtains again," he said.

Quickly Eberlin did so and turned to see Gatiss already undoing the string and laying the folder on the desk. Released from its binding, the file flopped open as if exhausted from the tension, and the two men simultaneously saw the single word scrawled on the cover.

ELSTER.

"Look outside," Gatiss said anxiously. "See if you can hear anything."

Quietly Eberlin crept to the door, opened it slightly and listened for a moment, then shut it, shook his head and returned to the desk. He stood watching the other man open the file, his heart racing, conscious of sweat forming on his forehead.

The first object among the small pile of papers that Gatiss pulled out of the file was a photograph. The story behind it was selfevident, and the reason for the hiding place sickeningly clear. The photograph, taken hurriedly by a flashbulb, depicted a man and a woman in bed. Both had obviously been surprised by the intruder and were gaping in horror into the camera. The woman, apparently quicker in her reactions, had attempted to put her hand over her face but had mistimed, so that only a blur beneath her chin betrayed the intention. The faces were clear and distinct but anonymous to both men.

"Blackmailer," Gatiss swore and threw the picture aside. "Bloody blackmailer."

Six more photographs in similar vein followed. All were of couples caught by some grub of a photographer in wretchedly obvious situations. At each one, Gatiss swore fiercely, but on the eighth picture he stopped openmouthed. Here was no illicit couple frozen in undignified postures. Instead, a man's handsome face smiled out at the two men, a face openly posing as if for a passport. But it was not only the innocence of the picture that surprised both Eberlin and Gatiss. It was the face itself. It was Oriental.

Eberlin stared closely as Gatiss passed it over to him with the words: "Recognize him?" Eberlin identified the man without hesitation. It was Lo Jui-ching, probably the most dangerous man in Red China, second only to Mao Tse-tung in the Politburo. Eberlin had heard a great deal of Lo's fantastic rise to power in the past ten years, and knew it was widely felt that Lo, and Lo alone, was the controlling force behind Red China's Secret Service, and worse, behind its Army. While in London, he had amassed a giant file on *Hai-Wai Tiao Cha Pu*, China's International Espionage Department, and the names of Lo Jui-ching and Li Hsien-nien, Lo's right-hand man, had appeared again and again. As far as Eberlin knew, Hai-Wai was split into two sections: *Ching Pao*, or the passive, fact-collating department, and *Teh Wu,* the actual operations branch. It was *Teh Wu* the British worried about. Worse, off-base doubles working for Peking couldn't be Chinese, for obvious reasons, and thus were usually nationals of the country in which they worked. It was disguising the needle in the haystack to look like a straw. "Lo?" Eberlin asked.

"Yes," replied Gatiss with a frown, and looked at Eberlin in puzzlement. "Greiser can hardly be blackmailing *him*?"

"Hardly. What's underneath?"

"More of them. Li Hsien-nien, Lin Piao–oh, and him. He's one of the Old Guard. King Sheng." Gatiss tapped the picture, then rifled through the remaining pictures. "Look at them. He's got pictures of almost the whole bloody Peking Intelligence."

"Yes, but they're not unknown. There's nothing here that's–" "Wait a minute."

"What?" said Eberlin.

Gatiss was standing dead still, staring at a photograph he had just picked from the file. For thirty seconds he said nothing as he studied the picture, his eyes wide, his mouth drawn tight.

"What is it?" Eberlin whispered anxiously.

Slowly, Gatiss turned toward him, his face tense and his eyes assuming an almost maniacal quality. Then suddenly he dashed the picture to the floor, strode to the mantelpiece and stared blindly into the fireplace. His body seemed frozen in a state of repressed anger and the room went cold.

"The bastard," Gatiss said finally to the air, and then fell silent.

Slowly Eberlin bent down, picked up the photograph and looked at it. It was an ordinary group picture of some of the Hai-Wai hierarchy. He recognized Lo in the foreground, and some of his grinning associates behind him. And then Eberlin's mouth gaped open and he had to turn away to prevent Gatiss seeing his reaction. Rotopkin had been right. On the phone, he had been right. His agony of the past fortnight was frighteningly over. Prominent in the back row of the picture, a neighbor's shoulder obscuring a part of the chin but little more, was a smirking familiar face. Younger perhaps but none the less recognizable.

Eberlin studied it for a long time, and found that all he could say was, "*Why?*"

Gatiss didn't answer. He seemed almost in a trance. Then, sluggishly bringing himself out of the catatonic state, he walked slowly to the desk and turned over the remaining objects in the file. One and all told the same pathetic story. A photostat of the man's bank account in a Swiss bank, the total touching five figures and indicating a regular withdrawal on the first of each month. Another photostat. Suddenly, Gatiss picked up the file, threw it violently across the room, and stood, breathing heavily, staring at the scattered papers.

"You know what all this means, don't you?" Gatiss said quietly.

"It means that Copperfield is Krasnevin."

Eberlin didn't reply, remaining suitably silent for the occasion.

Gatiss scooped up the pictures.

"Do *you* think he is?" he demanded.

Looking at the floor, Eberlin shook his head. Beneath the room, doors banged as light sleepers were disturbed by the noise.

"I don't know," he said. "But?" prompted Gatiss.

"I'm trying desperately to think of an innocent answer to all this."

"Don't try. It's Copperfield, isn't it? That's what it says." Eberlin nodded.

"It's Copperfield," he replied, and a girl on the floor below began to giggle.

* * *

Snatching up the file, the two men hurried downstairs, past the gauping faces of the whores and out into the sunlit street.

Neither said a word until they reached the hotel and the photographs were laid out once more on Eberlin's bed.

"He was in Gibraltar just before Nightingale was killed." "I know …" Eberlin said quietly.

"He even attended his funeral."

Gatiss spoke now without emotion, coldly analyzing the facts like a surgeon before an operation. "He's married isn't he?" "Copperfield?" Eberlin asked. "Yes."

"Yes, he is."

"How long I wonder has he been …"

Eberlin sighed. He suddenly realized he hadn't slept for the past thirty-six hours. It was beginning to tell on him. He lay on the bed wearily, beside the pictures, and lit a cigarette. Gatiss slowly collected all the evidence together, leveling it neatly against the mantel top, and walked to the door. Eberlin looked up.

"I'll contact Frazer. Tell him we found him," Gatiss said, and stood staring morosely into space for a moment. Eberlin noticed that it was seven thirty.

"Better pack your bag," Gatiss said finally. "We'll fly back tonight."

Then he was gone, rushing out of the room, slamming the door. For a while Eberlin heard Gatiss moving around noisily in the next room, and then, mercifully, he fell asleep.

15

Formula One (Zero G)

Who must die, must die in the dark, even though he sells candles.
–COLUMBIAN PROVERB

Life to me is like boardinghouse wallpaper. It takes a long time to get used to it, but when you finally do, you never notice that it's there. And then you hear that the decorators are arriving.
–ALEXANDER EBERLIN

WHEN he awoke, it was afternoon, and the room was like an oven. Starting up out of his fully dressed sleep, he staggered to the washbasin and submerged his face in three inches of cold water. Then, not caring to change, he left the room and stopped suddenly in the corridor. He was safe, he realized. The pressure was off, and there was nothing more he could do.

Gatiss's room was empty. The bed was stripped and only a small packed valise gave evidence of its inmate. Eberlin turned away and hurried downstairs where Prentiss was waiting with a scraggy young fräulein who ran away at the first opportunity.

"Afternoon, Eberlin," Prentiss said with a smile. "I heard all about it. Fantastic." And then, "I would never have guessed. Frazer's sure to get you a promotion now."

"Where's Gatiss?"

"Gatiss? Oh, he was here about an hour ago. Then suddenly he rushed off somewhere. You know Gatiss. Her name's Francesca by the way."

"Whose?"

"Oh, she's gone. Well, never mind." "You don't know where Gatiss went?"

"No idea. But he's been running about all morning. Are you going to eat?"

"No."

Eberlin walked out onto the steps of the hotel, screwing up his eyes against the sun. Putting on a pair of dark glasses, Prentiss joined him and stood, hands behind his back, whistling the second movement of Rachmaninoff's Second Piano Concerto.

"Oh he did say something about the Grand Prix," Prentiss said suddenly, splitting an octave.

Eberlin glanced at him. "What do you mean?"

"Well, I think he was going to go there later. I'm not sure why." Eberlin did and ran quickly down the steps toward the Mistrale. "Hey, don't forget we're leaving tonight," cried Prentiss, but Eberlin was already starting the car and roaring away toward the west of the city, cursing the sun, which he loathed in any city, and heading fast toward the Havel.

* * *

The Avus had been built by Hitler and ran for a distance of ten thousand meters as straight as an arrow, then banked into a curve at an angle near enough ninety degrees, to be bearable, and rejoined itself, so that from the air it looked like a sealed shepherd's crook. Along the length of the straight were trees, mostly poplars and elms which broke only when the road angled into that tight sharp bank, so that from the island inside the bank, the cars were hidden by trees until they suddenly appeared from nowhere and splattered themselves onto the banked turn like tomatoes hurled from a catapult, and hung static for a second before they roared off the curve and onto the level and out of sight once more.

It was without doubt the warmest day yet of the season and the attraction of the Formula One meeting and the sun had brought hundreds to the track where they were now sitting in style with bottles of beer in the concrete stands, or packed as best they could on the grass island surrounded completely by track and approached only by a single tunnel under the road. Standing here among the jostling Berliners and tourists and ice-cream stalls, one came closer to a race than on any other track in Europe, since the cars, traveling well over a hundred miles an hour, roared around one; only by revolving constantly could a spectator follow an individual car, and then dizziness would soon take one. And always there was that incredible brown banking of the track, like an immense Cinerama screen on which the blues, greens, reds and whites of the racing cars exhibited themselves for a second, seemingly hovering in the air, burning tires, top of driver's head, accelerator at maximum, only to be wiped clean by an invisible hand, leaving only a roaring in the ears and a nagging distrust for the law of gravity.

Eberlin stood on the grass of the island, smoking a cigarette and peering intently into the crowd for the familiar face. He had been there over an hour now, and three races were over, the last being won hands down by a British Lotus, much to the consternation of the crowd since it was the only foreign entry in that event. As a result there was only sparse applause when the dwarf green car sallied smugly over the finishing line. Eberlin didn't care either way. His only interests were Emmanuel Gatiss and an ice-cold Coca-Cola from the stall in the middle of the grass plot.

He sauntered toward it, pushing through the sweating crowd, his jacket over his shoulder now, and waited idly by the scarlet stand; listening abstractedly to the continual verbal Muzak of the loud speaker. Cars roared around him incessantly, throwing up a high-pitched whine as they hit the banking, then careened back onto the horizontal to his right. He drank the Coca-Cola thirstily from the bottle, and glancing up, noted the dozens of polizei in the Mercedes Tower watching the race with rapt attention. The whole place seemed crawling with police. Eberlin sighed, threw the bottle away and decided to find an empty foot of grass, lie down, put a copy of yesterday's *Daily Mail* over his face and forget everything. And then, for the second time, he saw Sobakevich.

There was no mistake about it. The crop-haired Russian was standing near the tunnel, staring intently into the crowd, one hand clasped tightly in his jacket pocket, the other picking at a spot behind his ear. He was watching someone, and it wasn't Eberlin. The crowd had grown now and the whole grass expanse seemed filled with restless, gauping spectators, oblivious of anything but the race. Three men nearby were filming the event with a camera lens longer than their arm, a couple were making polite love under a candy-colored sun-shade, and at Eberlin's feet a small boy, without any trousers on, was crying his head off. Eberlin glanced around anxiously, seeking to find the subject of Sobakevich's scrutiny.

At first all the faces seemed identical, but focusing his eyes in the direction of Sobackevich's gaze, he discerned Gatiss himself, sunglasses on his nose, standing like an emperor stag, arms folded, staring up toward the grandstand. The man seemed momentarily frozen, etched clearly against the smudge of the cars behind him, then he was gone, mingling in the crowd, lost from sight. To Eberlin it all seemed like a macabre duel, for he was suddenly alienated from the two men who were acting out their parts alone. Then Sobakevich was gone too, hidden in the sea of faces, and Eberlin began to push toward the tunnel, vainly trying to see either of the two men before it was too late. But it was. A sudden scream hit the air, rising strangely over the screech of tires and hanging coldly in the air long after the sound had faded. People began to push toward the middle, and voices were raised as the crowd, attracted almost telepathically by a huddle in the center, treading on each other and collapsing under each other, and then halting in a swelling throng in the middle of the green dried grass. The race was ignored and a man died.

Eberlin, drawn relentlessly to the new, unexpected and yet inevitable cynosure, pushed his way through the spectators, elbowing them aside, until he was within a few feet of the focal point of the crowd. He tried to peer over the heads but saw nothing but strained, curious faces, and then the police were jostling him aside and a gap appeared between the legs of the people and he saw him, lying on the grass, his face open to the sky, his crew cut standing out sharply on the pink scalp. It was Sobakevich and he was as dead as Queen Anne.

The wretched figure in the pseudo-American clothes was prodded and searched by the police, and then the body disfigured by a bullet fired to synchronize with the roar of a car, was covered with a length of yellow canvas advertising Lucky Strike cigarettes. Eberlin knew Gatiss had killed him, here in the crowd, in full view of all, and was probably standing a few yards away from the spot cleaning his sunglasses or admiring the view. He hurried away.

Suddenly, a voice behind him snapped in his ear, "Come on. Let's get out of here," and he saw Gatiss pushing past him and hurrying toward the tunnel. But the police were already there, blocking the only exit and pushing fleeing sightseers back onto the island.

Eberlin stopped, feeling himself being shoved and kicked by the excited crowd, and then, turning slightly, he caught a brief glimpse of Gatiss as two of the polizei moved toward him, searching all those about him. Then Gatiss had gone and Eberlin was seized by other polizei, searched and thrust aside. Then it happened, like an absurd farce.

Another tussle had broken out a few yards away and a man ran out onto the track. He was actually rushing up the banking, slipping for a second, then mounting the banking and scrambled to the top. Then Gatiss was running along the rim of the curve, toward the safety of the fields beyond. The spectators were in a panic and the grandstand as one man leaped to its feet. Eberlin stopped awe-struck and confused by Gatiss's action, but then he saw one of the polizei running out of the crowd too, his eyes set only on his prey. Oblivious of the race, the policeman clambered up the banking, one hand reacning for a gun, the other clutching desperately at the crumbling surface of the gradient. Then he stopped, ridiculously stopped halfway up the steep slope, and raised his gun to fire. Eberlin was being thrust forward by the crowd as he saw a red Ferrari hit the embankment from out of the trees and hurtle straight at the unsuspecting policeman. Someone shouted a name, obviously the policeman's, in warning, and he looked back. But it was already too late. The car hit him, hit him and gored him and tossed him in the air, and he landed, his back broken, in the gully of the bank. At the same time, as if in a macabre ballet, the Ferrari spun lazily upward, taking its time, hovered for a second on the rim of the slope in a farewell salute (tomato red car, large black number 7 on the side, driver watching the last few seconds of his life with amused curiosity) and then fell gently over the brim and exploded in private.

Gatiss had stopped momentarily on the top of the bank, frozen in silhouette like the sole survivor of a Grecian frieze, then he was gone, into the trees and away. As the roar of the crowd reached fever pitch, Eberlin saw his opportunity and slipped into the tunnel, now abandoned by the distracted police, and walked as casually as he could under the track until he saw the Deutschlandhalle.

Without looking back, he hurried to the Mistrale and sealed himself inside. Then, backing slowly into the street from the car park, he accelerated into Halenseestrasse and east toward nowhere and anywhere, his mind numbed by the events and his stomach, that impartial party to our actions, craving to be fed.

After driving blindly for an hour, he choked down a salami sandwich from a corner shop specializing in salami sandwiches, and drove slowly back to the hotel. It was now six twenty and Prentiss was sitting in the foyer with his coat on and an anxious look on his face.

16

The Passing of the Buck

Judas committed suicide because when he checked the thirty pieces of silver, he found there weren't any hallmarks.
–ALEXANDER EBERLIN

I have so much to do I am going to bed.
–SAVOYARD PROVERB

What do I do? I've told you. I collect noses from statues.
–ALEXANDER EBERLIN

HALF an hour later, they were collected by a brown Humber Super Snipe, owned by the British Army, and driven in relative comfort to Gatow Airport.

"Gatiss has already left," said Prentiss, lowering the window on his side of the car. "I expect Frazer'll get in touch with Berlin and straighten it out."

Eberlin nodded. He sat, his arms folded, looking out of the window at the last images of the city. He was beginning to breathe again.

On his left was now the entrance to the Avus, still suffering under the commotion of the afternoon, and beyond that the woods and the lakes beneath them. As the car turned right past the Radio Tower, he caught pleasant glimpses through the trees of white and yellow yachts drifting on the water, and heard buoyant, ecstatic feminine screams from the beaches below. He put a cigarette in his mouth and found he had run out of matches. Neither Prentiss nor the uniformed driver could assist him, so he sat, frustrated, for the rest of the journey with an unlit Senior Service in his mouth. But it was a pleasant drive, and he would be glad to leave Berlin for the last time.

"I bet you're glad to leave Berlin," Prentiss said with a smile. "In a way," replied Eberlin. "Are you sure you haven't got a

light?"

"Sorry."

"Why exactly are we going to Gatow Airport? It's purely military, isn't it?"

"Well, yes. Speed really. There's not another civil plane for hours and Frazer–"

"Frazer? You spoke to him?"

"Yes. Well, Frazer suggested we leave by kind permission of the Army. They often do that." He grinned to himself. "Went to a marvelous restaurant in Paris. Only a small place but incredibly good. Recommended to it by this girl I was with. Marvelous place for jugged hare. Owned by two brothers. No, three brothers. Specializes in game. Fantastic. I'll write the address down for you in case you get to Paris. It's in Boulevard Beaumarchais. Think it's called L'Enclos de Ninon."

Eberlin nodded politely and stared at the back of the driver's head. He thought, incongruously, about Caroline. He–

"Hey," he said suddenly. "What about my car?"

"Oh, don't worry about that. They're flying that back too." Prentiss touched Eberlin's arm. "Don't forget, you're pretty important to us now."

* * *

Gatow Airport is a sorry affair, much too dismal to be described save in the most offhand way. Three sheds, two hangars, two airstrips crossing in an X, fence of barbed wire, NO UNAUTHORISED PERSON ADMITTED ON THESE PREMISES and an air of utter depression. It is employed solely by the military, who take off and land as quickly as possible without being bothered too much by the environment. Recollecting it, one remembers only jumbled acres of burnt sienna, cold sheds and brown uniforms, as inviting as a grave.

Prentiss and Eberlin stood in a narrow waiting room on the edge of the airfield and gazed somberly at a DC 6 taxiing slowly to a halt outside. Some matches were offered to Eberlin, and he took them gratefully and sat down on a wooden bench next to a copy of *TitBits* and half a dozen soldiers in full kit.

Prentiss grinned and joined him, whispering in his ear: "Pretty hellish, isn't it?"

Eberlin agreed and avoided any conversation with the soldiers nearby. After a while, a sergeant walked stiffly toward them and clicked his heels on the concrete floor.

"Mr. George Dancer and Mr. Joseph Prentiss?"

Prentiss looked up with a self-conscious smile and nodded: then, with an attempt at etiquette, rose gauchely to his feet.

"Oh yes," he said. "I'm Prentiss, and that's Mr. Dancer." "Very good, sir. Sergeant Harris."

The sergeant offered his hand to both men.

"That I gather … is our plane?" asked Prentiss, making conversation.

"That is the one, sir. We should be leaving Gatow at twenty hundred hours. In about fifteen minutes."

"Oh … well … that's good."

"If there's anything you need sir, just ask." Eberlin looked up.

"Oh yes, sergeant," he said. "Do you have a telephone near here?"

"Personal call, sir?" "Yes."

"If you could follow me, sir." "Thank you."

Eberlin stood up and gave a quick smile to Prentiss. "Girl?" Prentiss winked.

Eberlin nodded.

"Promised I'd phone her before I left."

He pulled a face and followed Sergeant Harris across the waiting room.

At the end of the corridor hung three fire buckets. On the first was written SAND and inside was sand, on the second was written WATER and inside was water, and on the third was written FIRE. It was empty. Next to it however was a telephone booth. The sergeant nodded to Eberlin, then strode away, back down the corridor. Eberlin entered the booth and dialed Rotopkin. The preliminary codes and scrambling over, he said:

"I'm just leaving Berlin now."

"Good," replied Rotopkin. "It couldn't be better." "I suppose you know Sobakevich is dead.

"Yes. You've got to kill Gatiss for us. But not yet." "I couldn't do anything about it."

"What did you say?"

"I'm sorry. I was trying to light a cigarette and talk at the same time."

From where he was standing, Eberlin could see another aircraft through a window by the booth. It was being serviced, a dozen trucks fussing underneath it like seamstresses around the hem of a wedding dress.

"I must say," he said, "that the Copperfield thing has stunned everyone."

"I thought it might," replied Rotopkin. "I was worried in case it seemed too obvious."

"Not at all. We almost didn't find the file." He smiled. "Incredible, isn't it? Who would have thought Copperfield, fat Copperfield, was working for Peking?"

"He isn't," replied Rotopkin. Eberlin gave a slight gasp.

"What did you say?" he asked incredulously.

"I said he doesn't work for Peking. He doesn't work for anybody except the British. At least as far as I know."

"You mean–you framed him?"

"Had to," answered Rotopkin blithely. "Give you time to breathe. It'll take them weeks before they clear him–if they ever do. By then, we'll have you right out of it for good."

"But–" Eberlin began but didn't continue. Prentiss had appeared in the corridor and was gesturing toward his watch. Eberlin nodded, attempted a smile and pointed at the phone. Prentiss nodded with a grin and walked away. Eberlin was silent for a moment.

"I wish there had been another way," he said finally. "Supposing they don't accept Copperfield's protests of innocence."

"Let him worry about that. All the better for us. You'd better go anyway.

"Yes. The plane's waiting." There was a pause.

"You know," Eberlin said quietly, "all this wouldn't have happened if you hadn't killed Pavel."

"*I* didn't kill Pavel," came the surprised answer.

Eberlin gave a nervous laugh.

"Not you personally," he said. "I meant Kuzmich. If he hadn't been so–"

"Just a minute," Rotopkin snapped. "We did not kill Pavel."

"But you must have," protested Eberlin, his voice rising.

"I said we didn't. We thought *you* had got him out of the way."

"What? Me?"

The air was becoming difficult to breathe, and Eberlin suddenly began to tremble.

"Rotopkin–what are you saying?"

"Well, isn't it obvious? We were under the impression that you had told Pavel to go underground or whatever. Why do you think we've been–"

"You must be mad. I saw you–the Buick–I saw you there. You were taking Pavel's body away."

But he knew he was wrong.

"It wasn't us," replied Rotopkin. "I assure you it wasn't us." The door of the telephone booth suddenly swung open, and

Prentiss said cheerily:

"Come along, Eberlin, there's a good chap. They're waiting for us."

Then he saw Eberlin's face and added: "Oh sorry. She's like that is she? Tears and wailing. Well, try to hurry her up, and I'll see you in the plane. You've got a couple of minutes."

He grinned again, winked and hurried away. Eberlin stood dead still, the phone burning his ear. Then, his voice dry and broken, he said:

"If it wasn't you, then–it must have been the British." There was no answer.

"Rotopkin? Rotopkin! Are you still there?"

There was still silence, but he knew Rotopkin was listening. He was beginning to tremble again.

"If it was the British who killed Pavel," he said, "then–then they know. They know who I am. They've known all the time. Rotopkin–they *know*!"

His words seemed to be screaming in the air. "Rotopkin? Don't you understand?"

There was a moment's hesitation, then his countryman answered, his voice cold and final:

"You're dead, Krasnevin. You're dead." The phone went dead.

"Rotopkin," Eberlin shouted, but no one was listening. He turned in panic as a voice behind him said:

"I think we ought to go now, sir. Can't hold up the plane much longer."

Eberlin stared at the sergeant, still gripping the phone, incapable of doing anything. Harris leaned across and took the receiver from his hand and listened momentarily.

"Seems the party has rung off, sir," he said.

* * *

The waiting room seemed filled with soldiers, standing silently in line, neither speaking nor moving. Eberlin felt himself being led like a lamb down the corridor by the sergeant, his mind devoid of anything anymore. It had all been a bizarre game. It was all so clear now. Everything had fallen into place. He has been used, manipulated, exhibited by the British in order to attract the flies. He had given them, *given* them, Sobakevich and Henderson. And Greiser. And God knows how much more. And he had given them, before the race had barely begun, he had given them–Pavel.

At the corner of the corridor, he tried to run, only to collapse in a heap and be pulled to his feet by a sympathetic sergeant who knew nothing at all. And then he was led, surrounded by a hundred regiments no less, out onto the pathetically grubby airfield, warm in the summer evening, and forward, forward toward Prentiss, now standing at the door of the aircraft.

The strap was tightened around his lap and the cigarette stubbed out as he was dragged aloft, back to London.

"Marvelous planes these," said Prentiss with a smile. "Used to have a model once when I was a child, made out of plastic. Never worked. Still got it somewhere."

Faces peered at him, or the passenger in front, and the horrendous throbbing of the engines vibrated tightly against his skull. Beside him, Prentiss smiled and grimaced and chattered gaily about a million things, and all Eberlin could say, not in a vain attempt at dignity, but because he could say nothing else, was: "Copperfield's innocent."

And Prentiss replied, "Oh, we know that. Look, Eberlin, old chap, I don't smoke, so you can have my allowance of two hundred cigarettes if you like. For the customs, you know. It's worth it. One pound for two hundred. I mean, one can't turn a blind eye to that."

He scratched his nose. Eberlin closed his eyes.

"Do you get nervous in planes?" Prentiss was saying. "My aunt does. Sick as a dog everywhere. I used to be once, but now they're so fast. I mean we'll be in London in a couple of hours."

Then, glancing at Eberlin, he said, "Sorry. Was I rabbiting on?

Sorry about that. I suppose you're thinking about that girl." Eberlin opened his eyes and looked at Prentiss for a moment.

"I suppose Frazer and Brogue will be waiting at the airport for us," he said. "In London."

"Expect so. Oh, I don't know though. Will they be?" Eberlin nodded.

"Probably," he said and lit a cigarette.

Ahead of him he could see the rows of chattering soldiers, and the kitbags and coats stuffed on the rack above.

"How long have you been in the army, sergeant?" he said to Harris, offering him a cigarette.

Made in the USA
Charleston, SC
02 March 2015